THE TERRITORIES

Edited by

CHAD DUNDAS AND JONATHAN SNOWDEN

FIRST HYBRID SHOOT HARDCOVER EDITION PUBLISHED 2022

Cover Design by Marco Bucci

ISBN: 978-1-7349459-5-9

CONTENTS

WELCOME TO THE TERRITORIES

The Territories is an immersive, shared-world fiction project told in a series of connected novels, novellas and short stories set in professional wrestling's fractured territory days from 1983 to 1992. Our stories are told by different authors, in different styles and genres, but they all take place within the same world, set against the backdrop of the equal-parts gaudy and seedy underbelly of territory wrestling.

Thanks so much for taking the plunge with us on this first volume of stories. We hope to keep you entertained for weeks, months, maybe even years to come. In volume one, we're starting small(-ish) with a series of origin stories. We're proud of the authors we've brought together to kickstart this thing, and we hope to add additional intriguing and talented voices as we move forward.

As *The Territories* grows and evolves, you'll get to know our ensemble cast of colorful characters as well as the unique feel and attitude of our sixteen fictional territories. Some characters you might only meet once. Some will pop up again and again, in different times and places, as wrestlers come and go through various territories and promoters rule their individual fiefdoms, feuding with each other over money and talent. It's going to be a wild ride.

Again, thanks for joining us on this journey. We're excited for you to become part of The Territories. Now, read on, if you dare.

— Chad Dundas & Jonathan Snowden, series editors

THE BIG HOSS

(A NOVELLA OF THE TERRITORIES)

CHAD DUNDAS

Territory:
Frontier States Wrestling
(*Alberta, Saskatchewan, Montana, Wyoming, Eastern Washington*)
Summer, 1983

ONE
THINK HAPPY THOUGHTS

My God, summer 1983. Back when Mack Savage was still alive. Back when we still had the territories — and a man could still earn an honest living in professional wrestling. Sonny Da Silva had just taken over for his old man as the top boss out in New York, but nobody knew yet how big an asshole Sonny would turn out to be. We had Bucky Walters running Atlanta. Vic Valley in Minnesota. Fucking Hugo Schwartz controlled all of Texas. There were rules. Structure. A natural order to things. Not like today.

These days, I turn on the TV, I don't even recognize it anymore.

I look in the mirror, I don't recognize myself.

When I go in for my hip treatments, the nice-looking nurse with the barbed-wire tattoo gets me to hike down my pants so she can stick me with a needle the size of a No. 2 pencil. Just before she slides that big harpoon into my side, she always tells me: Think happy thoughts. Think about the best time you ever had in your life.

When I close my eyes, you know where my mind goes? Every time? Hand to God?

The summer of motherfucking '83.

I was all of twenty-two, twenty-three at the time, and I spent that whole summer working tag matches with "Maniac" Mack Savage in Frontier States Wrestling. Baby Jay Chevalier ran the territory back then, and he worked us half to death making every high school gym and bingo hall between Billings and Calgary. Sold out the Mule Palace three nights running over Fourth of July Weekend.

What a time that was.

It was Baby Jay's idea to put me and Mack together. I had been in the business about eighteen months. Green as goose shit but soaking it all up as fast as I could. Mack was on his way down from the big leagues for what turned out to be the last time. Of course, nobody knew that then. We all thought Peach State Wrestling or UWF would snap him back up, squeeze one last big run out of him. Meantime, Baby Jay figured he and I could give each other a rub. Mack was rehabbing from knee surgery but still headlining shows and pulling down main event money. He needed a partner who could handle most of the action in a twenty-minute match. Me? I needed somebody to take the new car smell off me, so to speak. On top of that, we both worked cowboy gimmicks, so Baby Jay thought it was a no-brainer

"What we have here is a symbiotic relationship," he said during one of our first meetings. "You know what that means? Like the little fishes that clean the gills on the sharks?"

"More like I'm the fairy godmother," Mack said, "and I gotta keep the princess alive until her foot gets big enough to fit the slipper."

And that's how everybody started calling me Princess.

Anyway, the Mule Palace.

Outdoor venue, right off the highway in Middle-of-Nowhere, Montana. We put twelve hundred people in the grandstand Friday, Saturday and Sunday. The main event each night was me and Mack against this heel tag team called The Great Depression. They were a couple of big dudes in overalls and newsboy caps. Kept their faces painted white, smeared eye-black down to the middle of their cheek-bones. I was never sure what they were supposed to be — ghouls, maybe — but those guys were great fucking heels. People hated their guts.

The Mule Palace mostly hosted livestock auctions and rodeos, so it had no locker rooms. Baby Jay set up these big white pavilion tents for all the boys. He had one for the babyfaces, one for the heels and one for Mack Savage. Since I was Mack's tag partner, I dressed out with him in his private tent. Baby Jay's guys would bring food in for us, drinks, whatever we wanted. Knowing what I know now, that shit probably didn't help my reputation with the rest of the boys, but back then I was too young and dumb to know any better.

That third night, the Sunday, the night we were going to have the blow-off with The Great Depression, I finally asked Mack what was up with his T-shirt. The first two nights he'd wrestled wearing a sleeveless black tee tucked into his trunks. The shirt said *Panda-monium!* across the chest in puffy white cursive writing.

"This?" he asked, looking down at the shirt like he'd just noticed he had it on. "Got it at the San Diego Zoo. Took the kids five years ago, maybe? Fuckers aren't as big as you might think. Even the giant pandas. One-eighty, 200 pounds for the males."

"That's fascinating, Sav," I said, "but what I mean is, why are you wearing it?"

I'd never seen him wrestle in a T-shirt before. For an old-timer, Mack still had a pretty great body. The boys used to call him "The Human Pharmacy," because he had the best hook-ups on anabolics *and* recreationals. People said once upon a time, before he made his money, he used to sell a little coke on the side, too, but I never knew if that was true. People used to tell a lot of stories about Mack Savage. All I knew was, the old man was yoked. Perfect body fat percentage, perfect tan, incredible vascularity well into his fifties.

Mack put one foot up on the bench I was straddling and looked around to make sure we were alone in the tent. "Promise me you won't breathe a word," he said.

"Who am I going to tell?" I asked. "You're the only one around here who doesn't hate my guts."

He sighed and bent to lace a boot, his face within whispering distance. "I'm off the gas," he said.

That sat me up straight. "You're off steroids?" I said. "What the hell for?"

He switched boots and grimaced. "Molly wants to have a baby," he said. "We've tried everything."

I'd been driving Mack Savage around Baby Jay's territory for two and a half months by that time, so I'd already heard a lot about Molly, his new wife. They'd met in '81, when Vic Valley booked Mack in his wrestler-versus-pro-football-player battle royale at the Rosemont Horizon. Turned out, Molly worked for the building manager. Or she was the daughter of the building manager. I forget. Anyway, it was a whirlwind sort of a deal, the two of them falling head-over-heels and getting hitched after dating just a few months. This baby thing was new information, though. Mack said he was pretty sure he'd made it clear to Molly before the wedding that he didn't want any more kids. But fourteen months into their holy matrimony she had swerved him, going absolutely baby crazy.

"I raised mine already," he told me, like I was the one he needed to convince. "My oldest is in junior college. You think I want to reset the clock *now*?"

I could see the bald crown of his head, monk-like, surrounded by tufts of bleached blond hair. For two solid decades, "Maniac" Mack Savage had been at the very top of the wrestling business — regional TV, closed-circuit, all that stuff — and he had three or four kids spread out over a handful of previous marriages. I knew there was alimony, child support, custody arrangements he had to abide. He told me it already ran him ragged keeping up with that stuff, but Molly wasn't taking no for an answer. She was jealous of the other wives, Mack said, the ones with the kids. It was getting to the point where she wouldn't leave him alone when he was home.

"I fucked up this time, Dally," he said. "This chick is too young for me. I can't take it. These old bones."

I'd met Molly once before and didn't think she seemed all that young, but I was no good at telling ages. Up to this point it seemed like she made Mack happy, and when Mack was happy, I was happy. The old guy had been good to me. It wasn't like anybody else was going out of their way trying to get me over.

Mack always liked to talk before a match. It was nerves, I guess. He had a lot to teach me, so I tried to listen to everything he had to say, but all this baby stuff was like a foreign language. Fact was, I couldn't have kids. My freshman year at Boise State, the doctor giving me my football physical diagnosed me with enlarged veins in my testes. A condition called varicoceles. I had to look it up in a medical book at the library and read it over and over until I had the term memorized. Basically, the doctor said it caused my sperm to mutate until they couldn't swim right. There was surgery you could get, but I wasn't thinking about that. I wasn't interested in kids or a wife or anything else that could tie me down. All I cared about was wrestling.

I was six-foot-six, 275 pounds and strong as an ox. Only two things I was missing were experience and a better body. I still looked like an offensive lineman, with a little pooch of fat that bunched up over my trunks. I knew I had a ton to learn, but I was a good worker — everybody said so. I could go forty-five hard minutes with minimal rest holds. I could work strong, sell like a motherfucker and was willing to blade myself wide open in front of twenty farmers at the local Grange Hall if that's how I was booked. Baby Jay saw something in me, which was why he paired me with Mack in the first place. It was an unpopular decision, I guess. Some of the other guys who had been in the business longer felt I hadn't paid sufficient dues. They resented me for it and would rib me any chance they got. But Mack knew Baby Jay had an eye for talent. That's why he consented to let me drive him.

"So, what are you gonna do?" I asked.

"What can I do?" he said. "Have another baby — if we can get something to stick."

Mack told me Molly rode him raw every time he was home, but so far they'd had no luck. He couldn't figure it out. Every time before, he'd knocked up his wives right away, two times on accident. So this didn't make sense. Molly was the earth mother type — mood rings and astrology and all that shit — so she made Mack go to this weirdo, holistic fertility clinic to get checked out. He said a witch doctor had rubbed him down with essential oils and gave him a shitload of big horse pills to take. These were all-natural supplements made from exotic herbs and roots with names Mack couldn't pronounce. The witch doctor guaranteed it would naturally boost his fertility, but Mack said the pills hadn't done a damn thing and tasted so bad he stopped taking them before the first bottle ran out. Finally, he'd convinced Molly to let him see a real doctor, at a real hospital.

As he talked, Mack pulled the Frontier States Wrestling heavy-weight title out of his duffle bag and draped it over the bench between us. Glistening gold plates bolted on sturdy black leather. A soaring eagle with the earth in its talons stamped in the center. Shiny brass snaps around the strap. Rumor was, Baby Jay made you put down a $10,000 deposit before he'd let you win the title, just to make sure nobody skipped town with the belt. He gave the money back — plus interest, so you made a nice little profit — when you agreed to drop the title to the next guy he picked out. The belt weighed twelve pounds and Mack complained about lugging it everywhere, but I wanted that thing more than anything in the world. Someday, after he got the call-up back to the big leagues, I knew I'd have my shot.

"Anyway, the new doc, the actual, medical PhD made me get off the 'roids," he said. "So for now I'm wearing the shirt. Can't have people seeing my little bitch titties."

"Pop the top," I said. "Show me." He hoisted up the T-shirt and let me look at his flat bronze torso. "You look the same as ever."

"I don't *feel* the same," he said. "I feel like the blueberry girl from *Willy Wonka*."

"I don't know who that is," I said.

"Just wait," he said. "Once you're a broken-down old mule like 'Maniac' Mack Savage and you got a litter of babies running around, you'll know every kid's movie by heart."

I clamped my mouth shut, because I hadn't told him about my medical condition. My eyes moved to his duffel bag, where the green canvas dopp kit he used to haul his drugs around poked out like an abscessed tooth. "What's gonna happen to your stash?" I asked.

He tucked his shirttail back into his trunks and snorted at me. That's how obvious the look on my face must have been. Plucking the dopp kit out of the bag, he tossed it into my chest. "Knock yourself out, kid," he said. "Maybe we can finally suck a little bit of the baby fat off of those abs." Then he looked around, scratched his head. "Where's my damn hat?" he asked.

"On top of my bag," I said, "where it always is."

TWO
THE BLOW OFF

Mack had been using "Blackout" by Scorpions as his entrance music since it came out the year before. It was a strange choice for a guy who came to the ring wearing a ten-gallon hat and swinging a branding iron over his head, but people went ape shit for it. The song fit the rock 'n' roll attitude of the "Maniac" Mack cowboy gimmick — with the way the guitar revved up at the beginning, to the crash of the first couple drum hits, to the way the whole crowd shouted "Blackout!" with the chorus. Everybody loved Scorpions.

Mack and I timed it so we came through the curtain just as the beat came in. It was always a kick to walk the aisle with him. Honestly, the feeling never fully left me. In all my years in the business after, I worked bigger rooms with bigger stars and drew bigger gates, but I never saw anybody more over than "Maniac" Mack Savage. His energy was pure joy. It filled the space as soon as the fans saw his face, plastered with his crazy, shit-eating grin. His eyes as big as saucers. You could have fifteen, twenty wrestlers on the card — big guys, small guys, heels, faces — it didn't matter. Mack always sparkled. The people just naturally loved the guy, and he loved them back. Later on in my career, I tried to steal a little bit of that vibe, to tell the truth.

Our last night at the Mule Palace the place came absolutely unglued before the people even saw us. They were packed elbow-to-elbow in the grandstand, with a few hundred more sitting in folding chairs on the dirt floor around the ring. Just the sound of the music had them running to the rail. I led the way, clapping and throwing up hook-'em horns signs with my hands, but the crowd looked right through me. When Mack busted out from behind the curtain, that big black branding iron thrust in the air and trademark glint in his eyes, they popped so loud I imagine God in heaven heard the screams. My arms were long enough I could slap hands with folks on both sides of the aisle by walking down the middle. I smiled my friendly sidekick smile, my head bobbing a little to the music, chomping gum, looking confident but focused on the big fight.

The Great Depression was already in the ring, wearing the engineer-striped overalls they favored as their gear. One of them carried a chunky miner's lantern in his fist. The other took sips from a jug of moonshine with three X's printed across the front of it. Damn, I wish I could remember those guys' names. One of them died, I'm pretty sure. In a car wreck? Maybe like '87? Otherwise they would've made it. They were that good.

I had to wait for Mack to finish his walk before I could get in the ring. Otherwise, The Great Depression would jump me and lay into me with their lantern and jug. The whole ordeal took — swear to God — eight minutes. Enough time to play "Blackout" twice all the way through. Mack ran down one side of the aisle giving high-fives to everybody at the rail and turned around to do the same thing back down the other side. He made sure he touched everyone. Pointing and smiling. Reaching into the sea of hands like a politician working a rope line. When he got to ringside, he made two full trips around, letting everybody get close to him. All the while I stood on the ring steps with one hand on top of the corner post, doing my best to give

The Great Depression the hairy eyeball. They glared back at me, the three of us all waiting like the only virgins at an orgy.

When he was finally ready, Mack dove headfirst under the bottom rope into the middle of the ring and jumped up swinging the branding iron around like a madman. The Great Depression bailed out onto the arena floor to avoid getting hit. One of them dropped his lantern on the way, and Mack kicked it out after them. I vaulted over the top rope, and then Mack and I stood back-to-back in the middle of the ring, me with my fists up and him holding the branding iron out like a fencing foil. The whole place going crazy for us. Well, going crazy for Mack. I should clarify: nobody gave a shit about me back then. Nobody even knew who I was.

Still, it was hard not to watch me out there. I was by far the biggest guy in the ring, and I could go. I mean, I could flat *go*. Before Baby Jay found me, I'd had maybe two dozen matches here and there, mostly working jobber stuff around the west coast. A couple matches for Danny Rich out in Portland. One hitch with NorCal Wrestling and Ray St. John in Oakland. I'd even made it out to Phoenix once, where Doc Slade had his boy Jimmy Ray tan my hide so bad during a strap match I swore I'd never go back. Trouble was, I was too damn big to be a good jobber. *Enhancement talent*, I guess Sonny Fucking Da Silva would call it now. Nobody wants to hire enhancement talent that makes their regular talent look puny by comparison. It was a dead end gig. I was getting frustrated, thinking about going back to school to finish my soc-crim degree, when Baby Jay saw me work a one-nighter for this little outlaw mud show in Colville, Washington and told me to move to Billings and work for him. Next thing I knew, I was on the Frontier States Wrestling payroll, driving for Mack Savage and working tag matches with him until his knee was well enough for him to go back to singles.

I couldn't believe my luck. The FSW territory was a little out of the way, but Baby Jay was making it sing in those days, running everything from Spokane to Billings, Calgary to Cheyanne. His normal circuit included mostly little towns that didn't get shit else for family entertainment, and he turned a nice profit doing it. Working for the guy was a sweet gig. I was surprised I landed it with such little experience. Baby Jay could be a condescending prick, but he was a good promoter. Of course, a few years after I left, he wound-up in a wheelchair, and things got pretty dark for him. Anyway, I never had many complaints. He drew good houses, paid you what he said he was going to pay you, and put the boys up in real hotel rooms — the Marriott or the Red Lion. None of the roadside motor lodge shit you got in some places. Plus, he even had a regional TV deal, which was considered pretty incredible at that time.

Only one thing pissed me off: Baby Jay had stuck me with this terrible good-guy gimmick. He called me "The Real Deal" Dallas Hostettler and made me wear plain blue trunks and cowboy boots with white swirls up the side. I had curly blonde hair and a mustache that wouldn't fill all the way in. I told Baby Jay I wanted to be a bad guy, and he looked at me with his cross-my-heart brown eyes and touched me lightly on the ribs in a way that made me flinch.

"Good-looking kid like you?" he said. "Play the babyface. The girls will eat you up. There won't be a dry seat in the house."

He was right. The girls *did* eat me up. Problem was, girls made up less than twenty percent of Baby Jay's crowd. The other eighty-plus percent were guys, and wrestling guys liked bad boys. Guys didn't want to be like "Real Deal" Dallas Hostettler. They didn't want to wear bland tights and boots with fucking sea swells on them. They wanted to slick their hair and roll cigarettes in the sleeves of their T-shirts like Marlon Brando in *The Wild One*. They wanted to wear black hats and have five o'clock shadow and chase people around with a branding iron like "Maniac" Mack Savage.

For now, I was putting up with being "The Real Deal," the cowboy nobody cared about. I knew if I kept my mouth shut and learned everything I could, my time would come eventually — and there was nobody better to learn from than Mack.

The first night at the Mule Palace, the Friday, we'd lost to The Great Depression in a mix-up. We played it like this: Mack tried to hit one of the Great Depression guys — I think it was the one with the lazy eye — over the head with a folding chair while I held him from behind. At the last minute, the guy squirmed out, and Mack hit *me* with the chair on accident. Then, while he was standing there looking dumbfounded like, 'Oh shit!' the other Great Depression member — the one who always smelled like Vicks VapoRub — drop-kicked him over the top rope. The first guy rolled me up for the one-two-three, and the whole crowd started throwing shit into the ring.

It got people pissed enough to come back on Saturday hoping to see us get our revenge. We did — with Mack hitting his elbow-off-the-top-rope finisher on VapoRub. People ate it up. "Blackout" started blaring, and me and Mack jumped up on opposite turnbuckles and pumped our fists in the air. In the middle of all the madness, Baby Jay hit the ring in his three-piece suit, carrying a stopwatch, waving his arms to cut the music and stop the whole thing. Once it quieted down, he took the mic and announced that the twenty-minute time limit had expired just as Mack had pinned VapoRub — so our team hadn't won after all. The match was declared a time-limit draw. People were livid. There's nothing folks who paid good money to see a wrestling show hate more than a fucking draw.

Sunday night was going to be the blow off. Me and Mack versus The Great Depression for the third straight evening — this time in a no-holds-barred match. The place was already lathered by bell time for the main event. To start the match, I locked up with Lazy Eye in the middle of the ring, and we opened with a little chain wrestling. This was something I was still getting the hang of doing. Lazy had to carry me through it, but he was good enough to make it look like I was getting the best of him.

Afterward, we worked through the standard stages of a wrestling match: From the part where the heels started to build heat by hitting me with a low blow or grabbing the ropes for extra leverage, to a couple of false comebacks by me, to the heel's cheating getting worse and worse until finally the big comeback, where Mack and I turned the tables on them for good. The formula worked like a charm, the older guys keeping things nice and simple for me, leading me by the hand right up to the big finishing sequence. Revving it up and up until the whole crowd was vibrating like a single, living animal, about ready to break through the ringside barriers. That's how hot they were to see me and Mack finally give The Great Depression what they deserved.

The end of the match was set up to look just like the finish from the first one, with me bear-hugging Lazy Eye from behind while Mack wound up to crack the guy's skull with a chair. All over again, Lazy Eye slipped away and bailed out of the ring just as Mack took a mighty cut with the chair. You could hear the whole crowd gasp. This time, though, I ducked out of the way, feeling the chair whoosh over my head. There was a tense moment where we both stared at each other. I pointed my finger in his face as if to say, "You better watch out!" The whole place was on edge, wondering if our alliance was about to implode.

Just then, VapoRub snuck up the ring steps and tried to club Mack from behind with his jug of spirits. I saw him and sprinted past Mack to knock VapoRub off the apron and onto the ground with an elbow smash. Mack turned and caught Lazy Eye also creeping into the ring and laid into him with the chair. The crowd whooped and counted every shot as the chair crashed down across the ghostly miner's back. I waited until Mack was done and then, just as Lazy got to his feet, nailed him with my patented running lariat, putting him right back down in a heap.

Mack said something to me but I couldn't hear him over the roar of the crowd. "What?" I shouted.

He came over and high-fived me. "Point at the corner," he said without moving his lips.

I pointed across the ring at one of the turnbuckles, and the frenzy ratcheted up even higher. Mack threw his hands up and spun a tight circle, then climbed the ropes while I dragged Lazy Eye to the center of the canvas. He crouched up there like a big cat, milking it, before he stretched up to his full height and pointed both fingers in the air.

When Mack jumped it was like the sky opened up. For a moment he was up there with the stars, airborne, before twisting his body in midair and coming down to lance his elbow across Lazy Eye's sternum. I hadn't even noticed how quiet the arena had gotten until the silence was shattered. The sudden boom of the crowd shook the ring. The ref slid in to count the pin, "Blackout" hit the speakers, and Mack and I hugged it out in the middle of everything. Standing in the eye of all that white-hot noise, it felt like we would both live forever and never grow old.

THREE
THE BIG RIGHT HAND

The next day was an off day, and we had a five-hour drive back to Billings in the rental car. The first few hours, Mack was quiet, staring out the window while I drove. I didn't mind it at first. Fact is, every now and then, it was nice when Mack would just let me be inside my own head. I was still climbing a steep learning curve, and every match seemed important to me. I'd sit there replaying each detail in my mind, analyzing it, thinking about what I'd done and what all the other guys had done. What had worked? What had sparked the crowd? What could I have done better? I was obsessed with wrestling. It was all I ever thought about.

After the match the night before, as soon as I got back to the hotel, I had pulled the drapes shut in my room and dumped the contents of Mack's dopp kit out on the bedspread. My hands shaking. My heart thumping. Mack's steroid stash didn't disappoint. It was a fucking treasure trove of performance enhancers. I saw blue tablets of Dianabol, clear vials of liquid Decca, little yellow Stanozolols that seemed to glow like summer sun. There were painkillers, too: Placidyl and Oxycodone, mostly. I sorted out little piles so I could commit it all to memory. There was even some stuff I didn't recognize

— and one thing I knew front to back in those days was drugs, brother. There were big-ass capsules, opaque and glossy midnight blue like some unknown pharmacist had scooped up the meaning of life and dumped it in there.

By morning, one of my eyes had swollen almost shut where Lazy Eye had potatoed me with a punch. It throbbed like a little heart. I thought about popping a Placidyl, but I knew Mack would be waiting for me to carry his bags out to the car. For the moment at least, I had to stay sharp. Couldn't have myself nodding off during the drive. Instead, I went into the bathroom and washed down a D-bol and a Stanozolol. Then I thought, fuck it, and took one of those big blue bastards, too. The mystery pill went down like rock, leaving a funny aftertaste in my mouth, but by the time I left the room, I felt like Superman.

After we got a couple hours into the drive, though, the warm glow in my stomach had gotten uncomfortably hot. It felt like somebody had mounted a crank between my shoulder blades and was slowly winding the tension tighter and tighter across my upper back. My knuckles were white on the wheel, fingers gripping it like a 500-pound deadlift. My teeth clenched so tight I thought they might turn to powder. Jesus, I thought, what the fuck had I taken? I hiked my shoulders, dropped them. Worked my jaw trying to loosen it. Sucked a big breath in through my nose and blew it out my mouth looking for a little release. Nothing seemed to work.

"Our team needs a name," I said to Mack, turning down the radio and glancing across the leather seats at him. I said it just to say *something*, hoping to pop the silence that in the last few minutes had settled over me like a goddamn lead blanket. He was still looking out the window, showing me the back of his head. I tried again. "We gotta get Baby Jay to come up with a name for our team."

Mack puffed a little laugh. "Our team has a name," he said, turning to let me see the white of one eye. "It's called *Appearing Live and In-Person: 'Maniac' Mack Savage. Tonight Only. Card Subject to Change.*"

"Fuck, man, what crawled up your ass this morning?" I asked. "We were great out there last night, Sav. We fucking killed it."

"I killed it," he said. "You stunk up the joint."

The crank on my back clicked a couple notches tighter. "What are you talking about?"

He had a gallon milk jug full of water clutched between his legs. It was one of his big things, making sure he stayed hydrated. He was always telling me it was the secret to staying young. Keep your skin tone, he said. Keep your muscles working. Yeah, that's your secret, I thought. That and a Brazilian bodybuilder named Mauricio who sells you a truckload of every muscle-builder known to man once a month. But I never said that out loud. Mack unscrewed the top of his jug and took a long gurgle of water, like he was trying to compose himself. When he spoke again his voice was a half degree more patient.

"You gotta learn to slow the fuck down, Dally," he said. "Let things breathe. You're always in a rush trying to get from one big power move to the next. You're big and you're quick, but so are half the young guys in Baby Jay's locker room. You want to catch Sal Da Silva's eye? Or Vic Valley? Or somebody in Japan? You gotta connect with the people. Tell a story out there instead of just showing everybody how strong you are, how high you can jump. And for God's sake, could you please stop punching people in the face every five goddamn minutes?"

I opened and closed a fist around the wheel. "But that's one of my signature moves," I said, trying not to sound like a teenager who'd lost his phone privileges. "The big right hand."

"Not anymore it fucking ain't," he said. "I never want to see you throw a punch like that again as long as we're partners. You understand?"

"Sav," I said, "I don't understand what you're so upset about."

He sighed the heavy sigh of a piano instructor whose student had bricks for hands. "For starters," he said, "throwing a closed fist is illegal in professional wrestling, and since you're the babyface, you got no business doing anything illegal. Second, have you looked at yourself in the mirror lately? You look like the baddest thing on two legs, my man. The crowd sees you, they think, 'Look at this big son of a bitch!' Guy like you hauls off and punches somebody in the face? That person ought to be six feet under. That person ought to be knocked the fuck out. So, when the audience sees you stomp your foot and pull up two inches short with one of your shitty-looking hill-billy haymakers, it looks like the lamest thing in the world. You might as well light it up on the side of the Goodyear Blimp: *THIS ... SHIT ... IS ... FAKE!*"

My stomach blanched and I clutched it with one hand, starting to wonder if the continental breakfast at the Edgewater in Missoula had been suspect. "Did you eat the eggs?" I asked. "Christ, those eggs might have been spoiled."

"Every time you do it, you're killing your heat," he said, rolling right along now, "just absolutely killing your heat dead."

"I knew I should've just had the fruit," I said, "maybe some yogurt. Yogurt is, what do you call it? Probiotic. Good for the stom-ach, Mary Lynn says."

"Every time you punch somebody and the guy doesn't fall down? He doesn't even get a black eye? You're telling the audience not to take you serious," Mack said. "So then, ten minutes later, when you do that big running lariat you like so much — guess what? It too looks faker than Liberace's codpiece. Why? Because you just spent the first part of the match teaching the audience that the shit you do in that ring is fake."

I belched up something acidic and swallowed it down. I knew he was right. This was the point where I should have nodded my head and said, "Yes, sir," and let it go. As a rookie, I had no business trying to argue ring psychology with the guy who won the 1977 International Wrestling Grand Prix Tournament in Japan while I was still in high school. But like I said, I was young and dumb. My stomach was going crazy, and he was starting to piss me off. "It's the 1980s, Sav," I told him, trying to laugh and look friendly while keeping watch on the twisting mountain road the rental car had started creeping up. "I'm pretty sure everybody knows wrestling isn't real."

He slapped his palm on the dashboard hard enough to knock the radio off its station. "Fuck what they know," he said, "and fuck what they say to the rest of their pencil-neck buddies at work or school the next morning. For two and a half hours from bell to bell, it's our jobs to convince those people fucking otherwise. And you know something? They *want* to believe."

"I might need to pull over," I said, "find a bathroom."

"When twelve hundred people pay their hard-earned money to drive out to the fucking Mule Palace to watch you wrestle, it ain't for the watered-down Cokes and shitty hot dogs, you understand me? It's because they *fucking love wrestling*," he said. "They're dying to fall in love with us. With *you*, Dally — and it's up to us to sell them that fantasy. Every single thing we do out there in that ring teaches them what to think. So, if they see you do something that looks fake, you're teaching them to think *everything* we do is fake. When they see you break the rules with your so-called big right hand? You're teaching them the rules don't mean a thing."

I felt hot all over. A trickle of sweat ran into one eyebrow. "The rules?" I said. "You're gonna lecture me about the rules? In pro wrestling? Give me a break, Sav."

"Without the rules, you have chaos," he said, starting to list things on his fingers. "And guess what? When chaos reigns, nobody gets to do their stuff. If the rules mean nothing, then the heels can't get heat. If the heels can't get heat, then the babyfaces can't get over. If the babyfaces can't get over, then we don't draw money. And if we don't draw money—"

"'*Then why is Baby Jay booking us in the first place?*'" I said, finishing his point for him. Every time Mack gave me a lecture about the business it always ended with him asking that question.

"Exactly," he said. "You're burying the referee on top of everything else. Show some respect for the man in the striped shirt, Dally. That's the least fucking thing you can do."

I had to chew on that for a second, starting to see his point even though it was the last thing I wanted. "He hit me first, though," I said finally, meaning Lazy Eye. "Potatoed the shit out of me right there in front of God and everybody. I owed him a receipt."

"Oh no," he said, lifting his water to his mouth and almost spilling it when the car hit a bump. "Don't go trying to blame this on Steve and Larry. They busted their asses trying to get us over."

Steve and Larry. *That* was their fucking names. "They take advantage of me," I protested, "because I'm the new guy. Low man on the totem pole. The shit-shoveler."

Mack hunted around the floor for the cap to his jug, couldn't find it and gave up. "Did it ever cross your mind," he said, "that maybe Stevie was trying to *help* you when he hit you like that?"

"Now you've lost me," I said. "How is punching me in the face trying to help me? I'd really fucking love to hear that one."

"Stevie," Mack said, "is creating desire." He tapped the knife blade of his hand on the dash to emphasize his points. "When a heel hits a babyface, the crowd gets hot. The people get riled up. They want to see the babyface get his revenge. They want to see him punch the jerk back. Right?"

"Right," I said.

"So," he said, "if *you* would just slow down for a minute and fucking *sell* the punch like you're supposed to, just let everybody catch their breath, then — when you try to punch the heel back — the ref can do his job. The ref could get between the two of you and hold you back. Because, like I just said, punching somebody with a closed fist is against the rules of professional wrestling, and the rules matter. You follow me? You don't get your chance for instant payback. And what does that do to the crowd?"

"It makes them want to see me hit him even more," I said, starting to get the picture.

Mack snapped his fingers. "Exactly," he said. "Hey, you're not as dumb as everybody says. Once you have that desire? Brother, you milk it. You tease it out as long as you can. Ten minutes? Fifteen minutes? It's a game of emotional keep-away. The fans want to see you punch that bastard, but every time you get close you get denied at the last possible second. You do that two, three, four times. You do it right up to the very point the crowd starts to get sick of it and is about to decide they don't give a shit anyway. You gotta *feel* the crowd, Dally. You gotta walk that tightrope. Tease them just enough to keep them on the hook and then — oh, blessed Jesus — then, when you finally do knock poor Stevie's block off, he goes down in the middle of the ring, spread-eagled, selling the bejesus out of it with his arms flung out and his tongue lolling out of his mouth, the place goes fucking bananas."

As he talked his goofy "Maniac" Mack grin spread across his face. The guy was truly a master orator. I felt myself shifting from annoyed to fascinated. From sick to exhilarated. If at that moment he had whipped out a timeshare contract on a condo in the fucking Antarctic, I probably would've signed.

"And then I get a rub," I said.

"And you get a fucking rub," he said. "So, like I've been trying to tell you this whole time, if you *are* gonna punch somebody in the face, at least have the fucking decency to protect the business and set it up the proper way. That way, when you do it, you get the reward, instead of getting exposed."

"Fuck," I said, mad at myself for being so damn green. "You really think they'd do that for me, though? The Great Depression?"

"I know they would," he said. "I know it like I know my own home phone number. Because they're the fucking heels, and that's their fucking job."

He slapped me on the shoulder so hard it stung. "Fuck," I said again. "You're right."

"Look," Mack said. "I'm going to tell you something I probably shouldn't."

I looked at him. Looked at the road. Looked at him again. "What?" I said.

He sighed. "Young Dallas Hostettler," he said, "you're going to be a big star in this business. A great big star. There's only one thing you gotta do until that happens."

"What's that?" I asked.

"Don't fuck it up."

"Yeah, Sav," I said. "I'll try that."

Fifteen minutes later I had to pull into a truck stop, run in, and puke my guts out in its piss-smelling bathroom.

FOUR

THE DUNGEON MASTER

A horn sounded behind us and snapped me back to the road. After we'd stopped so I could use the restroom, my stomach had settled down and I'd fallen into the rhythm of the drive. Mack had rolled over onto his shoulder, pressed his whiskers into the window and gone to sleep. I'd halfway drifted off myself — not sleeping, exactly — but retreating into my thoughts, going over what I could do to make it up to The Great Depression if I'd offended them. Maybe buy them a bottle of something or a six-pack before the next show. The sudden blast of horn startled me out of it. I checked the rearview mirror and swore under my breath.

I had to say Mack's name three times before he woke, groaning and kneading his bum knee with both hands. "Check this out," I said, nodding at the mirror.

He turned in his seat and peered out the back window. "Oh," he said, "look at these absolute dickweeds."

A white Cadillac — another rental, identical to our own — had come up fast behind us, was now riding our rear bumper. I recognized the pair of heads silhouetted behind the windshield and tried to move over to give them room. We had just passed Butte and were headed up the narrow highway to the continental divide, so there wasn't much space to give them. The Cadillac revved its engine and barreled up beside us, its passenger-side window gliding down. The pudgy, musclebound torso that leaned out belonged to Demian Rex.

"The fucking 'Dungeon Master,'" Mack muttered. "Just in time to fuck up a halfway decent drive."

That summer, Rex was Baby Jay's top heel. The whole program Mack and I had just finished with the Great Depression was designed to build to a singles feud between Mack and Rex over the FSW title. "The Dungeon Master" was a fireplug of a guy, under six feet but still probably 220 pounds. He kept his thinning, jet black hair pulled back in a short ponytail and wore a goatee dyed to match. Even back then he was on the old side, probably pushing fifty. Rex had been kicking around the business since the early seventies and had been working an occult bad-guy gimmick since spending some time with Sunshine State Wrestling down in Florida. He liked to paint an upside-down cross on the middle of his forehead and cake on eye-black until it made points by his ears. To the ring, he wore a hooded, fur-trimmed cloak over a black singlet with a purple lightning bolt blazing across the ass.

Now, Rex wore a black satin jacket with the name of a Tokyo steakhouse stitched above the breast. His black ponytail whipped in the wind as he hung out the open window. He clutched a foaming beer can in one hand. I glanced at the clock on the rental's dash and saw it was 11:30 a.m.

"Good morning, ladies!" Rex shouted over the wind. Behind him, I could see his sidekick, Wayne "The Warlock" Barrow, behind the wheel, grinning like they were about to spring the trap on some master plan.

"Fuck you, Gary!" Mack yelled back, loud enough that I was pretty sure the message got across even at seventy-five miles per hour and through the closed windows of our car.

Rex reared back and hurled the beer across the highway dividing line. The can clunked into the window next to my head, shooting froth all over the side of the rental. I swerved to the right, tires running into the gravel at the edge of the road, and slammed on the brakes, fighting to keep from going all the way into the ditch. The other Cadillac shot ahead of us. As it roared into the distance, Rex turned and flipped us the bird with both hands, his mouth forming cusses lost in the wind.

My heart was going a mile a minute, but when I glanced over at Mack to ask if he was OK, it looked like he'd barely moved. Hadn't grabbed the ceiling handle. Hadn't braced himself against the glove box. "Christ on a crutch," he said, almost smiling, "these mother-fuckers out here living their gimmicks."

"You want me to go after them?" I asked.

"Nah," he said. "We'll catch 'em soon enough. Rex has the bladder of a gnat."

He was right. About an hour later, we spotted the other Cadillac parked behind a gas station at the exit to Three Forks. He slapped my shoulder again and pointed, and I pulled off the interstate. When Rex and Barrow came out of the convenience store a few minutes later, we were waiting for them.

"Well, well, well," Rex said, wiping his hands on his jeans. "If it isn't Laverne and Shirley." He threw a few play punches into my gut as they got close. "That was some nifty driving, Princess. How's the old man treating you? He make you pack his adult diapers to every town? Get you to lick his boots shiny clean after each show?"

"Let the kid alone, Gary," Mack said. "He ain't hardly part of this."

Barrow was wearing a tight pink polo shirt tucked into khaki shorts. He stepped in front of Rex and chested up to Mack. "You got a problem, grandpa?" he asked.

Mack just smiled, looking into the middle distance and touching the tip of his nose with his thumb a few times. "You don't want these problems in your life, boy," he said.

Barrow sneered at him, but I could tell seeing Mack stay so calm gave him second thoughts. Barrow was a big guy, almost as big as me, and just as green. He had no doubt heard the same stories about Mack I had: like the time he burst a young guy's ear drum with a slap backstage in Charlotte. Or the time he fought off a mob in a Kansas City roadhouse using a broken off piece of table leg and a chain wrapped around his fist. Or the time Demian Rex accused Mack of messing around with his wife while the two of them were working for WOW Sports in Minneapolis in the late 1960s. As the story went, Rex had provoked a confrontation with Mack at the rooftop tiki bar of the motel where Vic Valley was putting everybody up. Rex had taken a swing, and Mack had tossed him over the safety rail, two stories down into the motel pool. Rex broke his nose on impact. After a fall like that, I thought the guy was pretty lucky not to come out of it worse off — but he'd hated Mack's guts ever since.

"Call your dog off this hunt, Gary," Mack said to Rex now. "Or I'll shred him like cheddar and sprinkle him on a taco."

I glanced at Rex, who was staring at Mack like he possessed red hot laser eyes. Some people inside the gas station had noticed what was going on and stood behind the big glass windows, watching us. Rex saw them, too. He grunted, giving in, and beckoned Barrow with a two-fingered wave. Barrow stared down into Mack's face for a few extra seconds before walking away. I threw a shoulder into him as he passed, causing him to stumble back a few steps.

"Watch it, fucker," Barrow snarled at me, but I just winked at him, filled with the urge to make him bleed all over that polo shirt.

"Young men," Rex said. "Don't quarrel amongst yourselves. Not in front of regular folks."

Barrow gave me the same hard look he'd given Mack, but eventually returned to Rex's side. As they walked away, Rex turned back to me and called: "You ever want to be more than a glorified bellhop for this old goat, give Baby Jay a call. I'd be glad to smarten you up myself."

I wanted to tell Rex to go fuck himself, but I squeezed my teeth together. It wasn't my place. There was an order to things. If a couple of veterans had heat with each other going back fifteen years and neither of them could get over it, who was I to say anything? If Mack needed me, I had his back. That was about as far as my involvement went.

We got in the car, and Mack nudged me with an elbow. "Back it up," he said. "I want to see the looks on their fucking faces."

I threw the rental into reverse and coasted back twenty feet so we could see the two heels as they approached their Cadillac where it was parked behind the gas station. When they rounded the corner and saw it sitting in the dirt on four flat tires, Mack reached across me and blared the horn. Rex and Barrow spun around, their faces in knots, and it was Mack's turn to extend two middle fingers out his open window.

"Long way back to Billings, boys," he shouted. "We'll see you fucking idiots at TV, if you make it!"

I laid some rubber on the concrete as we took off for the interstate ramp.

FIVE
A VIOLATION OF MY RIGHTS

I had a girl in Billings named Mary Lynn Fawcett. She worked as a nurse at the big hospital downtown. The two of us had met one night after a match where VapoRub had clubbed me with his miner's lantern and I'd gone into the ER to get some stitches over my eye. We'd been dating a couple months since then but had both agreed we weren't looking for anything serious. Mary Lynn had a career and a fifteen-year mortgage in Billings. She was not interested in being a wrestler's wife. I couldn't blame her, and I was fully committed to the traveling life, so we were just wading around together in the shallow end of things. Keeping it casual, as the kids say these days.

Mary Lynn was smart and not afraid to tell me when she thought I was fucking things up with Mack and the boys, and I appreciated that about her. Another good thing: she was not a wrestling fan. That — along with her work schedule — meant she never bugged me about coming out on the road, getting tickets to shows, or hunting for autographs. We hung out on nights when I was in town to tape TV or when Baby Jay had a show booked at the Metra. The evening after our blowoff with The Great Depression, after I had dropped Mack off in the suburbs, I drove straight to her house.

We each drank a beer sitting at Mary Lynn's small kitchen table while I told her about Baby Jay's three-night stand at the Mule Palace and our matches against the heel tag team of undead prospectors. When I told her how Demian Rex and Wayne Barrow had almost driven us off the road, she grabbed my forearm in a way that sent a little wave of electricity through my body. I listened to her stories about the hospital — how the male doctors treated her like the hired help and the patient who had come in high on amphetamines with a knife in his chest and asked for her number before he was discharged.

"I was one of those patients once," I said. "Asking for your number, I mean."

"You didn't so much ask as sweep me off my feet," she said. "And once I found out you weren't going to get me pregnant, I knew you were the man for me."

She meant it as a joke, so I grinned even though part of it stung a little bit. Yes, I'd asked Mary Lynn out on a date just before they'd turned me loose from the E.R. that first night, a black caterpillar of stitches over one eyebrow. She'd agreed, and we'd hit it off right away. After four dates she'd invited me back to her place for the first time, and when I produced the ancient lambskin rubber I carried around in my wallet, she'd just grinned and told me it wasn't necessary. She'd already snooped through my personal file. She knew all about my varicoceles and didn't care. Mary Lynn didn't want kids, said she couldn't imagine bringing children into a world where the Iranian Ayatollah, the soviet Russians and the Red Chinese were just going to end up blowing us all to kingdom come. Anyway, since we had both agreed we didn't see our thing as a serious, marrying-type proposition, it was no big deal.

"You used my private medical information against me," I said to her now, in mock protest. "That's a violation of my rights."

She stretched her leg and prodded the crotch of my shorts with her freshly pedicured toes. "It doesn't feel like you're overly concerned about it," she said.

We went to the bedroom and made love on top of the bedspread.

Mary Lynn hated being on the pill — it messed with her hormones — and my medical condition just meant that so long as we both kept up our pledges to be exclusive, we didn't have to use protection. This was not much of an issue for me. I wasn't like a lot of the young guys who wanted to go out after the shows and meet women. I'd rather have a few beers with Mack, make sure he wasn't going to get himself into any trouble, and then head back to my room so I could get to the gym bright and early the next morning.

Afterward, we lay nude together on the bed watching the low ceiling fan wobble over our heads. I told her about Molly, Mack's wife, and how badly she wanted to have a baby. Mary Lynn made a sad face when I started to tell the story but laughed when I got to the part about Mack going to see the witch doctor.

"What a time to try to start a family," she said. "With nuclear power plants melting down in East Germany? They're hanging teenage girls on the streets of Tehran, did you know that?"

I did not know that, but it didn't surprise me that Mary Lynn did. She was a bit of a news junkie. Her coffee table was always stacked with the latest issues of *Time Magazine*, *U.S. News and World Report* and *The National Review*. I never messed much with that stuff myself, except when I thought it could help me with wrestling. "Last I checked, this is still the U.S. of A.," I said. "Right now, the biggest threat to our freedom is that Mack says Molly keeps asking to invite us over for dinner."

"That might be fun," Mary Lynn said. "I'd like to give this Mack Savage a piece of my mind."

"Word on the street is they might be swingers," I said. "We go up there, there's no telling what we might get ourselves into after the pork chops and corn on the cob."

"Don't make me barf," she said. "It's bad enough you have to drive that old fool all over the mountain time zone."

"Mack's a good guy," I said, "he's just a stickler for tradition, is all."

"He treats you like his own personal bellhop," she said. "You're a grown man, Dallas, not some boy scout who still needs to learn to tie all the right knots. I'll never see how all those fans could pay their hard-earned money just to see a gimpy old graybeard like Mack Savage and not even give you the time of day. You, my red-hot lover."

I felt myself blush. "There's a little thing called paying dues, Mary Lynn," I said. "Mack has been a wrestling legend since you and I were in grammar school. He's had classic matches with all the great ones — Poppy Rose, Sam Styles, probably even old Joe Varga once upon a time. Guy is practically royalty."

"A hundred years ago, maybe," she said. "I just don't think Mr. Chevalier or any of these other local yokels fully understand what they've got in you."

"And what is that?" I said.

"Sweetheart," she said, "I'm a keen observer of the male species and have been my whole life. They don't come any bigger or better looking than you. Plus, you've got a brain."

Now I felt a little fire in my belly. "Well, it's not even really me the people are seeing out there," I said. "They only see 'The Real Deal' Dallas Hostettler, the boringest cowboy who never roped a steer."

"Are you familiar with Henry Kissinger?" she asked.

I let that question hang there for a second. "Vaguely," I finally decided to say.

"Mr. Henry Kissinger once said, 'It is not a matter of what is true that counts, but a matter of what is perceived to be true.' What I mean is, you could be the most interesting man in the world and nobody would ever know it unless they get the chance to see the real you. I think that seems like an awfully difficult proposition with your good buddy Mack Savage sucking up all the oxygen in the ring."

I sighed. It would have been impossible in that moment to try to explain to Mary Lynn all the things Mack was doing for me. We had been talking about it for weeks but she refused to see it. I suppose it's always hard for people who aren't involved in the business to get the whole picture. Hell, sometimes it's hard for the boys themselves to see it. But right then, I felt tired. I wanted to drift off for a few hours before I got up to go to the gym and then to TV.

"I'll tell you what you do," she said. "Tomorrow at your TV taping you walk right into Mr. Chevalier's office, and you tell him the world needs to see the real Dallas Hostettler, not the manufactured version some out-of-touch wrestling promoter came up with to try to swindle thirteen-year-old girls out of their lunch money."

"I appreciate your confidence in me," I said, "but I'm just not sure I'm the right person to deliver that message. Especially considering Baby Jay has also been in the wrestling business about as long as I've been alive."

"The task of the leader is to get his people from where they are to where they have not been," she said. "You know who said that?"

"I'm going to go ahead and guess it was Henry Kissinger."

"That's right," she said and kissed me on the lips.

"Maybe you're right," I said. "And anyway, this is all just for a little while longer. Once Mack's knee is fixed, he'll defend his title against Rex, and he and I will go our separate ways."

"And where will that leave you?" she asked.

"I suppose I'll learn as much as I can while I'm here and when my run in FSW is done, I'll go work another territory. Hopefully, one of the big ones. Peach State Wrestling down south or WOW Sports in Minnesota or the Texas Wrestling Alliance, maybe even UWF out in New York. We'll see what happens."

"And then you'll be gone," she said.

The tone in her voice was more matter-of-fact than upset, but suddenly it felt like a balloon full of tension had inflated in the room. It hovered over us, bumping against the ceiling fan. I felt like I'd made a mistake, said the wrong thing, somehow wandered into some territory I should have avoided if I wanted to keep this night light and friendly.

"We always knew how this was going to go, Mary Lynn," I said, as gently as I could.

"I know that," she said, "but it doesn't mean I can't feel sad about it."

"Yeah," I said. "Me too, I guess."

After that, we lay there in silence until Mary Lynn got up and went to take a shower.

SIX

TEN FEET TALL AND BULLETPROOF

It turned out the gas station where we'd stranded Rex and Barrow had an air compressor onsite, so they made it to TV on time the next day. Still, they were fucking hot about it — staring daggers as Baby Jay called the four of us into his office to talk about the booking for the next few weeks. Baby Jay had bought a warehouse on the outskirts of Billings and converted it into a studio to shoot his weekly wrestling show. He'd hung sparkling gold floor-to-ceiling curtains over the building's corrugated siding and scored a couple of old bleachers from a local high school that was remodeling its gym. The warehouse was a shithole and hot as fuck in the summertime, but it looked great on TV.

"How's that knee?" Baby Jay asked Mack as we all piled into the office. "Everything shipshape and squared away?"

I think Baby Jay had been in the Navy at some point. Guy used a lot of nautical expressions. His office was just an eight-by-eight square framed into the back of the warehouse with studs and particle board. It looked like maybe at one time the place had been a body shop and Baby Jay hadn't bothered to take down the decorations. There were ten-year-old calendars emblazoned with the logos of tire companies and tool manufacturers. A tattered poster showing a woman in a pair of cutoff jean shorts leaning low over the open hood of a muscle car, holding a socket wrench in both palms and winking at the camera. Something about being in there gave me the creeps.

"Getting better every day," Mack said, even though I knew the knee still bothered him like crazy. He stretched his leg out and it made a loud cracking sound.

"We full speed ahead on this singles program?" Baby Jay asked, eyes jumping between Mack and Demian Rex. Rex and Barrow stared at the floor, expressions like they'd rather eat hot dog buns filled with turds than look us in the eye.

"I don't know, boss," Mack cut in. "I could probably take another week."

"Another week?" Baby Jay said, tipping his head back on his shoulders. "Mack, you're killing me here. You're absolutely choking the life out of me."

"We got plenty of time," Mack said. "It's early days yet."

"We've got the Metra booked for end of summer. I already put down a deposit. We need to put five thousand asses in those seats."

"If we book it nice and slow, do things the right way, we'll have them eating out of our hands," Mack said.

"OK," Baby Jay said, holding his palms up like he was trying to think. "OK. We'll do another tag match. Rex and Barrow against Savage and the Princess. It's got to be a hot one, though, fellas. It'll have to have the people climbing up the walls. Can we hack it?"

Everybody nodded.

"Fuckin' A," I said. Maybe I put a little too much force into it. They all turned to look at me. That morning I'd set a new personal best on the bench press at the gym. I had started getting used to the pills Mack had given me. They didn't burn my guts quite as bad anymore, and they made me feel ten feet tall and bulletproof.

"Good," Baby Jay said. His eyes lingered on me a beat longer than the rest, like maybe he could tell something was different about me. When he broke his gaze away, he turned it on Mack and Rex. "What about you two fuckin' idiots? Can we get through a hot little singles run here without nobody getting tossed off a fucking motor lodge? Without nobody getting their fucking rental car vandalized? We're professionals, yes? We'll do what's best for business? What gets everybody's little kiddies the best Christmas they ever had by the end of this year of our lord, 1983?"

"Sure thing, boss," Mack said.

"Sure," Rex said, "assuming everybody minds their manners."

The way he emphasized the word "everybody" brought Mack up out of his seat. "You've got a lot of nerve, you know that, Gary?" he said.

Rex stood up and then the two old-timers went nose-to-nose in the middle of the booker's office. A couple of aging lions snorting and snapping their jaws. "You think I'm scared of you, Savage?" Rex asked, hiking up his shirt to show the thin pink scar along the lower part of his abdomen. "When they already slashed me with a knife?"

Rex was always going on about how The Dungeon Master gimmick had gotten him so much heat that at one point some mark had gone after him with a blade. The scar didn't look like much to me, if I'm being honest. Just a little nick barely visible underneath his tan. It could have just as easily been a catscratch as anything else. At that moment, I didn't have time to contemplate it. Barrow flew up out of his seat and shoved Mack so hard he stumbled back against the wall on his bum leg. The whole little structure shook, one of the old girlie posters ripping loose from its thumbtacks.

I shot to my feet and grabbed Barrow by his face. I squeezed and watched his eyes bug out. Then everybody was pushing and shoving, a tangle of arms and legs and shouts. Too many clowns stuffed inside a jack-in-the-box. The office door flew open, and Steve and Larry from The Great Depression started pulling us apart. I let them drag me halfway out before I let go of Barrow's face. Saw a thin trickle of blood running down from his earlobe.

"Fuck you, Hostettler," he screamed, but more out of pain than anger. When I looked back at Baby Jay, he'd jumped all the way up onto his desk to get out of the line of fire and crouched there with his hands hanging down around his feet like some kind of chimpanzee.

It took a while to get everybody calmed down and herded behind the backstage curtain so they could let fans in for the TV taping. It only took about fifty people to fill the two bleachers, and FSW could almost always draw that many back in those days. The building was small enough that it looked packed on TV. There were some characters that turned out for every show. A pair of sisters who dressed like nuns. An old grandpa with Coke bottle glasses who occasionally had to be restrained by the ushers to keep from going over the rail after the heels. One really fat guy who always got the same seat. A guy who wore an actual, honest-to-God barrel instead of a shirt and pants.

That week's half-hour show had two matches and, to be honest with you, I don't remember them. The point of the episode was to build to the last two minutes, when Demian Rex and Wayne Barrow hit the ring to cut a promo kicking off their feud with Mack and me. They sent The Great Depression out first to break up whatever match was underway and clear the ring. Then Rex and Barrow made their slow walk from the back, their dark, orchestra theme music playing on Baby Jay's shitty in-house sound system. Rex had the fur-trimmed hood of his robe pulled up over his head and carried a wooden staff carved in the shape of an Egyptian ankh. The staff was taller than he was. As I watched from a spot behind the curtain, I thought I would've asked Baby Jay to get me a shorter staff — one that didn't make me look so tiny. Barrow came in behind him wearing a dog collar and with his hair plastered down over his face so it came to a point in the middle of his chest. Couple of weirdos.

It took them a full minute to get to the ring, pausing to give a couple of kicks to the jobbers The Great Depression had tossed over the ropes. When they got there, Barrow slumped against one turnbuckle like a sulky teen. Steve and Larry loitered in the back doing their part, looking massive. When Rex asked for the microphone, Baby Jay did a good job acting scared, like he didn't want to hand it over. Finally, Rex stormed over and grabbed the mic out of his hand.

"Shut up, cretins," Rex said to quiet the scattered boos. "Shut up, and tremble before our assembled greatness."

The only light in the house was the spot mounted on the ceiling of Baby Jay's office. It held Rex in its white-hot cone while Barrow and The Great Depression stayed in the shadows. Even I had to admit, it lent a fairly creepy feeling to the climax of the show. Mack stood next to me behind the curtain, and I could still feel waves of anger coming off him. He hadn't had much to say since the tussle in the office.

"Now, you feeble mortals know the mighty 'Dungeon Master' Demian Rex has spent most of his life consorting with dark spirits," Rex said. He'd brought his voice down half an octave from normal, a gravely rumble by the time it was transmitted through the speakers. He went slowly, enunciating every word. Truth was, he was pretty good on the mic.

"Look at this third-person motherfucker," Mack mumbled beside me.

"As of late," Rex said, "the dark forces of the shadow world have been filled with discontent. The spirits are restless — so upset are they by the current state of affairs in Frontier States Professional Wrestling. As such, the various ghouls and ghosts who commune with us during our regular rituals and seances have filled my mind with sinister thoughts. I am tormented beyond belief. Haunted by images so ugly and violent they bother even me. And, cretins, let me tell you, it takes a lot to trouble 'The Dungeon Master' Demian Rex."

The crowd, which had been sitting quietly, rapt by Rex's speech, gave that last line a couple of laughs, but Rex silenced them with a chop of his hand.

"Quiet!" he yelled. The force of it made the audience sit back in their seats and prompted Barrow to leave his perch in the corner. He and The Great Depression slowly began to close ranks until they formed a half circle around Rex, their faces eerie in the light of the spot. "I can't eat! I can't sleep! The spirits have entrusted me with an unholy mission. They won't let me rest until I put an end to the things that distress them. So now I've got something to say."

Up to this point, Rex had kept his hood pulled up. He'd been talking down into the microphone like a drunk looking for wisdom in his drink. Now, he swept the hood off and threw back his head, revealing a face caked in white make-up, with deep black circles around his eyes and a blood red pentagram drawn across his forehead. Even I caught my breath a little bit.

"'Maniac' Mack Savage!" He crowed, bringing his voice up to a thunderous boom. "Drag your sorry carcass out here and face me. And bring along that big gorilla you call a bodyguard, 'The Real Deal' Dallas Hostettler, while you're at it."

The crowd gasped. I don't think they saw this coming. Personally, I didn't care for the way Rex put a little extra sneer around the words "Real Deal," but that was our cue. The audio guy gave it a few seconds to let the tension build and then the opening riff of "Blackout" blared across the studio. When Mack and I ducked through the curtain, the cramped building came alive. People ran up to the flimsy railings, waiting to slap our hands, but for the moment we stayed on the small, elevated stage just beyond the curtain. Mack had this thing he could do with his eyes — they seemed to take on an extra sheen. Baby Jay scurried up to hand him another microphone, and the crowd could hardly contain itself as he lifted it to his lips and said, "Well, well, well, if isn't 'The Dog Catcher,' Demian Rex. You got something you want to tell me, boy?"

That's how easy it was for him. Just a simple line like that and it had the whole place hooting like it was the funniest shit they'd ever heard. I looked at him and mouthed the words, "Dog Catcher?" He just shrugged. In the ring, Rex was livid, slapping the ropes and stalking back and forth as Barrow and The Great Depression tried to calm him down.

"Savage," he said, then had to take a few more seconds to get himself together. "Savage, you broken-down old halfwit. You've angered the forces of evil with the way you've paraded around with that championship title these past few months. You're arrogant, Savage. You're careless. I tried to have members of my flock take care of you, but you used that big ape next to you — just like you've used everyone else in your life — and you escaped by the skin of your teeth. Well now, Savage, I see I have to handle things myself. I'm full of the power of my spirits, full of power from the beyond, and I'm going to harness it, I'm going to use it, and I'm going to take that Frontier States Professional Wrestling title from around your waist and bring it home to my dungeon family, where it rightfully belongs!"

Mack looked at me and winked. "Is that so?" he said.

"It is so," Rex said. "I challenge you to a match, Mack Savage, next month at the Billings Metra Arena — and I demand that it's a steel cage match, to keep your big bodyguard from saving your bacon one more time. I'll have your head, Savage! I'll pry that massive cranium right off your shoulders with these two hands!"

Mack stepped down off the stage onto the concrete aisle. "Well, in that case," he said, "I accept!"

The mic made a loud THUMP and then a screech of feedback as he dropped it and took off for the ring. I was a step behind him, pushing past The Great Depression to get my hands on Barrow. He and I started brawling against the barrier and he let me have a couple stiff ones in the ribs. That was fine; I had them coming after the confrontation in Baby Jay's office. All the same, I put a little extra oomph on it when I planted one of my boots in the middle of his stomach. Over Barrow's shoulder, I could see Mack and Rex having a similar throwdown on the floor against the ring apron. I pushed Barrow back until all six of us were just a tangle of arms and legs. A second later, the whole locker room emptied out through the curtain.

It was a complete schmoz. Rough hands tried to drag Barrow and I off each other, but we were locked together in a death embrace. A young babyface tag team with rock 'n' roll bandanas tied over their heads had isolated The Great Depression near the ring steps and were getting after them with punches and kicks. Mack and Rex had crashed into the announcers' table, sending one of Baby Jay's TV guys sprawling out of his chair. From somewhere in the mass of bodies, I could hear Baby Jay himself yelling into his mic about pandemonium breaking loose. Barrow and I were brawling near the barricade, and just as I let the other guys pull me off him, I saw we were right in front of the old grandpa who came to every show. The guy was staring at Barrow like he wanted to kill him. Then he reared back and threw a full tub of popcorn. The wrestlers pulled me back, the tub whistled by my head and hit Barrow square in the face, sending an explosion's plume of yellow kernels into the air.

It was, to put it lightly, a mess. The younger guys all had to stick around after the taping to clean up, while the veterans went home. We had a drive into North Dakota the next day, so everyone else was in a hurry to get out of there. I took my time pushing a wide broom around the ringside area, so it was just me and Baby Jay left in the studio by the time I sauntered over and knocked on the doorway to his office.

When he saw me standing there, he threw up his hands like he thought I might be there to cause more trouble. He knew I wasn't, but Baby Jay liked to pull your leg. "You know," he said as I came in and sat down, "they say Ace Easton, the booker down in Los Angeles, keeps a .38 special in his desk?"

"That a fact?" I said.

"Of course, Ace runs a slightly different kind of business than I do," Baby Jay said and waggled his eyebrows like Groucho Marx. "More unseemly characters coming in and out, if you catch my drift. Anymore, though, I'm wondering if he isn't onto something, keeping a bit of iron handy."

"About that," I said, "I wanted to say I was sorry, boss, about earlier. What happened in here was uncalled for. The booker's office ought to be sacred, and —"

I stopped when I noticed him smiling at me. "I'm just messing with you, sailor," he said. "Shit, this isn't the first time a couple of hardheads have had a dust-up in here. The point is, what happens inside these four walls stays here, you understand?"

I nodded to say I did, and then we sat there staring at each other for a moment before Baby Jay cleared his throat. "Is there anything else I can do for you, son?" he asked.

The old metal chair squeaked as I shifted my weight. "So, it's Mack versus Demian Rex at the end-of-summer blowout show," I said.

"That's right. That's the draw."

"Where will I be while all this is happening?"

Baby Jay laughed. "Well, you'll be in Mack's corner, of course," he said, "standing by to make sure no members of Rex's nefarious dungeon family can sneak up and do anything — I don't know — fuckin' nefarious."

"And what about after?"

"I'm sorry?"

"What about after?" I said again. "What happens to me after Mack's knee is healed up and he goes back to full time singles competition? Do you have something in mind for me? Some creative direction I should be getting ready for?"

Baby Jay blinked and ran one palm all the way from the top of his head to his chin. "Mr. Hostettler," he said, like a professor lecturing an arrogant freshman. "Can I ask you something? How long have you been in this business?"

"About a year," I said. "Year and a half."

"About a year, year and a half," he repeated. "Would you say you've learned a lot?"

"Sure," I said. "Mack has been teaching me —"

"Well," he said, "I can see there is one virtue you have *not* yet learned — and that is the virtue of patience."

"Oh," I said, swallowing, "OK."

"Patience is perhaps the most important trait for a young wrestler trying to make his way in this business," he said.

"I see." My face started to get hot.

"You know I have twenty-one wrestlers under contract in this territory right now?" Baby Jay said. "Every one of them is after me to be part of the next hot angle. What's happening after summer? What's happening in the fall? It's like keeping a dozen plates spinning at all times. If there were two of me, I couldn't keep up. So, you want to know what FSW has planned for you after the summer? The honest to God truth is, I have no idea."

"I understand," I said, though it felt like somebody had pulled the plug out of me and let all the air out.

"Dallas, you're a good kid," he said. "You've handled everything we've thrown at you so far. But you're so damn wet behind the ears you look like we just pulled you out of the surf. Just, you know, relax a little bit. Things will happen for you if you sit back and let them."

"Yes, sir," I said. "I just thought—"

"And, well, the beauty of it," Baby Jay said, "is if you don't like how we're booking you here, there's a great big world out there. A lot of territories. If you think you could do better somewhere else, I'd be more than happy to shake hands, cut you loose and wish you the absolute best in your future endeavors. Is that the direction you want to go with this?"

Well, shit. This wasn't how I'd seen this conversation playing out in my head. "No sir," I said. "I think I'm in a pretty good spot here, all things considered."

"At least we agree on that," Baby Jay said. "Now beat it, kid, before I have to open up my bottom drawer and whip out my six-shooter."

SEVEN
A PACK OF SMOKES

There was a cowboy bar called Duelin' Dalton's where Mack liked to go whenever we worked Bismarck. The bar's owner — an actual dude named Dalton — kept an autographed eight-by-ten of Mack behind the bar and always made sure our drinks were fresh. Mack usually soaked up the attention like a champion hog at the county fair, but two nights after our TV taping with Rex and Barrow, he was fucking morose. He smiled for pictures with some girls early in the evening, but after a couple whiskey shots with beer backs, he sank into himself. Quiet. Not like the "Maniac" Mack I knew at all. I always had a hard time keeping up with his drinking, but that night he was throwing them back at about a three-to-one pace compared to me.

"What's the matter with you?" I asked, after watching him stare at a spot on the bar between his hands for a full minute. There were little pinpricks of stubble up and down his forearms.

That night, we'd wrestled a young heel tag team called the Disaster Brothers. Just a couple of guys in black bodysuits and yellow masks. Crunch and Dasher, or some shit like that. The gimmick itself was just a placeholder while Baby Jay tried to figure out what else to do with them. I have no idea if either of them ever caught on in the business, just that the Disaster Brothers was only a thing for a grand total of about eight months. That night, Mack and I had handled them pretty easily, with him hitting his elbow off the top rope on one guy just as I folded the other guy into origami with my running lariat. But as Mack scored the pin fall on his Disaster Brother, Rex and Barrow hit the ring and laid a steel chair across my back. They'd gone after Mack next, but he saw them just in time and scooted out under the bottom rope. After that, Rex and Barrow had stomped on me for a while before Rex got on the mic and taunted Mack, saying he'd take the title from him during their match at the Metra.

When I asked Mack what was bothering him, I felt a tickle of worry scoot down my back. I assumed it was something I did — or something I didn't do. I was afraid he'd launch into another lecture about how I didn't sell this move properly or didn't anticipate that swing in the crowd's attention. But instead he rolled his big, melon head in my direction and peered at me like a cowpoke trying to find his way through a rainstorm.

"Baby Jay is going to job me out to Demian Rex," he said.

For a second, I thought I'd misheard him. "What?" I said. "Like hell he is."

"Think about it," Mack said, sounding even drunker than I'd thought he was. "Who got the upper hand at TV?"

"It was kind of a draw, I guess," I said.

"And who ended the night on top tonight?"

"They did," I said, feeling one hamstring throb where Rex or Barrow—I didn't know which—had stomped me for real. "But that don't mean nothing, Sav. Baby Jay's just building heat for the title match."

"Bullshit," he said. He started ticking points on his fingers again. "Our tag match next week will end some kind of fucking noncommittal way, count-out or disqualification or time-limit draw. Week after that, probably you and Barrow have a match where you go over."

I had my beer halfway to my lips, but I set it down. "Me and Barrow?" I said. "In a singles match?" It had been a long time since

I'd had a singles match, let alone one where I had been booked to go over. Just the possibility of it made me feel like my heart had cracked open and let a bunch of sunlight out.

"Fucking shut up and listen to me," Mack said. "Yes, you'll go over, and we'll end the show in the ring while Rex and Barrow hightail it out of there and the whole place goes crazy. It'll get everybody charged up to watch the big show at the Metra, and then," he dragged his thumb across his throat, "the big swerve — and that'll be the end for 'Maniac' Mack Savage in this neck of the woods."

"You're just being paranoid," I said.

"It's paint-by-numbers booking," he said. "It's booking 101."

"Baby Jay might be a lot of things, but he ain't dumb," I said, "and it'd be dumber'n hell to take the title off you and put it on a guy like Rex."

"Baby Jay thinks I'm too broke down to be the lead dog anymore," he said. His eyes were red. He slammed back a shot and then squinted down the barrel of his half empty beer. "Maybe he's onto something."

"Screw that," I said. "I won't let it happen."

He laughed. "What are you gonna do?" He asked. "Turn it into a shoot? Use one of those long monkey arms to reach out and trip Demian Rex at the exact right moment? You crack me up, kid. You're all right."

"You ever hear of Henry Kissinger?" I asked him.

"Dally," he said, cutting me a look, "I swear to Holy God in heaven if you lay any of Mary Lynn's greeting card bullshit on me right now I will kill you where you sit. Just let an old man wallow in his misery."

He slammed another shot.

"Hey," I said, "you're the champion of FSW. You're Mack fucking Savage. You ever consider acting like it?"

For a second he looked like he might knock me off my barstool even without me handing out any Henry Kissinger quotes. Then a sly grin broke across his face. "Get the car, Princess," he said, polishing off the dregs of his beer. "Let's get the hell out of here."

I sat out in front of Duelin' Dalton's with the motor running for five minutes, but Mack never came out. When I pushed through the double saloon doors into the barroom, I found it deserted except for the bartender and a couple of women shooting pool. I went into the back hallway and poked my head into the restrooms, but they were empty. There was a rear exit at the end of the hall that took me out into the parking lot where I'd gone to get the car in the first place. Dark and quiet now. A couple hundred yards out I could see traffic storming by on the interstate. I had visions of Mack wandering out there and getting hit by a car. I turned to head back into the bar when I caught sight of his two cowboy boots sticking out from behind the soda pop machine at the far end of the building.

I walked over and leaned over him. Mack lay on the pavement, his head and shoulders pushed against the bar's exterior rear wall. It looked like he'd slipped into the narrow gap between the soda and cigarette machines and gotten himself wedged in there. I said his name and he looked up at me, an expression on his face like he'd put himself down for a nap and wanted to know why I would disturb him.

"Fuck are you doing?" I asked him.

He looked around, noticing the sides of the two machines for the first time. "Trying to get a pack of smokes," he said. "Fell."

He grabbed my hand and I wrenched him free, sat him down on a parking block while I fished out my wallet and bought him a pack of Marlboros. It didn't look like he'd hurt himself too bad. Maybe scraped up one elbow, but that could've happened during our match with the Disaster Brothers. I put one of the cigarettes between my lips, lit it, and then handed it to him. He hauled himself up and made it three steps before he almost fell again. I fit myself under his arm and half dragged him back to the Cadillac.

"You're a good friend, Dally," he said to me as I swung him down into the seat.

"You're drunk, Sav," I said.

"Still."

When we made it back to the motel, I pulled the rental right up to the door of Mack's room. It seemed like he'd gotten heavier during the ride. It was tough to get the motel door unlocked with him hanging off me like he was. After dropping the key twice, I'd finally got the damn thing halfway into the lock when the door flew open and we found ourselves face to face with Molly, standing there in the doorway wearing a pink satin robe open over a set of black lingerie.

"Fucking hell," I said. "You scared the shit out of me."

She stood there in the doorway smiling at us like we were the sorriest couple of assholes she'd ever seen in her life. "Surprise," she said to Mack, who was so close to passing out he barely noticed she was there.

She stood aside while I lugged him in and stretched him out on the bed. The TV was on, showing an old movie. There was a paperback detective novel open on the bedside table and a Virginia Slim burning in the ashtray.

"Must have been some party," she said.

I tried not to look at her. "I'll just get his bag from the car," I said.

When I brought the bag back, Mack had rolled onto his stomach and seemed to be asleep. Molly had retrieved her cigarette and stood smoking against the far wall with her backside propped on the edge of the air conditioning unit.

"Sorry about this," I said, setting the bag in the room's small closet, making sure Mack's hat and the velvet sack he used to carry the title belt were laid out neatly on top.

"He's going to kill himself, you know," she said.

"How's that?" I said.

"He's going to kill himself," she said again. "Maybe not in the traditional way. Not in the slit-your-wrist-in-the-bathtub sort of sense, but he'll get the job done eventually."

"He just had one too many is all," I said. I didn't want to look at her in just her robe and underwear, so I kept my eyes on the floor. "All in all, I don't think he's too bad off."

"You don't see him the way I see him," she said. "He comes home from the road, he can barely get around the house. Drags himself from the bed to the hot tub and back again."

When I finally did look at her, the expression on her face was so sad, it made my skin feel like it was burning, a thousand degrees. Back then, I bet she was only mid-thirties, probably a good twenty years younger than Mack, but something about her seemed older to me. She made me feel like I was just a big, dumb kid. "Well," I said, hitching my thumbs in my belt loops in a way I hoped didn't look as sheepish as I felt. "It can be a pretty rough business, I suppose."

"He had to see a doctor about his kidneys," she said. "I bet he didn't tell you about that one, did he? His liver function's not great. That knee is bone-on-bone."

"Yes ma'am," I said, not sure what else to say. I was starting to feel like I needed to get out of there.

She pushed away from the air conditioner and stubbed her cigarette out in a cut glass ashtray. The smells of the smoke and her perfume were strong in the air. She went to a suitcase and pulled out a set of plaid flannel pajamas. "Back when I first met him?" she said, nodding to where he lay sprawled on the bed. "Why, I thought he was the most dashing, exciting man I'd ever met. But this life is just taking him apart piece by piece. I tell him to stop it. I beg him, really, but it's no use. This is the only thing he's ever known. He says to me, 'What's Mack Savage without that ring? Just some old cowpoke who never worked an honest day in his life.'"

"I really don't know if it's as bad as all that," I said. "He's still got some good years left, I think."

She practically laughed at that. "Years?" she said. It looked like she was searching her mind for some reasonable way to respond to my stupidity but couldn't find it. "Well, thanks for getting him home. He's lucky to have you."

"Yes, ma'am," I said again. "Sorry you got all dressed up for nothing."

She smiled at that, at least. "Good night, Dallas," she said, heading for the bathroom.

"Good night."

I hauled ass out of there. Got five steps down the walkway toward my own room before I noticed I still had Mack's key clutched in one hand. Fuck that, I thought, do no go back there. In my own room, I unzipped my jacket and sat on the edge of the bed, feeling like I couldn't get enough air in my lungs. Mack's dopp kit was on the bedside table and I rifled through it until I found a benzo cap. I bit a corner off it and stretched out on the bed with my shoes still on, promising myself I would still make it to the gym in the morning.

I was going to need to lift something heavy.

EIGHT
THE HOT TAG

The next week at TV, Baby Jay announced he wanted our tag match to be a double DQ. The four of us were in his office again, working out how it would go. Mack and I had spent the rest of the previous week working the Disaster Brothers, doing different variations of the same match and the confrontation with Rex and Barrow in Bismarck, Fargo, Grand Forks, and Minot, before heading back to Billings. Molly stayed with us the whole way, riding in the back of the rental car, eating with us at restaurants and hanging out backstage during events. If she felt strange or embarrassed about airing her concerns about Mack to me that night at the motel, she never let on. At TV, when Baby Jay started making plans for the double DQ, I glanced over and Mack arched one eyebrow at me as if to say: *I told you so.*

I still wasn't sure he had it schemed out totally right. Every time I looked at Rex, it made me feel physically ill. It was hard to believe Baby Jay would willingly put the strap on this fat little balding dude who looked like the drummer from a bad heavy metal band. He was just as old as Mack, if not a few years older. Meanwhile, his sidekick Barrow was as big as an ox and just as dumb: the guy had a hard time remembering the simplest series of moves. *Tackle, drop down, leapfrog*—five times out of ten Barrow would get lost somewhere in the middle. The other five, even if he made it through the sequence, he'd be so terrified of fucking up, he'd be as a stiff as a robot running out of oil.

The way Baby Jay wanted to play it was this: Near the end of our TV match, we'd do a ref bump. I'd hit Rex with a lariat, and then Mack would drop the elbow on him for good measure. Mack would go for the cover, but there would be no ref to count it and, meanwhile, Barrow would club me over the back with a folding chair. When Mack saw that, he'd lose his shit and go after Barrow with his branding iron. The referee would come to just in time to see me lying on the canvas, Barrow holding the chair and Mack swinging at him with the iron. He'd call for the bell, rule the match a double disqualification — and we would all brawl it out until after the show went off the air.

"Simple enough," Baby Jay said, clapping his hands. "Any questions?"

"I don't like it," Mack said. "It makes us look weak."

"Savage," Barrow groaned, "have you ever had a booking you didn't bitch about?"

"It makes you look weak, too, you dumb sack of dicks," Mack said. "All this business with the chairs and the branding irons. Are we not professionals? Can we not build heat with a simple wrestling match? If people wanted to see all this weaponry, they'd have dinner at Medieval Times."

"Easy now," Baby Jay said. "Let's not get into another pier six brawl situation here. My heart can't take it."

"It's your damn branding iron," Barrow muttered under his breath.

"I said, shut it," Baby Jay said. "This is how we're doing it. We've got a twelve-minute TV main event to work with here, not a fucking James Clavell novel. We're doing the ref bump, chair shot, and branding iron. That's my call, and last I checked I was still running this territory. People will love it. Right after the show, we'll announce

Barrow versus Hostettler for next week and ten percent off tickets to the Metra for the blow off for anybody who buys right now at the FSW box office. We'll have money flying out the windows. It'll be like a goddam money tornado in here."

"Me and Barrow?" I said. "Next week?"

"How about that, Princess?" Baby Jay said, chucking my chin with his knuckles. "First singles main event for both you little diaper babies, if I'm not mistaken."

Barrow and I locked eyes, and it felt like something unspoken passed between us. We didn't like each other, but that had more to do with shit between Mack and Demian Rex than anything personal between the two of us. I thought he was a dumb fuck. He probably thought I was conceited and pampered and got opportunities I didn't deserve. Maybe we both had a point. Behind his flinty stare, he nodded to me, each recognizing the opportunity we had in front of us. The TV main event on the go-home show before Baby Jay's biggest card of the year. It blew anything either of us had done in wrestling up to that point out of the water. Plus, there would be tape. Tape that we could send along to other bookers in other territories when our runs ended in FSW. It was all there for the taking, and we'd be a couple of goddam fools if we let two bickering old men egg us into fucking it up somehow. I nodded back at him.

When I looked at Mack, he had his head down, fiddling with the dials on his expensive watch. I remembered what he'd predicted to me that night in the bar in Bismarck and felt a rush of guilt beneath my excitement, knowing it was all coming true. Still, Baby Jay wouldn't really job him out to Rex, I thought. I looked at the other veteran, who seemed oblivious to Mack's funk. He looked from me to Barrow, grinning like a proud father.

"It truly brings a tear to my eye," Rex said, "to see you dipshits grow up so fast."

"Let's go, Dally," Mack said, hefting himself to his feet.

That night, we went on last, right after the Disaster Brothers defeated the Great Depression in a short tag match. Baby Jay was trying out the Disaster Brothers as babyfaces, and it seemed to go pretty well. The crowd was hot by the time Mack and I hit the ring. Rex and Barrow were waiting for us, coiled up together in the far corner like a couple of rattlesnakes. Mack's knee was close to being one hundred percent, so he said he wanted to start things off. That was fine by me. The upcoming singles match against Barrow was still be-bopping around my head, and I relished the chance to stand on the apron and soak up the atmosphere.

Rex and Barrow spent the first half of the match isolating Mack on their side of the ring. It was classic tag psychology stuff. They kept Mack grounded, making quick tags and mixing in a couple of hope spots where he either got off an offensive move of his own or got close to making it across the ring to tag me in, only to have one of the heels drag him back. I had to admit, Rex and Barrow worked pretty well as a team. Rex plodded around the ring like a little penguin, but his power moves looked impressive. When he tagged Barrow in, the younger guy would vault into the ring over the top rope.

With about two minutes left in the match, Mack finally hit Rex with a solid knee to the midsection and broke away, diving across the ring to slap my hand for the hot tag. The crowd went off like fireworks, and I hopped over the top rope to let Barrow know he wasn't the only one who could do that. I hit Rex with a full speed running lariat and in the process knocked the referee into a turnbuckle and flat onto his back. With the ref out, I turned and gave Barrow, who was still on the ring apron, the big boot right to the face and sent him twisting to the floor. I double-pumped my fists in the air, and the roar was so loud I thought the windows might blow out. The crowd lifted me up and carried me on its shoulders, filling me with a kind of pride I'd never felt before. It put a warm charge in my belly and a tingling from my fingertips to my scalp. I wanted to stay in the moment, let it guide me like the current of a river from one high to the next.

Then I heard the guy who wore the barrel instead of a shirt yell, "Kill that son of a bitch!"

I looked over my shoulder and saw Mack climbing to the top

rope, making slow progress on his bum knee. Rex sprawled in the middle of the ring, arms and legs flung out, eyes closed. From the corner of my eye, I saw Barrow pick himself up off the floor and go hunting for a folding chair. What happened next, I still can't really explain.

Barrow tossed the timekeeper aside and snatched his chair, causing a swell of jeers from the people around the ringside area. I turned away, pointing my finger at Rex to tell him that's what he got for messing with Savage and "The Real Deal." I waited for the impact of Barrow laying that folding chair across my back, but it never came. Instead, I heard a loud *CRACK!* and turned to see Barrow up on the ring apron. Instead of sliding back into the ring to hit me with the chair, he'd jumped up and whacked Mack across the thigh, ass and lower back. Mack, who perched unsteadily on the top rope, didn't know the shot was coming and it knocked him off balance.

He reached down to try to steady himself but couldn't hold it and pitched forward, ass over everything. One of his legs — the good one — got tangled in the ropes and he came down in the ring with his full weight on the other, surgically repaired knee. His yelp was clear as day over the crowd noise. I watched the leg buckle and had to swallow back my dinner at the way it contorted. Mack fell forward against the ropes, then down to the mat on his ribs and shoulder. No break-fall, nothing, just down like a sack of potatoes. To this day, it was one of the worst falls I've ever seen. He groaned and clutched his knee with both hands in a way that told me he was really hurt. Hurt bad. Of course, the crowd didn't know any difference. They went right on screaming.

Barrow hopped back down to the floor, and I took two steps to follow him, intent on going out and beating that man to death with my bare hands. Then I felt Rex rush up behind me and hit me with a double-axe-handle across the back. I reared up, selling it despite the chaos, and Rex grabbed a handful of my hair. He turned me to face him. "Go down, kid," he said into my ear, just before he popped me with a smooth uppercut.

I flopped onto my back and rolled to my side, turning so I could see Mack crumpled in the corner. His eyes were pinched shut, one tear leaking out. Above us, Rex beckoned Barrow back into the ring, and they lifted their fists in the air as the boos plummeted down around them. I rolled onto my hand and knees and spoke into a place between my forearms. "Mack?" I said. "You OK?"

"I'm fucked up, Dally," he said, somehow not moving his lips, though I could tell he was in agony.

"Can you get to the iron?"

"I ...," he tried straightening his leg and winced. "I don't know."

"I'm gonna call for the doc," I said.

"No," he said. "Fuck that. I can do it."

He grabbed the middle rope with one shaky hand and dragged himself to a sitting position. Rex noticed and steered Barrow so the two of them were facing the opposite way, jawing with fans in the front row. Mack reached down and snagged the branding iron from where he'd leaned it against the corner of the ring. He moved slow, like it was taking everything he had just to pull it up and lay it across his lap. His face was pale and slick with sweat. For the first time since we'd be riding and wrestling together, I saw what Molly saw in him — a guy nearing the end. Hooking his fists around the top rope, he took a deep breath and yanked himself to his feet.

The crowd popped huge when Mack vaulted up, and I saw the crazy "Maniac" Mack look come back into his eyes. I stood too as he hobbled across the ring, swinging the branding iron over his head with one hand. At the last moment, Rex and Barrow spun around and saw us coming. Rex dropped flat and rolled out under the bottom rope, Mack just barely missing him with a wild cut. I grabbed Barrow by the shoulder and potatoed him right across the bridge of the nose with a closed fist. He cried out and stumbled back, a rope of blood splattering on the canvas.

"What the fuck, Hostettler?" he said.

I took a step toward him and cocked my fist. The crowd went crazy for me to hit him again. "Get out of here you dumb son of a bitch," I growled. Barrow was already moving, hopping down from the ring and to follow Rex as they retreated up the ramp. Mack was standing at the edge of the ring, triumphantly holding the branding iron high and leaning heavily on the top rope. I went to him and he threw an arm around my shoulders.

"I'm fucked, Dally," he said. "My leg is gone."

I looked at the ring steps and the long walk back up to the curtain. The noise in there was still deafening. "How we gonna get you out of here?" I asked.

He winked at me and grinned at the audience. If you didn't know, you'd think he'd just won the fight of a lifetime. "Slowly," he said, "and real damn careful."

NINE
THE THING THAT KILLS ME DEAD

I'd promised to take Mary Lynn out for dinner that night at a restaurant called The Bucking Horse. It was the sort of place where the waiters wore fringed vests and the chandelier in the center of the dining room was fashioned from a big, old wagon wheel. If you wanted honey on your biscuits, they'd bring a ladder out and pour it down from about eight feet up. I don't know what the point of that was, exactly, but it was a pretty cool trick. I liked the food and had been looking forward to spending some time with Mary Lynn, but after the TV taping, going on a date was honestly the last thing I wanted to do.

I'd ridden with Mack to the hospital and sat there while the doctors checked him out. Their initial suspicion was a pair of major ligament tears and maybe some additional tissue damage from the impact of falling off the top turnbuckle. Since it was the same leg he was already rehabbing from surgery, they didn't seem to want to say too much about what kind of recovery he might make. The surgeon who'd done the initial operation came in to see him while we were there and said he'd like to get him back under the knife as soon as possible. Mack did his best to come off as upbeat, even though I knew he must be crushed. Smiling and nodding along with all the doctors. I'd called Molly to tell her what happened, and she'd driven down to be his ride home.

"I don't understand it," I said as I helped walk Mack to the car. "What the hell was Barrow thinking?"

"Kid just blew an assignment," Mack said. "It happens. Got mixed-up and thought he was supposed to bust me with the chair instead of you."

"You think Rex might have put him up to it?" I asked. "As a way to get back at you?"

"Fuck no," Mack said. "Gary will always hate my guts, but he's been a stand-up guy in this business for twenty-five years. If he still felt like he had a score to settle, we'd do it in the parking lot after a twelve-pack like a couple of gentlemen."

"What do you think Baby Jay will do?"

He blew the air out of his chest. "I don't know," he said, "but we're gonna have to convince him I can still go, Dally. We gotta make it to that final match and get him to see even a version of Mack Savage with a busted knee can draw more money as FSW champion than the damn 'Dog Catcher.'"

"You sure you can even wrestle on it?" I asked. His leg was wrapped in a thick white bandage, and he carried a pair of crutches across his chest.

"I'll be fine," he snapped. "I can hack a little dinged-up knee for a couple weeks. It ain't like I never done it before."

I nodded, but even as he said it, I knew what he was really thinking. Another surgery was a big expense. If Mack had to come off the road and sit out for an extended period, he'd have no money coming in, no way to make a living. He didn't strike me as the kind of guy who had a stash squirreled away for emergencies. One thing I couldn't have known at the time but understand all too well now was the desperation that took over in him as he began to think about it. A wrestler who is facing a long layoff — or an old wrestler who realizes he's maybe facing the end — suddenly becomes an expert mathematician. You start adding up the mortgage, child support, medical bills, electric bill, water bill, garbage bill. You start thinking about that Rolex you haven't taken out of the box in years. Your old fishing boat and who might make an offer on it. You think, with a terrifying tightening in your throat, of the insurance office boss in Tampa who once said he could get you a job if you ever needed it. Would that guy still remember you, after that night drinking piña coladas out of cups shaped like the heads of Hawaiian gods? The way he'd made the job offer and then you'd both laughed at how ridiculous it was, because of course the gravy train of wrestling would roll on forever-and-ever-amen.

After Molly and Mack drove off, I sat in my car and swallowed a handful of pills from the dopp kit with a can of beer. I was depressed and beat up and needed a pick-me-up. A few hours later, sitting across the dinner table from Mary Lynn, I felt better but still wasn't convinced Mack could pull off the rest of our feud with Rex and Barrow. He was a tough old bastard, but the doctors had damn near laughed at him when he suggested he could keep up his regular work schedule. The way I'd seen him moving around the ring after Barrow had knocked him off the turnbuckle made me inclined to agree with them.

"The worst part is," I said to her as we ate tater skins as our starters, "I was supposed to wrestle Barrow next week at TV. Now, it's possible Baby Jay will just scrap the whole angle."

"Didn't you just say you broke that man's nose?" she said.

"He's fine," I shrugged. "But if Mack can't go, or if Baby Jay decides he wants to change the booking at the last minute, Barrow and I might both be out of luck. Baby, for a long time I thought it was my big break to hitch my wagon to Mack Savage this early in my career, and now I'm wondering if it's going to be the thing that kills me dead before I even get started."

She reached across the table and gripped my hand. "You're way too good for something like that to happen," she said.

I grinned at her. "How would you know?" I said. "You've never even seen me wrestle."

"Because I believe in you, stupid," she said. "If it doesn't work out here, you'll land on your feet somewhere else."

"Somewhere else," I said, "is not where I want to be."

"At least we agree on that," she said.

It was the first time we'd admitted to each other that maybe the thing we had going wasn't a just-for-fun summer fling after all. There was a moment where we stared at each other, flushed and pink in the light of the wagon wheel chandelier. Mary Lynn took a long drink of wine and laughed. "If I tell you something," she said, "will you promise not to get a big head over it?"

"That sounds like a dangerous proposition," I said. "I will make no such promise."

"You're looking extra great these days," she said. "I mean, you always look good to me, but whatever new workout routine you're on — it's working."

"It's that new stuff I got from Mack," I said. "Actually, that reminds me." I pulled out of my pocket one of the big blue football pills that had been rattling around loose all over the dopp kit when I got it. "You have any idea what this is?"

She squinted at it. "I'm a nurse," she said, "not a pharmacist."

"Whatever it is," I said, "it makes me feel like I can walk on water."

I saw the waiters coming with our meals and washed the pill down with a slug of beer. They served us medium-rare steaks with rice pilaf and buttery sprigs of broccoli. I was famished and had to pace myself, knowing the pill might make me sick unless I took things slow. While we ate, I listened to Mary Lynn talk about her work, laughing at the story she told about a doctor the other nurses suspected had lost his house and was secretly living at the hospital. He was always there, she said, sleeping at odd hours in the lounge, showering in the locker room-like areas. Someone had seen him changing his clothes from a suitcase in the trunk of his car. She was so funny and beautiful — and so much smarter than me — I was filled with sadness at the notion I might have to leave her when my FSW run ended.

For dessert, we shared a piece of chocolate cheesecake, though I only had a few bites before setting my fork down. Something like that, I knew it would go straight to my abs. Mary Lynn had had a few glasses of wine by the time she said, "I'd like to, you know."

"Like to what?"

"See you wrestle," she said. "It'd be a shame if you become a big star and I have to tell my grandkids I never even went to a show when I had the chance."

Another pang of sadness hit me. I didn't feel like a big star. I wasn't sure I felt like a guy who was *ever* going to be one. Plus, imagining a world where Mary Lynn went on to have grandkids that weren't also mine set my mind down a path I didn't want to follow too far. I covered it with a grin. "Well," I said, "we can surely do that. That can surely be arranged."

"Can it?" she said. "Even to this big-deal TV taping where you're going to wrestle the evil Mr. Wayne Barrow?"

"Of course," I said. "Baby Jay always comps a couple tickets for the boys, and I've never used any of mine. We'll have you right down there in the front row."

"Oh no," she said. "Not there."

"It's the best seat in the house," I said.

"I don't want to make a spectacle of myself," she said. "With the rest of your terrible friends ogling me all night."

"Mack is the only one of them I would call a friend," I said.

"Still," she said, "I want to be tucked away somewhere nice and inconspicuous in the bleachers."

"That's silly," I said, "but we can do that, too, if that's what you'd like."

"Then it's a date," she said, and lifted her glass.

My beer bottle had been empty for a half hour, but I picked it up and we toasted across the table. The glass made a gentle *ping* as they touched. My heart double-clutched in my chest. Right then, I wished I could stop time, just freezeframe the whole world, so I could live in that moment forever.

Forty years later? I still feel the same damn way.

TEN
BABY JAY SPEAKS

Baby Jay Chevalier stood in the white dot of a spotlight inside the FSW ring, the crowd in his makeshift warehouse TV studio as quiet as a bunch of sinners in church. Waiting for him to get on with it. After a few moments of solemn contemplation, he pressed the mic to his lips, a worried look on his face.

"It has come to my attention," he said, "that we have a problem on our hands. A very big problem, my friends. You see, last week on this very program, the Frontier States Wrestling Heavyweight champion, 'Maniac' Mack Savage — a man who has held that position with the utmost dignity and distinction for the last six months, a man who has done absolutely everything there is to do in the sport of professional wrestling, a man that frankly I would be happy to have either of my sons grow up to be like — was heinously injured at the hands of 'The Dungeon Master' Demian Rex and his unholy squire, 'The Dark Warlock' Wayne Barrow."

The crowd booed, and Baby Jay nodded along gravely, as though he too could barely grasp the inhumanity of it all. "Let me tell you, ladies and gentlemen," he said, "Mack Savage is as tough as they come. I saw him earlier today, hobbling around on crutches with his knee in a brace. He still wants — no, he still *insists* on defending the title for you people against Demian Rex next Saturday night at the Metra right here in Billings, Montana—"

A surge of cheers sprinkled through the audience. "I know, I know," Baby Jay said, holding his hand up for quiet, "but I have to level with you, as the Chief Operating Officer of FSW, I have concerns about whether Mack Savage is physically capable of going one-on-one with an animal like Rex in his current condition. So, you can see, we have quite the conundrum on our hands."

Some more boos.

Baby Jay paused and put both fists on his hips and pressed his chin to his chest like this was something he'd thought long and hard about. When he finally lifted the mic back to his face, the crowd was rapt. "Mack Savage, would you come out here, please?" he said. "And bring your tag team partner, 'The Real Deal' Dallas Hostettler, with you, if you would."

"Blackout" hit the speakers, and I ducked through the curtain so I could hold the flap for Mack. The cheering didn't falter when he stepped through on his crutches. One leg was trussed-up like a newborn baby, but he still had that look in his eyes. Our walk to the ring took even longer than normal, and then I had to sit on the second rope while he gingerly stepped through.

"Now, Mack," Baby Jay said over the applause. "Mack, the first thing I want to do is thank you for the class and sportsmanship you've brought to the FSW title. It's never easy when one of our champions suffers an injury — but, unfortunately, I have to make an announcement tonight about the future of that title and about your scheduled match with Demian Rex. At this time, I'd like Rex and Wayne Barrow to also join us here in the ring."

The crowd booed some more as the lights went out and the creepy organ music that always accompanied Rex and Barrow to the ring began to play. The two of them walked out wearing their fur-trimmed robes, hoods thrown back, expectant smiles on their faces. They made no notice of the jeers from the audience. It felt a little crowded in the ring with all five of us standing around, but we tried to keep our distance, eyeing each other from opposite sides. "I want all you men to know I've thought at length about this," Baby Jay said. "It's clear that the title match between Mack Savage and Demain Rex can't go off as scheduled. It just wouldn't be competitive, and it wouldn't be fair."

"No!" Mack said. "No, I'm fine. I can take this turkey!" He didn't have a mic, but the people could still hear him.

"This morning I put a call in to the National Wrestling Council's board of directors about how we should handle the situation," Baby Jay went on. "Frankly, NWC President Mick Klinger advised me to strip Mack Savage of the title and move forward with a tournament for the vacant championship."

This brought a cavalcade of boos down from the crowd. People jumped out of their seats, shaking their fists. Mack practically leapt off his crutches, balancing on his good leg and shaking his head so hard his hair whipped back and forth. Rex rubbed his hands together with glee.

"But I'm not going to do that," Baby Jay said, bringing a sudden silence to the room. "I'm not going to do that. It wouldn't be right, and it wouldn't be proper." He was a good talker. He took us up and took us down with the rise and fall of his voice. "Here's what we *are* going to do. It's clear we can't have Rex and Savage wrestle as scheduled, not as a one-on-one match. So, tonight, we're going to be making a little change. How about we make things a little bit more interesting? How about we make next week's title match a three-way dance?"

Everybody in the ring looked around at each other. The crowd, too, seemed caught off guard. There were some scattered cheers, but it was more like a murmur that spread through the audience. "We've already got 'The Real Deal Dallas' Hostettler and 'The Dark Warlock' Wayne Barrow scheduled to fight it out in this week's main event," Baby Jay said. "So, let's spice things up. The winner of tonight's match between Hostettler and Barrow will gain entry as the third participant into next weekend's title match between Rex and Savage at the Metra! If Hostettler wins, he'll be there to back-up Savage. If Barrow wins," Baby Jay shrugged, "then I'd wager the FSW heavyweight title will belong to The Dungeon Family by next week. Either way? Game on, gentlemen. Game on!"

ELEVEN

ONE-ON-ONE

Barrow and I started our match slowly, with a few headlocks and shoulder blocks. We were both big guys, so each time one of us took a back bump, it shook the whole ring — loud in a room made mostly of concrete and steel. We traded chops in the corner, and Barrow laid into me with some good ones. He still sported matching black eyes and a swollen nose from where I'd punched him the week before, but he'd been easygoing and pleasant in all our pre-match meetings. The guy knew he'd fucked up. He'd gotten confused during the tag match and knocked Mack off the turnbuckle when he should've slid back into the ring and gone after me. But I'd talked to him enough to satisfy myself that Mack was right — that Barrow hadn't done it on purpose. He was either the world's greatest liar, or there was no conspiracy. To this day, I believe what he did was just a screw-up.

It's funny how shit like that works out sometimes. Just a split-second brain fart, a spur-of-the-moment mix-up by a guy who never went on to be much in wrestling, and it ends up affecting the rest of your life. It's almost enough to make you believe in the grand fucking order of the universe, you know what I mean?

Here's the thing about Barrow, though, that I learned the very first minute of being in the ring with him: the guy actually wasn't a bad worker. He was quick and smooth, and when I picked him up for a vertical suplex, he floated up there like a goddamn feather. It was the first big power move of the match, and when I sent him crashing down to the canvas, the crowd exploded in a way they never had for me before. Not without Mack being in the ring, too. The fans wanted badly for me to beat Barrow, not only to pay him back for what he'd done the week before, but so I could get myself into the title match and back Mack up against Demian Rex — to make sure it was Mack and not "The Dungeon Master" who walked out of the biggest event of the summer with the title still around his waist. It was a good feeling to hear them cheer like that for me. It had me sky-high.

With Barrow down, I double-pumped my fists to keep the crowd going, then pointed and winked up to the back corner of the bleachers where I knew Mary Lynn was sitting. It had been a kick to have her backstage all afternoon. The boys seemed to take to her easily and — even though I didn't like the way Baby Jay looked at her when I introduced them, like he was measuring her for a new suit — it made me happy that she seemed pleased to be there. I had secretly feared she might hate every minute of it, but she was talkative and great all day. She was even a good sport when one of the guys from The Great Depression pulled out his wallet and started showing baby pictures. It was the first time in a while the rest of the boys treated me like another human being. Nobody even called me Princess.

Mack and Rex had both come to ringside for the match, and when I put Barrow down with that suplex they both reacted like I'd made the final out in the World Series. Mack pounded on the ring apron and threw one hand in the air to urge the crowd to cheer louder. Rex turned away like he couldn't bear to watch, shaking his head and taking a little walk to get himself together. I could tell Mack was in pain and feeling down. He'd mostly kept to himself before the taping, hanging out in the private dressing room Baby Jay kept for him in the back of the building. He'd popped out for a minute to grab a plate of food and say hello to Mary Lynn, but that was it. When I'd gone in to see him, he was sitting with his bad leg propped up between two folding chairs. A can of Budweiser in one hand. I thought he might be excited for me, have some advice on how to handle my first main event match, but he mostly just nodded or grunted when I said something. Before I left, he shook my hand and said, "I'll see you out there."

Now that the lights were on and the bleachers filled, he was back to his normal self. He paced back and forth on his crutches next to the ring, shouting encouragement and whipping up the crowd. It was good to know he was out there. It gave me strength.

When I grabbed Barrow by the hair to pull him up, he threaded his legs through mine and rolled me into a small package. Dude was quick, I have to say. My ankles went over my head and the whole room gasped as the referee counted: One, two — and I kicked out. Barrow sprang up and shook his finger at me, warning me not to take him lightly. I used the middle rope to pull myself up, and then we stood there in the middle of the ring, eyeing each other like gunfighters. From outside, Mack started pounding out a slow rhythm on the mat. The audience picked it up and pretty soon the whole room was reverberating with the sound of it: Thump. Thump. THUMP. THUMP-THUMP-THUMP. Slowly getting louder and faster until it exploded into a furious ovation. That's when I knew for sure we had them.

We were young and green and — technically speaking — it wasn't the prettiest match I ever worked, but it might have been the purest. Before this, Mack had told me how it could feel when you were out there and everything just clicked, but I'd never experienced it. For whatever reason, that night in Billings, Barrow and I had the magic. The crowd was hooked, and as we went along, you could feel the tension and anticipation building toward the finish.

Baby Jay had given us fourteen minutes, an eternity in television wrestling back then. It was a lot to trust a couple of rookies with, but we had worked with him earlier in the day to make sure it came off well. Since Barrow had trouble remembering long sequences, we'd decided to call most of the action in the ring, with me acting as the ring general. It was my first time calling a match. Most other times, I'd been in there with veterans like Mack and Rex and had let them guide the way. Now, it turned out I had a knack for it. I could feel the rise and fall of the crowd, the drift and drag of their attention. I had Barrow use his speed to avoid most of my big power moves — ducking out the way at the last instant and then doing something sneaky and underhanded to slow me down. A kick to the knee or the groin, a thumb to the eye. A couple times when I hit the ropes, Rex snagged my boot with one hand and tripped me from the outside. The ref always just missed it. Mack would go charging around the ring on his crutches and the crowd would cheer, hoping to see him finally get his hands on "The Dungeon Master."

The last time it happened, Mack finally got close enough that Rex hightailed it out of there. Mack gave chase and the two of them disappeared between the bleachers into the bowels of the warehouse. With just the two of us left in the ring, Barrow softened me up with a couple punches and then hoisted me onto his shoulder for the power-slam he'd been using as his finisher.

As he started across the ring, preparing to drive me down into the canvas for the one-two-three, I scooted out the back. I slipped behind him, landing on my feet and gave him a stiff shove to keep his momentum going. I hit the ropes and just as he turned around to confront me, I nailed him full speed with my lariat. Caught him so hard it turned him almost completely upside down. The crowd went crazy. I covered him and the referee counted it out. One-two-three. The bell sounded, and a split second later, The Great Depression hit the ring, interrupting my victory celebration before it could even get started. VapoRub and Lazy Eye leveled me with punches and kicks, and after taking a few seconds to recover, Barrow joined in, too.

With Mack off chasing Rex, there was no one to have my back. Even as the ring announcer declared me the winner, those three big bastards beat me senseless. I tried to get up, and they beat me down again. One of the Great Depression guys brought a chair into the ring and beat on me with that for a while. They kept it up until the crowd started throwing trash into the ring. Once they'd had their fill, they all stood over me and raised their fists, taunting the crowd and daring anyone who was man enough to come in there and challenge them. It was a bittersweet way to get the win in my first TV main event. I'd earned my way into the three-way title match the next weekend at the Metra, where I'd be able to help swing the odds in Mack's favor against Rex. But we were going off the air in the go-home show with me getting stomped-out by a bunch of mid-carders. That part rubbed me the wrong way.

When I knew it was safe, I cracked my eyes open and looked out into the back rows to find Mary Lynn. She was leaning forward in her seat, gaze fixed to me, one hand covering her mouth. I guess the heels had been making it look pretty good when they put me down. In truth, some of those chair shots did hurt like a motherfucker. But I chanced a half grin in her direction and just a tiny wink before Barrow put his boot onto the side of my head and shoved me down again.

TWELVE
JUST TO SEE HOW IT FEELS

A few days before the big show at the Metra, Baby Jay threw an end-of-summer barbecue for the babyfaces and their families in a local park. A bunch of the territory's ongoing angles would wrap up that Saturday, and afterward many of the guys would be moving on to other places. For a lot of them, it was the last chance to get together before the show. I didn't yet know if I was going to be one of the guys pulling up stakes and shoving off. Aside from the regular booking meetings, Baby Jay and I hadn't talked since the night he told me the story about Ace Easton's gun. I was also dragging my feet on contacting other promoters about finding a spot for me in the fall. Mack was mostly staying home, doing what he could to rehab his knee, so he wasn't around to give me advice. I was flying solo.

I'd asked Mary Lynn to come to the barbecue with me and was surprised when she agreed. We brought potato salad in a big orange bowl and set it on the picnic table with the rest of the spread. We all must have been a pretty strange sight out there together, a bunch of beefy dudes and pretty women cracking beers at one o'clock in the afternoon. Seeing all the other boys gathered like that also made me realize how isolated I'd been that summer, riding only with Mack.

Several of the families already seemed to know each other, and I saw a few wives pulling each other away for private sidebars. Kids paired off to chase each other through the trees. I had visions of dinners, bowling alley trips, backyard pool parties — none of which I'd been invited to. When I looked back at Mary Lynn, I noticed her focus had drifted off to the other side of the park, where a few moms had stopped to stare at us while their kids played on the slide and jungle gym.

"Hey," I said. "Hey. You all right?"

Her eyes snapped back to the moment. "Sure," she said, "just a little tired. Maybe I'm fighting off some kind of bug."

"You want me to get you a seltzer water or anything?"

"Sure," she said, "that would be nice."

When I came back with the drinks, I found Baby Jay had corralled her against the table of sides. He was wearing thong sandals and shorts. The two of them were in the middle of laughing at something he had just said. "What's funny?" I asked, handing her the seltzer and cracking a beer for myself.

"Nothing at all," Mary Lynn said. "I was just telling Mr. Chevalier here about an article I read recently in *Time Magazine* about the national cattlemen's association's efforts to open up more public lands for grazing."

"This little lady seems to have quite the head for business," Baby Jay said.

"She's a smart cookie, all right," I said, grinning and feeling stupid, getting the distinct impression something was going on here I wasn't quite catching.

"The article was accompanied by quite a striking photo," Mary Lynn said. "A ranch hand working a field full of longhorns. This big, tall galoot in a black cowboy hat with a bull rope slung across his shoulder. I have to admit, he cut a pretty dashing figure."

My cheeks began to sting, but I shut it down, telling myself I refused to become jealous over a picture in a magazine. "Talking about agriculture at the babyface barbecue," I said. "Who would've thought?"

"It's refreshing talking to somebody who's head isn't just full to bursting with wrestling," Baby Jay said. "So, of course, I had to ruin it and ask whether the beautiful Ms. Fawcett here had ever considered trying her hand in our business."

I nearly laughed at that one. Mary Lynn was all of five-foot-two, five-foot-three. She didn't look like she could wrestle a bumble bee, let alone another person. She saw my expression and grinned, patting my chest with an open palm. "Not as a wrestler, silly," she said, "but maybe — I don't know — as a valet?"

"A valet?" I said. Suddenly I felt like an idiot, repeating myself. I was one step behind whatever they'd been discussing, and I couldn't keep up. "For who?"

"For you, genius," Mary Lynn said, with a laugh.

Were they pulling my leg? "You're pulling my leg," I said.

Baby Jay shrugged. "Idle talk, maybe," he said. "But you have to admit she has a certain look about her, don't you?"

"Sure," I said. "But —"

"If there were a wrestler I knew," Baby Jay went on, wheeling right past my protests, "let's say a young fellow who we all agreed had every physical tool but had so far struggled to — how should we put this — connect with an audience, well, I might recommend he try something a little bit unorthodox. But what do I know? I've only been in the wrestling business my whole entire life."

I looked at Mary Lynn, and she made a point of covering her grin with a swig of her bubbly water. I knew then that she was just putting me on. Before coming to watch me wrestle Barrow at TV, she hadn't wanted anything to do with it. She had her own life, her own career. There was no way under the sun she'd want to join up with Baby Jay's traveling carnival, even in a part-time role. I started to feel better.

.   .   .

AT THAT MOMENT, a horn sounded and Mack's big Cadillac pulled up to the curb fifty yards away, Molly behind the wheel. Mack was out before the car could even stop, grinning from ear to ear, walking without his crutches to the back of the car to haul a big red cooler out of the trunk.

"Excuse me," I said to Baby Jay and Mary Lynn and hurried over to give him a hand.

Mack waved to some of the older guys. He had a big black brace on his injured knee. The cooler he was trying to wrangle looked like it weighed a hundred pounds. "Let me help you with that, partner," I said as I got close, voice loud enough so that everyone could hear. Then quieter, just between the two of us: "What are you doing, Sav?"

"What?" Mack said. "I brought beverages."

Molly stood with the driver's side door open, looking worried and helpless.

"You're gonna shred whatever is left of that knee, if you're not careful," I said. "Where are your crutches?"

"I'm fine, Princess," Mack said. "You want to carry the cooler, be my guest, but I've already got one nursemaid trying to play mother hen. I don't need another one."

His words were slurred. I took him lightly by the arm and leaned close. "What are you on?"

He jerked away. "Nothing," he said. "Just a six-pack of Budweisers and a couple of Placidyls."

"Jesus, Sav," I said, "you look strung out. You got a lot on the line here, brother. You really want to show up to the family picnic looking like they wouldn't let you into Studio 54?"

"That's rich," he said, "coming from a guy who put on fifteen pounds of pure muscle tapping into the goodies from my private stash."

He poked me lightly in the ribs. He hadn't meant it as a compliment, but I felt a rush of pride at how I looked. I'd been hitting the gym like a madman getting ready for the match with Barrow and our end-of-summer three-way. I was bigger than I'd ever been, more toned, lower body fat percentage. I hoisted the cooler out of the trunk and lugged it across the grass, him limping along next to me. It was slow going with me not wanting to leave Mack in the dust. As we walked, he nodded and greeted people by name, shaking hands with a few of the boys. I could feel Baby Jay's eyes tracking us. It made our progress feel twice as tedious.

When we finally got to the picnic table, I heaved the cooler up on top. I could see the relief in Mack's face as he rested his butt on the table to get some of the weight off his leg. Mary Lynn and Molly had found a spot on a couple of lawn chairs near the horseshoe pit. I thought of what Molly had told me that night in the motel room, that Mack would rather run himself to death than admit the end was near. Everybody was eyeballing Mack between sips of their drinks, cataloging how he looked, how he was moving, the drugged-out look in his eyes. Baby Jay fiddled with some meats on the grill, but I could see the wheels spinning in his head. Fuck, I thought. You fucked up, Mack. You should've just stayed home.

"How you feeling, champ?" one of the boys asked him. A small crowd had drifted over to the picnic table, just like it always did wherever Mack went.

"Hell, I'm all right," he said. "When those TV lights come on, I'll be A-OK." Nobody responded to that, so he said it again. "When those TV lights come on, I'll be A-OK."

I was about halfway into my second beer when Mary Lynn told me she wanted to go home. She still wasn't feeling good, she said, and was starting to think maybe she'd eaten something bad. I hadn't had a burger or a piece of chicken yet, but I didn't complain. Sitting there watching Mack tell stories and pretend to be OK had gotten old fast.

As we walked to the car, she slipped one arm around my waist. "Great news," she said, "Molly and Mack invited us to dinner on Friday night."

"No shit?" I said. "Fun."

"She's pretty worried about what will happen if he has to come off the road."

"I'm sure Baby Jay will come to his senses," I said. "Still no better man in this territory to be the champion than Mack Savage. Hell, he'll probably make a mint next year." Even as I said it, I wasn't sure I believed it anymore.

"I don't think that's what she's worried about," Mary Lynn said.

We got to the car and she unfolded herself from me. "So, you going to let Baby Jay talk you into a career in the squared circle, or what?" I said.

I meant it as a joke, but she didn't answer. There was something serious in her face when I looked at her across the roof. "What?" I said.

"As a matter of fact," she said, "he offered me the opportunity to accompany you to the ring on Saturday night."

"Accompany me?" I said. I snorted another laugh. "And what did you say?"

"I accepted," she said. "Just for that one night, of course. Just to see how it feels."

I didn't know what to say to that. I nodded slightly. "Well," I said. "If you're sure. Crowd can be pretty rough. Especially to a good-looking woman."

"I guarantee you it's nothing I haven't heard before."

I wasn't at all sure how I felt about that, but I'd had my fill that day of trying to talk people out of their damn fool ideas. We climbed into the car, and I cranked the AC as high as it would go.

THIRTEEN
A FUCKING SHOCKING TURN OF EVENTS

As soon as I got to Mary Lynn's place the following Friday night, I could tell something was wrong. I'd dressed for dinner with Mack and Molly in one of the two collared shirts I owned, my best pair of jeans and boots. I felt like the cock of the walk, but after Mary Lynn took the flowers I'd brought for her and put them in water, she barely looked at me. The silence hung in the air like skunk spray. She went into the kitchen and started pulling plates out of the dishwasher, putting them away, even though she already had on a yellow dress and matching pumps. I thought, does that really need to be done *right now*? To keep myself from saying something, I went to the little makeshift bar she kept in the front room and fixed us both a drink.

"You're not nervous, are you?" I said, trying to keep my voice light. "Don't be. Mack and Molly both think you're an absolute doll."

She said nothing, just kept clanking and crashing dishes into cabinets.

"Hell," I said, "it's not the Ayatollah again, is it? Something you saw on the news?"

"I need to talk to you," she said, banging cupboards shut like she was trying to get ready for the dinner rush at a busy restaurant.

"Come out here and tell me, then," I said, not wanting us to have to shout at each other across the entire apartment. "I fixed you a cocktail."

She came as far as the fringe of the living room carpet. I raised my eyebrows and offered her the drink, but she shook her head. Oh boy, I thought, standing there with an ice-filled glass in each hand. Here it comes. The "we both know you're leaving soon, so what's the point of carrying on?" talk. The big kibosh. I took a drink from the glass in my right hand. I'd mixed a vodka tonic pretty strong. It burned going down. The look on her face was pinched, but more nervous than angry.

"I'm pregnant," she said.

That turned my skin hot and prickly. Something flopped in my stomach. I took a sip of the drink in my left hand, trying to calm it. That drink tasted twice as strong. "Whose is it?' I asked.

Her shoulders turned bright red and dropped like she might cry. "It's yours, of course," she said. "I haven't been with anyone else in over a year."

Another sip. The vodka went down smoother this time. "That don't make any sense, Mary Lynn," I said. "I have the varicoceles."

"I know that's what you told me," she said, her tone implying that maybe I'd lied about it. "But I guess you're in better working condition down there than we thought."

"This is really happening?" I said. "I mean, are you sure you're standing there right now swearing to me there hasn't been anybody else?"

"You're a shit, Dallas, you know that?" she said. "There hasn't been anybody else. I'm in love with you."

"Well, I'm in love with you, too," I said. It had been true for a while, but this was the first time either of us had admitted it. "But, Mary Lynn, this just can't be."

"Oh, that's great," she said. "Just what a girl dreams of hearing from the future father of her child."

"Honey, baby, no," I said, going to her and wrapping my arms around her. Awkward with both drinks in my hands. "I'm just surprised is all. It's a fucking shocking turn of events."

She leaned into me. It felt good. "It's not what I wanted, either," she said.

I looked down her back and saw where the condensation from the two glasses was making a spot on the back of her dress. "It's a goddamn miracle, is what it is," I said, feeling the moment lift me. "It's a blessing. Something I never could have hoped for me. A baby? From these loins? Amazing."

She pulled back to look at me. "You really think that?" she said.

"Sure," I said, still not quite convinced that's what the tangle of emotions inside me was saying but going with it. "Sure I do."

She kissed me hard on the lips and then pushed into my arms again. We stood there swaying in the living room, the two glasses sweating in my hands for what felt like a long time. Inside, my mind was going crazy, running down every conversation with every doctor I'd ever had. Slowly, an idea began to form in my head. Putting the pieces together of what had occurred here. A revelation, you might say.

"Wait just a damn minute," I said. "Wait just one motherfucking second."

"What is it?" she asked, expression going back to worried.

"Get your coat," I said.

I drove to Mack and Molly's house as fast as I dared with a couple of vodkas in me. Pretty sure the tires screeched on a couple of the turns. Mary Lynn had to tell me to slow down twice, that I was acting like a maniac. I leaned on the doorbell until Molly answered, pushed past her and found Mack sipping a beer in an armchair in the living room. His bad leg was resting on the coffee table. The TV was on, but I paid no mind to what he was watching, shaking the dopp kit he'd given me in his face.

"What is this?" I asked him.

He looked at me like I'd lost my mind. "What the hell are you talking about, Dally?"

I dug around in the kit until I found one of the big blue horse pills I'd been taking and I held it under his nose. "This," I said. "What is this shit, Mack?"

His eyes crossed as he focused on it. "How the fuck should I know?" he said.

Molly and Mary Lynn had come in after me and Molly stooped to see what we were looking at. "Why, that's one of the fertility pills we got from Guru Goldblum," she said. "What are you doing with it?"

"You mean the witch doctor," I said. "The kook with all the unorthodox methods."

She put her hands on her hips. "He's a perfectly legitimate holistic healer," she said.

I turned to Mack. "You put a bunch of black-market baby-makers in with all the rest of the drugs you gave me?"

Mack put his palms up like he'd been accused of stealing the last cookie. "I don't know," he said. "Maybe. I keep all my shit in one place."

"Mack," Molly said, "You told me you took all those pills."

"I took most of them," he said.

"The hell you did," I said. "I've been popping these things like candy since you gave them to me. There must have been two dozen of those damn blue boulders in there."

"So what?" he said, taking the dopp kit from me and hefting it like he might complain that I'd nearly cleaned out his stash. "I didn't hear you bellyaching when you maxed out your bench press every single week this summer."

"Mack," Molly said, like she was warming up to get righteously pissed.

"This was fucking irresponsible, man," I said.

"You *told me* you took those pills," Molly said.

"They tasted like a stray dog's asshole," he said. "I couldn't keep them down. I still don't see what the big deal is."

"I'm pregnant," Mary Lynn said. "That's what the big deal is. Dallas and I are going to have a baby."

That caught them both off guard. They looked at each other and then back and forth between the two of us. Mack busted out laughing. "Congratulations!" he said, hoisting himself off the couch and wrapping the two of us in an awkward hug. "Let's celebrate. Hell, I think we got some fancy champagne somewhere in the basement."

"We're not done talking about this," Molly said.

"Oh, my dear, I have no doubt about that," Mack said as he ambled across the room and disappeared down a set of stairs.

The rest of the night is a blur in my mind. I remember we had ribs for dinner and that they were delicious. Molly had cooked them in the oven first and Mack finished them on the grill. We drank a lot. All except Mary Lynn, but she was a good sport about it. Mack and Molly both laughed and applauded when she told them she was going to walk me to the ring on Saturday night. Slowly, it began to dawn on me that, of all the women I'd ever known, there were none I'd rather raise a child with than Mary Lynn. Turned out, that hunch was right about a thousand times over during the next four decades.

At some point, we paired off. Mack and I wound up smoking cigars in a couple of lawn chairs on the back deck. Molly and Mary Lynn had gone down to the basement game room, with Molly promising to show Mary Lynn how to be a nine-ball hustler. Mack told me again how happy he was for me, and I told him I was starting to get used to the idea. The truth was, I couldn't stay mad at the old son of a bitch. He asked me if Mary Lynn and I were going to get married, and I admitted I hadn't thought it all the way through yet. I said I guessed we would.

"Little Dallas Hostettler," Mack said, "growing up before my very eyes."

"It all feels very sudden," I said, "but I guess I'm starting to get my mind around it."

"My advice," he said. "It's best to stop before you raise an entire army."

"What about you?" I asked. "You guys still trying?"

"We were," he said, "but after this fuck-up with the pills it might be awhile before we're sleeping in the same bed again."

We sat in silence for a bit after that. The cigar made the inside of my mouth taste like an ashtray, but Mack seemed to be enjoying his. It felt like the thing to do — smoke cigars together on a momentous night. "What about tomorrow?" I asked. "You have any notion what Baby Jay is going to do?"

He cut me a look out of the corner of his eyes. "I have a few ideas," he said.

"Anything you'd care to share?"

He laughed. I couldn't tell if it was a nice laugh. "You may have become a man in the bedroom this summer, young boy," he said, "but you're still as green as grass when it comes to the wrestling business."

"I'm not sure I understand what that means," I said.

"You'll figure it out," he said. "One of these days."

FOURTEEN
THE SWERVE

Baby Jay put off the final booking meeting until just a couple hours before showtime. He was alone in his makeshift office in one of the Metra's small side rooms when Mary Lynn and I got there Saturday night. I'd ended up drinking too much with Mack the night before, was still hungover and dreading this meeting. When Baby Jay saw me, he smiled and waved us in. He was already wearing his best suit. Front of house was sold out, he said, including the floor and standing-room tickets he'd added at the last minute.

"I'm loving this look," he said, nodding at the sunglasses I'd kept on and the gallon milk jug of water I had balanced on my knee. "This business will make a rock star out of you yet, kid."

"Heaven forbid," Mary Lynn said.

"OK, first item of business," he said, lifting a bottle of orange juice he had on his desk. "Mazel tov to the both of you. I hear there's yet another little Frontier States Wrestling fan bound for the world soon."

We both nodded and thanked him for saying so. Mary Lynn squeezed my elbow, and I wondered how the hell Baby Jay had heard about it so soon. "Where are Mack and Rex?" I asked. It was weird they wouldn't be there for this.

"I already talked to them," Baby Jay said. "Everybody's on the same page, you can count on that."

"Everybody except me," I said, going for a smile. "I still don't know what we're planning."

Baby Jay grinned back at me, letting me know he thought he was being very indulgent of everybody's feelings that day. "I guess that's why we're here," he said. He came around and sat on the front corner of the desk, the way he always did when he had something to discuss with the talent. Guy was only about five-foot-eight, but it always felt like he was looming over you when he perched up there. "Dallas, I want you to know this isn't a decision I've come to lightly. I've given it a lot of thought over the last few weeks. It's not going to be an easy road for everyone, but I've come to the conclusion it's the best thing for business."

"Oh no," I said. "You're jobbing Mack to Demian Rex, aren't you?"

"Kid," he said, like a genius who constantly had to explain himself to idiots. "Nobody's been closer to Mack than you this summer, and I understand that. But I also know you've seen that he's not in a good place right now — and I'm talking emotionally *and* physically. He looked like a damn zombie at the barbecue last week. Guy had to take a whole bottle of painkillers just to get from the car to the picnic table. You think a guy like that is gonna be able to make Fargo, Pierre and Calgary next week to defend the title? Not happening. It's tough, but that's the truth of the matter."

"You're exaggerating," I said. "We were at Mack's house last night, and he didn't seem too far gone."

I looked at Mary Lynn, hoping she would back me up with at least a nod, but she sat stock still. Her eyes said she was starting to pick up what Baby Jay was saying.

"I know you love the old man," he said. "I do, too, but being FSW champion is more than dragging your carcass to the ring and letting your younger, stronger, better-looking partner carry you through a fifteen-minute match. I need a guy who can do the local morning show without falling asleep halfway through the interview. I need somebody who can show up at KB Toys and sign autographs for three hours. I can't have a pill freak as the poster-boy for my business. I worked too hard to get FSW to this point to let Mack Savage — or anybody — sully our good name."

I almost laughed, but my heart was flapping in my chest. I'd never talked to Baby Jay like this before. "You're worried about kids at a toy store?" I said. "You really think Rex is going to be able to do shit like that? You think 'The Dungeon Master' can go to the mall and pose for pictures with toddlers on his lap like some kind of damn Santa Claus? Good luck with that. You'll have parents dragging their bawling kids out to the car by the dozens."

Baby Jay took off his glasses and polished them with the handkerchief he used as a pocket square. His body sagged, as though my own personal stupidity had settled like a weight on his shoulders. He held the glasses at arm's length, inspected their lenses, blew warm air onto them, wiped them again and put them back on his face. "Not Demian Rex," he said. "You."

I sat back in my chair so hard its two front legs rocked up off the floor. "What are you talking about?" I said.

"I'm talking about you, you big dumb hayseed."

Mary Lynn leaned over to me. "He wants to make you champion, Dallas," she said.

"I know that," I said. Then to Baby Jay: "You want to make me champion?"

"I don't *want* to," he said, "I'm doing it. Tonight, in the match, you're going over."

"Wait," I said, "slow down. What about Mack? What about Rex?"

"Mack," Baby Jay said, "is a fifty-three-year-old man who needs his second complete knee rebuild in four months. He's finished, kid, he just can't see it yet. And Rex? Nobody loves 'The Dungeon

Master' more than me, but that guy's never really been anything more than a mid-card draw. He's great when he's chasing, you know what I mean? But it'd be promotional malpractice to let him try to run with the title. I might as well put a bunch of money inside my favorite suitcase, douse it in gasoline and set it on fire."

"But I'm not *even* a mid-card draw," I said. "Nobody gives a shit about me."

"That's where you're wrong," he said. "Maybe nobody gives a shit about 'The Real Deal' Dallas Hostettler, but I've been watching you, kid. You might be the best pure athlete I've ever seen out there in the ring — and you're getting the hang of the psychology and pacing. Everything else, we can fix. We'll repackage your gimmick, give you a new look. With the beautiful Miss Mary Lynn by your side, it'll be aces. Six months from now, you'll be as popular as 'Maniac' Mack Savage ever was."

"I'm not ready," I said, feeling embarrassed for it but also knowing it needed to be said. "Maybe six months from now. Maybe a year from now. But right now? Tonight?"

Baby Jay threw up his hands. "Life ain't a fucking taxi service, Princess," he said. "You don't get to call down and order your opportunities whenever you feel like it. They come when they come. You either climb in and take the ride or you stay on the fucking curb."

"We'll do it," Mary Lynn said.

"Of course we'll do it," I said, hoping my face wasn't as red as it felt.

"I should fucking hope you will," Baby Jay said. "Jesus Christ, I've never had to twist a guy's arm to get him to become the goddamn champion before. I better not be wrong about you, Dallas. I'm sticking my neck out here. A long way out."

"You're not wrong," I said, "but what about the deposit on the title belt? I don't have that kind of money."

"The deposit is bullshit," Baby Jay said, waving his hands. "Nobody's put down a deposit on a wrestling title since 1975. If you run off with my belt, I'll just call Vic Valley and he'll send some guys out here to kill you. That's how it works."

"Got it," I said. It started to dawn on me that I wouldn't have to leave town. That I wouldn't have to find a new place to live, to prove myself to a whole new locker room full of guys. At least not yet. "What about Mack and Rex? They're good with this?"

"They'll do it," he said, "and that's all that matters."

I walked out of there feeling lightheaded but somehow like my arms and legs weighed a thousand pounds. The backstage hallways were full of people getting shit ready. A few of them were already looking at me like they knew that I was going over that night. I told Mary Lynn to head to our locker room, that I would meet her there in a few minutes. She gave me a worried look, but I told her it would be alright.

"I gotta go find Mack," I told her.

FIFTEEN
CIRCLE OF LIFE

The sound of the door clicking shut brought his head up. He was alone in a locker room built for a basketball team. It felt cavernous in there. Empty. Every step I took across the room echoed like I was walking into a cathedral. He already had his gear on — a pair of wild-print orange tights I knew said MANIAC across the ass — and was strapping his knee brace onto his bad leg. The dopp kit I'd given him back at dinner lay on the bench next to him, and next to that was the FSW title belt. The belt drew my eyes like a beacon.

"What do you want?" he asked, before I'd even got halfway. He sounded like a guy confronting the neighbor who'd shot his dog. It put a lump in my throat.

I waited until I was sitting down on the bench across from him. "I wanted to make sure we're good," I said. "You signed off on this? You'll go through with it?"

"I should slap you in the mouth for even asking me that," he said. There was something lazy about the way his head moved when he looked at me. I couldn't really see his eyes behind his mirrored shades, but I could tell they were hurt. Maybe a little crazy from the drugs. I wondered how many of those painkillers he'd taken.

"You know this wasn't my idea, Sav. You know damn well I had nothing to do with this."

"What difference does that make?" he said.

"Baby Jay wouldn't take no for an answer," I told him. "He said it's my time."

Something about that struck him funny. "Oh, I bet you argued real hard against the idea," he said. "I just bet you did."

I wanted to tell him this was just business, but I knew it would sound hollow. "Believe whatever you want," I said. Then I hesitated and asked: "You want to talk about the finish?"

"No," he said. "I don't want to talk about the fucking finish. We'll handle it out there. At least we can do *that* like a couple of professionals."

"Fine by me," I said. "Well. OK. I guess if there's anything else you want to say to me, go ahead and get it off your chest."

For the first time, he looked unsure of himself. He tipped his head to one side and cracked his neck loud enough that it echoed on the concrete walls. "I think Molly's going to leave me," he said finally.

His voice had an awful hollow sound when he said it. It made me realize a couple things: First, that as beloved as he was, Mack didn't have much else in his life besides wrestling and Molly. Second, that maybe right at that moment, I was his best friend. "Fuck," I said. "I'm sorry to hear that. You sure about it?"

"She don't know it yet," he said, "but the scent is in the air."

"Sav," I said, putting my face a little closer to him. "You need to get your knee fixed, brother. Do your rehab. Have that baby. A year from now, you'll be right back here winning this bad boy back from me. Mark my words."

I rapped my knuckles against the big eagle on the front of the FSW belt. It snapped him out of his reverie. He grinned at me again — that mean Mack Savage grin with tobacco grit all over his teeth. "You know what, Dally?" he said. "This business is a fucking cesspool. It snatches you up while you're still just a young buck. It gives you a little taste of the good life — the money, the girls, the fucking high of the crowd — and, for a while, you don't even notice the years racing by. When the next guy shows up? The guy who's gonna take your place? He don't show up with a knife in his hand. He shows up all smiles asking, can he carry your bag for you? Asking, can you teach him everything you know? Everything you learned in your life of blood sweat and tears? In your life of getting your fucking ribs broke in Tijuana? Dislocating three fingers in Puerto Rico and getting a fucking animal doctor to snap them back in place? Having the fucking Maharajah bust your ankle in a match out in Detroit? And you know what? You agree to do it, because — fuck it — some old-timer did it for you a million years ago, you know what I mean? Because it's the fucking circle of life. You get to be my age? You can see the end coming. You can see it coming down Main Street like the fucking Fourth of July parade — and somehow, when that dagger slides into your back, it's still a fucking shocking experience. Somehow, it still all happens sooner than you think. You get on the other side of it? This life? All this shit? It feels like a pretty fucking short ride. You sit around wondering what the hell you even done it for."

He was right, but it was the kind of wisdom you can't really appreciate when you're young. Now that I've lived it myself, I wish I could go back and throw my arms around him. Just give that son of a bitch a big bearhug and tell him everything was going to be OK. But in the moment, I bristled. "Sav," I said. "I told you, it's not my call. Baby Jay wants to put the title on me. What am I supposed to say? No?"

"For all I know, the three of you had this schemed-up against me from the beginning," he said. "Mary Lynn is gonna come in as your valet now? A pretty lady shows up just in time to help you spread your wings and get over as a big-time singles star? That's really convenient, isn't it?"

"This isn't you," I said. "You're not acting like yourself."

"I could understand if it was Rex," he said, leaning back in the chair as if he hadn't heard me. Like he was talking to himself. "At least Rex knows his stuff. At least Rex can wrestle his way out of a wet paper sack. But you? The Little Princess? How am I not supposed to be insulted by *that*?"

"Fucking stop calling me that," I said, feeling something crack loose in my chest. "You know what? I came in here to have it out with you face-to-face. I thought you might be happy for me. I thought you might take it like a man."

"You're not ready," he said, as plaintive as I'd ever heard him. "You're going to fuck it up."

I thought about telling him maybe he had a point, that I'd said those very words to Baby Jay not half an hour ago, but I was already pissed off, and the way he said it pissed me off more. It made me reflect on the times I'd carried him through matches that summer, doing all the work while he stood in the corner shaking his ass for the crowd, making the girls squeal. The times I'd carried him to his motel room afterward, him too shitfaced to walk, me listening to his stories, his so-called life lessons in the business. Hanging out in his locker room smelling his old sweat socks and his beer farts, schlepping his bags, making sure his hat and title belt were where he could find them. Now he wanted me to hold his hand and talk him through his divorce, and *then* he wanted to sit there and run me down? On the biggest night of my career? The biggest night of my life? Nah, I decided, that wasn't happening.

"Well, if I did fuck it up," I said, "wouldn't that just make me the next 'Maniac' Mack Savage?"

He hit me harder than I expected, flying out of his chair with a full body tackle I hadn't seen coming. I toppled backward off the bench and the two of us landed in a heap on the concrete floor. He was still quicker than a hiccup, and I was lucky his knee was jacked-up. His leg brace got tangled up beneath the bench and I managed to get my feet under me. I heaved him up, grabbing two fistfuls of his *Panda-monium* T-shirt and pushing him against a row of freestanding lockers. The whole thing boomed and tipped, falling like a giant domino against the far wall. It must've made a hell of a sound, but the two of us were too blood-crazed to hear it, like a couple of pit bulls trying to get their jaws around each other's throats.

He threw a short hook into my floating ribs, but I was too strong for him. He couldn't twist free of my grip. I took him off his feet with an old lineman trick I liked to use back at Boise State — basically a swim move with a little foot sweep the referees never saw. He clattered down again, and this time I was on top, raining down punches as the door flew open and a bunch of the boys came pouring in.

It was good timing for me, I guess. All they saw of our fracas was me with Mack pinned to the floor, beating the tar out of him. It took three of them to pull me off, and even as Baby Jay got between us, trying to hold us back, we clawed at each other like animals. Mack's sunglasses had come off, and for the first time I could see the yellow whites of his eyes, as big as dinner plates in his head. A little blood trickled from the corner of his mouth. We were both huffing and puffing. My ribs ached, but other than that, I was all right. Demian Rex slipped his arms underneath mine, and I let him pull me back.

"Easy, ladies," he said. "Relax. Relax."

Baby Jay and the guys from The Great Depression had Mack corralled at the other end of the bench. The big empty room was suddenly full of bodies and loud voices. It was stiflingly hot in there. Everybody was grabbing at me, talking at once. I could see it on their faces, though: this look of awe at having to stop me from beating Mack's ass. Mack, on the other hand, was a mess. His hair was wild, blood smeared across the shoulder of his T-shirt. He looked crazy, huffing and puffing, spit flying out of his mouth.

"Look at this place," Baby Jay said, with the tone of a man already thinking about his security deposit. "For fuck's sake, save some of it for the ring, boys."

Barrow came to help Rex, and the two of them had almost got me out of the room — me, making a show of trying to resist but really letting them walk me back — before Mack called out my name.

"Hostettler," he said, easily getting free of The Great Depression but not coming any closer. "Just do one goddam thing for me, would you?"

"What's that, Sav?"

"When it comes time for you to give me that lariat? Don't you hold nothing back," he said. "If I'm going out, I'm going out on my shield."

"Brother," I said, "you can take that to the bank."

Then, I let the two heels push me out the door, watching Mack's red face disappear as it swung shut behind us.

SIXTEEN
THE BIG HOSS

The ring was full of broken bodies. Mack lay spread-eagled in the middle of the canvas, his face unrecognizable behind a mask of sticky blood. Demian Rex slumped in one corner, his chin lolling against his chest. Barrow had collapsed near the ropes with his arms flung up over his face as if trying to defend himself from more of my blows. After taking a moment to collect myself, soaking up the locomotive roar of boos coming from the audience, I strolled over, put my boot on Barrow's side and rolled him out under the bottom rope. His body sounded like a raw turkey when it landed on the concrete. Baby Jay came up to hand me a microphone, and one of his stagehands put something heavy in my other hand. I looked down and realized it was the Frontier States Wrestling heavyweight title belt.

I lifted that fucker to the heavens.

Let the boos pick up even more steam.

"Quiet down now," I said, in as reasonable a voice as I could muster. My heart was still going a mile a minute. "Hush. Hush. You're gonna want to hear this. I got a few things to say. There, that's better. Can you hear me now? Damn, you all should see your faces. Don't look so surprised, people. Don't look so shocked. Nothing that transpired in this ring here tonight should surprise you. Not in the slightest. This has been a long time coming. For six months I've been here in FSW. For the last three months, I've traveled up and down these roads with that man, 'Maniac' Mack Savage, from town to town and outhouse to outhouse and every single bar and restaurant in between. Yeah, brother, I seen a whole lot of this country, and I seen a whole lot of your dirty, stinking faces out in those seats. Night after night after night in this ring, breaking my body down to nothing. Bleeding. Sweating. None of you two-bit hillbillies ever gave me the time of day, did you? No. You were too busy cheering for Mack Savage. Cheering for your hero. Well, look at him now."

Mack's chest was heaving up and down with every breath. We'd gone forty hard minutes leading up to the finish and, at the moment of truth, when the whole crowd expected me to lay out Demian Rex so Sav could pin him, I'd turned and hit Mack with my lariat like a runaway train. The silence of it was the most amazing part. That second or two after people saw me slam my forearm across his chest where they couldn't believe it. Now, he wasn't moving. A little bloody bubble formed on his lips and popped.

"Mack, brother, I guess we had some fun, man," I said. "I guess we closed down a few bars. We had some parties, old man, and I'll always be grateful for that. But there comes a time in every man's life when you gotta sit back and you gotta take stock. You gotta ask yourself a few questions. You gotta wonder: what about me? How come I'm the one doing all the work? How come I'm the one taking all these ass-whippings and *handing out* all the ass-whippings and I ain't getting none of the rewards? How come everywhere we go, the people all *love* 'Maniac' Mack Savage and don't nobody — don't *nobody* — spare one second for 'The Real Deal' Dallas Hostettler? For me, I guess that moment came last week. Last week, when Wayne Barrow and those animals in The Great Depression had me laid out in the middle of this ring, beating the absolute snot out of me. And where were you? Where were you, Mack? You were nowhere to be found, brother. You were too busy off somewhere chasing down

Damian Rex. Too busy to care about your ol' buddy Dallas, huh? Well, you know what? After I thought about it and thought about it, I decided that stuff ain't right, man. It ends right now. Right here."

One of Baby Jay's cameramen had come into the ring with a hand-held and I looked right into the lens when I said the next part.

"I ain't never been nobody's fool, Mack Savage, and from this moment forward I ain't nobody's toady, neither. I ain't nobody's babysitter. I ain't here to hold no hands, and I damn sure ain't here to kiss no babies. From now on, Mack, you're on your own. And you know what? So am I. I ain't never sticking my neck out for anybody else ever again. Not like I done for you. From now on, it's all about me. I'm looking out for number one. Sure, you can boo if you want to. Yeah, let me hear all them boos. All that hate just gives me strength. That just lets me know I finally done something right for a change. I finally done something for myself.

"So, listen up. Listen to me now. I guess you could say there's a new sheriff in town in FSW. A lot is going to change around here, starting with one thing. From now on, that guy ain't none of you ever gave a crap about? 'The Real Deal' Dallas Hostettler? That guy is dead. He's dead and gone, and he ain't never coming back. If any of you country bumpkins or wannabe tough guys out there want to address me, want to get my autograph or say one stinkin' word to me, you all can start off by calling me 'The Big Hoss.' 'The Big Hoss' Dallas Hostettler is here, brother, and the world ain't never going to be the same again.

The crowd didn't know how to take any of this. They were booing me like crazy, but I could also tell they were a little bit fascinated. I pointed out through the ropes at Mary Lynn, who was standing there beaming up at me from ringside.

"Hey, man, hold on. Hold on. Listen. I want you all to meet somebody. Mary Lynn, come on in here, darling. Come on up here. Let me get these ropes for you. Yeah. Alright. You all seeing this? Take a good look. Take a good look at the only friend — the only *true* friend — I've ever had in this business and the only true friend I'm ever going to need again. I want to introduce you all to my new manager, Miss Mary Lynn. Isn't she something? It's just me and her now. I don't need no 'Maniac' Mack Savage. I don't need no 'Dungeon Master' Demian Rex. I sure as hell don't need any of you people, but I have a funny feeling you all are going to be needing me a lot more starting right now. I just need the beautiful Mary Lynn, here, and I need this title belt. That's all.

"So, tonight, out here in front of God and everybody, I want to make this thing official. Hold on, now, I gotta get down on one knee. I just had a hell of a fight. I'm still moving a little slow, but I'll get there. Any of you ever try doing a whole wrestling match with a diamond ring tucked in your tights? No? I didn't think so. I can't recommend it, if I'm being honest, but I have a feeling it's gonna be worth it.

"Mary Lynn Fawcett, could you find it in your heart to be my wife? Would you marry me? Would you marry the champ?"

Nobody else knew this part was coming, and that made it just about the best moment I ever had in my career. Mary Lynn saw that big rock in my hand and her eyes got wet. She looked around at the crowd like she wasn't sure if she should believe it. Some of the fans were clapping now, in spite of themselves. Everybody loves a proposal. Then Mary Lynn nodded her head, came over, and kissed me. A nice, long one for the cameras and the people. Letting everybody get a good look.

"Yeah, that's right," I said, as we broke it off. "That's what I was hoping. Now, that's a good night, people. That's a good night. That's how you do it. You're looking at the new power couple of professional wrestling. You're looking at the new breed, right here. Now, we hate to disappoint you. We hate to send you home with sour feelings. But me and Mary Lynn got some more business to attend to backstage. Thank you all for coming. We'll see you next week."

SEVENTEEN
LET'S GO HOME

Nobody ever called me Princess after that.

Following our dust-up in the locker room, I never spoke another word to "Maniac" Mack Savage, besides a simple head nod or a "How you doing?" when we crossed paths at some get-together. He and Molly never had that baby. They called it quits about — I don't know — '85, I guess? She ended up hitting it big in real estate. Last I heard, she owned a string of commercial spots out in Seattle. Had a chain of nail salons that turned a good profit. Mack just couldn't quit the wrestling business. It wasn't in him to stop. He just kept going and going, washing up in every territory that would have him until he'd wore out his welcome just about all over. After that, he did Japan. Did Mexico. Worked smaller and smaller rooms until finally I saw him on a VHS cassette tape wrestling in a backyard at some kid's bar mitzvah. Just a bunch of folding chairs set out in the grass around a sad little ring. The people there still went apeshit for him the way they always did, but it was fucking awful to watch. You could smell the desperation through the Memorex.

He never took the time to get his bad leg fixed. Never really rehabbed it the way he should've, and near the end he could barely walk on it. Must have been on a steady diet of cortisone shots just to make it through the matches. His skin sagged. His voice was like a cloud of dust. Wrestling does that to some guys. It eats them alive. Once they feel the rush of it — that warm feeling you get from the crowd and the girls and the beers with the boys afterward — they realize nothing else in life will ever come close. They don't know what else to do with themselves. When father time comes knocking, they panic.

Mack died in 1990. Heart attack out on his boat on Lake Mead. He'd been living alone down in Vegas the last few years, I guess. I heard the boat sat out there in the sun almost a whole day before somebody found him. Even today, I can't fucking let myself dwell on that part of it. How does a guy like Mack Savage, one of the true kings of this business, die alone and then sit there roasting until some jet skiers come along and find him all bloated and burnt to a crisp from the heat? That's unfathomable to me. It's just fucking sad. Sometimes, I'll be minding my own business, watching TV or out riding my Harley, and I'll see something that reminds me of it, and all of a sudden my skin gets cold. A dark mood settles over me. I start thinking maybe I could've done something. Maybe I could've at least called the guy. Reached out. Tried to help him. But I know Mack never would've taken my calls. A guy like that won't let anybody help him. He's on his own path, and wherever it leads — that's where he's gonna end up. Breaks my fucking heart.

Demian Rex wrestled another twenty years but somehow got out of it with most of his faculties intact. When he finally did retire, he cut off his hair, ditched the vampire dye job and started a car dealership in Rapid City. Gary Steinberg's Crazy Deals. I used to see his commercials on TV, with Rex yelling into the camera and tossing money into the air and shit like that. Hard to believe it was the same guy who used to paint a pentagram between his eyes and scare little kids during our Sunday matinees. As much as I hated him back then, he turned out to be an all right guy. Used to send us Christmas cards every year, though I think we all lost track of each other after a while. I don't even know if he's still alive, to be honest.

Wayne Barrow never figured out the mental side. He always looked like a million bucks, though, and rode that for a few years. We used to go out for beers whenever we crossed paths. I used to help him out when I could. Gave him the phone numbers for the promoters I knew who might be willing to take a flier on him. Mid-90s, he gave it up and went into bodybuilding. Won some trophies. Got his butt kicked in a few strongman competitions. I think a heart attack got Barrow, too.

The Great Depression were so fucking talented, but like I said, there was that car accident. Steve or Larry, whichever one of them it was, got all fucked up. Otherwise, New York or Atlanta would've snapped them up and made them into something. They could've been pretty huge, if you ask me. Just needed to tweak the gimmick a little bit here and there. But sometimes that's how it goes.

Baby Jay, man, what a sad story. I never would've seen it coming, either. A few years after I left the territory, he booked himself to take a piledriver from some young kid who probably had no business even being in the ring. Of course, the kid fucked it up, and Baby Jay wound up in a wheelchair. After that, he got into all kinds of crazy illegal shit. Drugs, gambling, hookers, extortion. Straight mafioso stuff. Fucking became a pretty scary guy for a long time. I knew lots of the boys who got in trouble with him, got in hock and couldn't get themselves out. But I ain't saying no names and you did not hear that shit from me.

Me? I wrestled twenty-two years before my hip gave out and Mary Lynn made me hang up my boots. Every day, I thank my lucky stars I have her in my life. Without her, I might've turned out just like Mack. The two of us were fortunate she got into the business, I guess. She took a shine to it right away. Turned out she's got a real mind for creative. Most of the best angles I had in my career were at least partly Mary Lynn's idea. We spent most of the rest of our careers traveling together, her acting as my manager and me becoming champion most every place we ever went.

People still put the promo I cut that night in Billings on the internet. I heard some of Sonny Da Silva's agents will show it to the younger talent when they're trying to learn how to work the mic. After that night, I traded in my blue tights and sea-swell boots for all black. Black hat, black tights, bull rope draped across my shoulders for good measure. That part was Mary Lynn's idea, too. We stole the look right out of that photograph from *Time Magazine*, the one she told Baby Jay about. When fans saw me coming down the aisle dressed like that, especially with Mary Lynn wearing her matching hat and puffing on the big stogie she adopted as her trademark, it got a reaction. People just loved "The Big Hoss," man. That, or they hated him. Either way, it was money in our pockets. We never had a hard time getting booked.

A few weeks after Mary Lynn found out she was pregnant with our first, I went and saw a specialist who told me there was nothing at all wrong with my testes. Guy reviewed my medical file and said he couldn't explain it. Theorized it was possible the old doc back at Boise State had messed up my original diagnosis. Of course, I knew it was also possible that Molly's and Mack's witchdoctor hadn't been so totally full of shit after all, that those pills Mack had slipped me had done something to my insides, but I kept my mouth shut about that part of it. Mary Lynn and I ended up having four girls and raised them mostly on the road. Our oldest — Victoria — whom we conceived right before I won the FSW title, is an actuary now. Ain't that some shit? All our girls done good, to be honest. They had their ups and downs just like anybody growing up, but they all turned out to be solid citizens. That makes me prouder than anything I ever did in wrestling.

In my forties, I ended-up signing with Universal and going to work out in New York for Sonny Da Silva. Of course, by then he'd mostly broken up the territories. Ran the old-timers out of business. Turned all the boys into "sports entertainers" in some kind of half-assed effort to juke the state athletic commissions. Fucking Sonny. I never saw eye-to-eye with that prick. Not even after he put me in his rinky-dink little hall of fame back in — when was it — 2016? Flew me out to the city, put me up in a suite at the Four Seasons. Trotted me out the night before WrestleFest with all the other has-beens to give my little speech, hand me my little trophy. I was there four days, and I never said a word to Sonny Da Silva. Not word fucking one. He made himself real rich — a *billionaire*, as he'll be the first fucking person to remind you — but I'll never forgive him for what he did to this business.

Holy hell, though, the money was good. It was more like working at some suit-and-tie corporate gig than a wrestling show, but times change and you have to change with them. I did the whole pay-per-view thing, did every WrestleFest about ten years in a row. They made a bunch of action figures for me. Put me on T-shirts. Even put me on a goddam ice cream bar. It was quite the life, I suppose, and truth be told I had some good times running around with the other old-timers who were still working there in the late 1990s. Guys like Kevin Cumberland, who had become one of Sonny's primary booking agents after his brother, Jason, left the business. Never felt as pure as the early days, though. Plus, Sonny was always hanging around slithering like a fucking snake. It felt like a relief when I finally got out.

These days, Mary Lynn and I got ourselves a gym and a little wrestling school out in Denver. Title and insurance and everything are all in her name, but it's my picture on the sign out front. People come to us — just kids, really — and we turn them into wrestlers as best we can. We try not to rip people off too bad. Some people you've probably heard of have come through our gym, and I feel proud every time I see them on TV or see them on the internet. The only thing I ever promise them is honesty. If I don't think you're going to make it in the business, I'll tell you to your face. If only so you can save your-self the time and money. If I think you've got what it takes, I'll do my best to bring the best out of you.

I tell people right off: a lot of the stuff you saw me do out there in the ring, I stole it from Mack Savage. There's no shame in that. I tell these kids, pay attention to the people you think are better than you. If you're lucky enough to know them, ask for their advice. See what they do well. You can't take everything, but you can borrow little pieces here and there. For me, a lot of my facial expressions, body language, ring psychology, it's pure "Maniac" Mack. Funny, because at this point, most people probably think of that stuff as belonging to "The Big Hoss," but it wasn't mine in the first place. I think of it as the great knowledge of the business passing on to the next generation. If I'm lucky, maybe the next big star will steal some of my stuff and make it their own and, in that way, they'll keep it alive. I tell these young kids, I wish Mack could be here to teach it all to you himself, but he ain't because the business ate him up and then he died. That's something they'll each have to learn about when the time comes.

Sometimes in the gym, when the students are out there doing their drills or doing air squats or burpees or any of the other terrible bullshit we make them do, the whole room fills up with the sounds of wrestling. That's probably when I'm the happiest. I like to close my eyes and breathe it in. Feel my fingers on the canvas where I'm standing next to the ring. Feel my feet inside the old wrestling boots I haven't put on for quite a while. Smell the stink of it. I imagine I can still hear his voice. Maybe on some long-lost Saturday night out at the Mule Palace or somewhere. The two of us covered in sweat and out of breath as the crowd goes crazy chanting his name. We'd have the whole world right where we wanted it and he'd look at me, give me that crazy "Maniac" Mack wink and say, "All right, kid. Let's go home."

I repeat that to myself a few times, letting the experience wash over me. Feeling his presence and the times we had. All of it still as real as the day it happened. I linger a minute in it because I know pretty soon, it'll all be gone. I take a moment to remind myself how fortunate I am. I'm an old man now, and not everybody gets the chance to say that. For sure, I'll take it over the alternative.

Then, when I'm ready, I open my eyes.

And I'm still here.

THE LAST WILL AND TESTAMENT OF JOE VARGA

JONATHAN SNOWDEN

TERRITORY:
Peach State Wrestling
(*Georgia, spreading nationwide*)
1984

Start at the beginning.

That's what my daddy always said. The key to a good story. Of course he was a dumb fucking drunk, so who the hell knows, right?

Anyway, starting at the beginning isn't as easy as it sounds, because where that is, I can't exactly say.

Is it a trailer park in Dothan where I grew up, a good spit away from Florida? The cracker part, not the part with the beaches where you might go for spring break.

Maybe it's college, when I drank my way right out of a wrestling scholarship at the University of Iowa, all that corn, both the stalks and the whiskey, driving me a little bananas until a chance at a national title went up in the flames. Right alongside all the bridges I burned.

Or was it the day the great Joe Varga pulled me from that fire and taught me just how little I actually knew about physical manipulation of the human anatomy? Mostly by twisting my head in directions it wasn't supposed to go, taking the idea of straightening me out literally, I guess.

Was it my second failed marriage? Or the third, those two glorious weeks with a Las Vegas stripper I'd met working for Ace Eaton in LA, tits so silicone firm you could use them to hammer a nail, if you were so inclined.

Where was I?

The beginning. For me, this particular story begins and will hopefully end in a wrestling ring, the only place I've ever truly belonged, even when I hated it. And boy *did* I hate it sometimes.

In this case it was a rickety old thing in Phenix City, Alabama, hard as a dick in a titty bar, if you excuse my French. I was wrestling Wayne McCollough, a muscly kid Baby Jay Chevalier had given up on in Billings. And with good reason. He had the look of a wrestler, or at least the Flex Boulder kind of TV wrestler, the kind who earned his keep on the pointy end of a needle, if you catch my drift.

The kid was on the juice is what I'm saying, muscles like the comic book hero he surely thought he could be. Was even wearing these spandex pants, red, white, and blue like he was about to salute the flag, tight enough that you could tell if he was, if you catch my drift. But six years in the business, and he was still running through the steps in his mind, a high school kid at his first dance, just trying to look cool and poised and normal and fucking it all to hell. Dumb as a box of rocks.

He had all these moves he wanted to try, hopeful that the Bobby Jacobs name, faded and cursed as it was, might get a tape of this thing in the hands of the dirtsheets or maybe into a VCR in New York with Sonny Da Silva sneaking looks between lines.

Who the hell knows what he thought. He was young enough to

still dream, which is good for him, but I was way past pretending, content to work this headlock for a while, feeling out where we might go, testing the crowd to see just how little they would tolerate us doing.

"C'mon, fight, you peckerwoods!"

Music to my ears, though I could feel Wayne's tension growing, worried about losing the crowd just as I was sure I had a firm hold. A headlock is a thing of art. If you do it right, you can ride that thing for a good ten minutes, hit the finish, and then hit the bar. So I'd let him up, give the audience and the boy hope, then hip toss him back down to the mat, a little smile letting those rednecks know that I knew that they were getting pissed off and that I surely didn't give a single fuck. That wasn't me being an asshole. Or, I guess, just me being an asshole. Like I said, this was art, and my art was making these drunk dipshits mad enough to care about Wayne McCollough beating the hell out of me in the end.

Strangler Lesko had become the biggest star in wrestling with this headlock back in the 1920s or some shit, and I cranked it hard enough to make him proud, the way they did in the olden times, before MTV and the remote control made us an instant-gratification society.

When a man had to think about dragging his ass out of his chair to change the channel on the boob tube, he was more patient. Judicious. You can put up with a lot so as not to have to get out of the chair to spin that dial. These remote control motherfuckers? They want that hit of dopamine right damn now, want to see someone jump off the top rope or chop each other's chest into hamburger. And they most definitely did not want to see me hold this kid in a headlock.

"Booo! You suck Jacobs."

Lesko had perfected his on a giant wooden head with springs inside, the kind of thing you did when you had a 22-inch collar, weighed 250 pounds, and all your buddies were damn tired of getting their ears squeezed into cauliflowers. I only knew this because old

Varga had the damn thing in his office, creeping everyone out and reminding him of better times. Anyway, the result was Lesko getting so strong that he could grab that headlock on an old boy, put some pressure right on the jaw and make just about anyone put their own shoulders on the mat just to escape the pain. *That* was wrestling.

Where was I?

McCollough. Phenix City. Well, just so you don't think of me as a bully, let me assure you that I didn't put a real hard squeeze on him, these being supposedly more civilized times. At least I didn't until he tried to yank away before I was ready, trying to get his stuff in, like the world needed to see another stiff meathead throw a clunky clothesline or come off the top rope with a double-axe handle so hard you'd almost prefer the actual axe. And lord knows I didn't want to take a single flat back bump on that hard-ass ring for $50 and a handshake.

"Man, what the fuck?" he said, muffled a little on account of my forearm covering his mouth. It was kind of a stage whisper but loud enough that someone snickered in the audience. Fucking greenhorn couldn't even kayfabe calling spots in the goddamn ring.

"Hey kid, just stay where I put you. Let it breathe."

"Fuck that, let's *do* something." Grown man throwing a damn hissy fit.

Long story short, he tried to pull himself out of my headlock, like for real, confident his big, watery, chemically-enhanced muscles would overpower me, pot belly, miles on the road, and punches on my bump card making me look like fresh meat, I guess. But there's strength you get moving iron up and down and strength you get moving men against their will. And he was going nowhere fast. But he was persistent, even popping me in the mouth with his elbow as he flailed around.

It was the blood that turned me. Every man has a monster inside. Mine just happens to be a little scarier than yours, you know? So when I felt that trickle of blood on my chin, I lost myself for a second. I let go of that headlock, like the kid wanted, but kept the position. I needed that to lay in the crossfaces, one after another straight across the kid's face. It was the third or fourth one that broke his beak. By the fifth, the little ref was trying to grab a hold of me, claiming a violation of the rules. I'm not an unreasonable man, so I met him in the middle, grabbing the headlock again, his blood now coating my forearm, and I gave him a little squeeze, and the referee told us to get to the finish already, damn it.

That's when I saw her familiar face where she had certainly not been before. You don't miss a woman like that. Fourth row, as beautiful as ever in her Anne Taylor, eyes puffy, tears still there if you looked close enough. She looked at me. I looked at her. And I knew.

The old man was dead. And my life was never going to be the same.

JOE VARGA HAD BEEN a man's man, a tuft of hair on his thick chest, muscles supple and lithe in an era when wrestlers tended towards the beer belly and barrel chest look. Wrestling is a smoke and mirrors show, but Varga was as real as they come. He'd had to be.

For years he carried the five pounds of gold, a dainty championship belt that declared *he* was champion of the entire world. He'd go from town to town, country to country, putting that prize up against the local promotion's top star. Sure, we were all part of the famed National Wrestling Council. But each area of the country was its own fiefdom, each one ruled by a bigger piece of shit than the last. Sixteen heads of the same snake, he'd called them, the promoters who ran the wrestling racket.

"I went in there every night ready to fight," he'd told me once. "I always wanted one of those sons of bitches to try me. Not a one of them ever did though. Not after Birmingham."

He'd usually take the other fella down early in the match, like I'd done McCollough now that I think about it, and hold him there just to show he could, let the other guy feel his strength and how easily he could take each and every one of your joints and end life as you knew it.

There was always a fear that someone would go into business for himself in the old days, taking the world title off an unsuspecting champion in what the old timer's called a shoot — one of those times when wrestling got a little too real. His mentor had been Lesko himself, and he'd actually done it back in 1931, roughing up some dumb football player in front of 5,000 people in Detroit, taking the belt from the New York Syndicate to an upstart group out of Chicago. Squeezed that man's head until he had turned onto his back just to escape the pain, squeezed it until it felt like it was going to pop like a pumpkin in one of those Gallagher shit shows me and wife number two had seen at the Sahara.

The old man and I bonded over it, that ability to take another man and bend him to your will. He'd taught me all the basic shit you need to work a wrestling match, the drop downs, the back bumps, the way you can throw a punch that looks mean as all hell but wouldn't move a hair on an old lady's head.

But he'd also taught me things I'd never learned on a wrestling mat in school, the way you could hook a man's finger just so if he didn't want you to take a hold of his arm, how you might turn a front facelock into a choke hold with just a slight shift of your hands, how to control a leg and rip out the knee in just seconds, the other fella all but crippled by the time he even feels the hurt.

Pain was our business, and we'd train it day and night. He'd take money from guys to teach them how to wrestle, then put them in the ring with me to find out how badly they really wanted it. It wasn't pretty, but it was what he knew, a business of tough men and not prancing sissies like young Sam Styles, our current illustrious world's champion, feather boas and big bumps obscuring what old Joe thought was a shocking lack of anything resembling actual wrestling.

Where was I?

Joe Varga was dead. I had just let big dumb Wayne McCollough pin me with a lariat that had a little extra on it I probably deserved.

And Lana was following me to the back, because no one stopped a woman who looked like that from going anywhere she wanted to be.

"Bobby. Bobby! Will you slow down?"

But I couldn't. Because slowing down meant hearing the news I'd only guessed at. It meant making it real. It meant everything I'd wanted to say to the old man had died with him. And it meant I'd have to look into the eyes of a woman I'd never stopped loving, look at her and know she could never be mine, and look at her and know it was a situation of my own making.

I went on not slowing down all the way out the back door, all the way to the parking lot, grabbing my bag and keys and praying my $50 would still be there when I went back later to collect. But there was a little Mercedes convertible parked right behind my beloved Bronco, blocking me in.

Outmaneuvered, as always, by a goddamn Varga.

Sorry, Stevens. She was Lana Stevens, thanks to Rod "By God" Stevens, my former partner and best friend, and didn't that just fucking burn, you know?

Lana was wearing flats and not heels, so I hadn't really gotten comfortable on the hood of her car as she barrelled into view, somehow making teary-eyes and barreling sexy. There was no preamble or softening of the blow.

"He's dead."

"I know."

And then she looked at me the way she did. Didn't say anything. Just looked. She saw it all. A 37-year-old man going on 60, 30 extra pounds around the middle, $127 in the bank account, drinking and fucking his way to an early grave. Worn slap out.

"Lana, I...."

I didn't know what to say. In a television studio I could talk like a chatterbox, threatening to break somebody's arm and do them in at the Civic Center, brother. But what do you say in a situation like this? I was suddenly slower than molasses, mouth open like one of those honest-to-god morons, bless their souls.

Joe Varga had taken me in. Into his home. Into his family. He'd molded me into something, called in all his markers to give me the kind of break almost nobody ever got, then watched as I shot it all to hell. I was lost, my own thoughts getting the best of me, 15 years of memories all washing over me at the same time.

That's when she pulled me into a hug, surprising the hell out of me, I've got to say, blood and sweat all over her white pantsuit, her tears on my chest as I held her tight. She'd lost her daddy, and here I was thinking about myself. Isn't that just damn typical?

We were thick as thieves back in the early times, Lana, Rod and me. She'd sneak over after classes and watch us workout in old Joe's barn, sweat dripping as we did our Hindu squats or rolled in the ring, practicing what we'd learned that week. Then she'd sneak out of the house at night, when we'd hit the one bar in Winder, Georgia, a sophomore at the University of Georgia but happier with two dipshit pro wrestlers than she was at a fraternity party or knitting circle or whatever the fuck girls did at college.

That girl could drink, and she could laugh, a little snort that came up from her soul. She was Joe's whole life since her momma had passed, and she got away with everything but murder. He had one rule: she couldn't date any of the boys. But that line got erased like all the others one night in Athens at the 40 Watt, when we'd snuck off to the bathroom and done what young and stupid kids did. When she showed up at the matches the next night in Dawsonville to watch me pin Rod with the Varga Press, it was on my arm.

"Daddy, I love him."

And that was that. Joe just shook his head in the way old folks did when they knew you were fucking up but also knew there wasn't a damn thing they could do about it.

We'd been married just six weeks later, in life and on broadcast worldwide on FantasticVision, Bucky Walters himself introducing us to the wrestling fans in Georgia in the days before the channel beamed worldwide. Me and Rod had been a tag team then, Stevens and Jacobs, the "American Dream," fighting the Franklin brothers, meaner in real life than they were in the ring, which was no small feat. We were young and handsome and in charge of bringing in the blowjobs. That's what wrestling promoters called young female fans, because that's the promise their presence offered, both to the fans and the boys in the back. Classy right?

Some wrestlers attracted the hard cases, heavy drinking dock workers and shit, there to see blood and guts. We were there to soften the crowd, grab the attention of the girls who had just given up on Tiger Beat. They would bring in the young men, dressed to impress in their jean jackets, hair just so, in case the girls got themselves worked up at the matches, all that naked flesh leading to a backseat quickie in the parking lot.

Where was I?

Lana.

It felt like she held me in the parking lot for half an hour, even if it was really more like thirty seconds. Or maybe I held her. We held each other, I guess, neither wanting to let the moment go.

"Bobby...you know he loved you right?"

"I know."

But I didn't. Not really. I hadn't spoken to the old man in years. Not since I'd crashed our marriage and my career, not since he said he'd end me in this business, not since he went about making sure he succeeded, calling all his old cronies to put in the word that I couldn't be trusted. Not that I didn't do my part to help, stuck now working a succession of outlaw mudshows willing to risk the old man's ire to be able to put my name on the posters they'd tape up all over town.

She seemed tired, and I guessed she was tired of talking about it, too, even fresh as it was. Lana was still beautiful. Her hair was blonde, but when the sun shone on it, it turned auburn, a memory of a day at Myrtle Beach hitting me suddenly like a brick. She was thirty-four, but she looked younger, especially when she was happy. She didn't look so young right now.

"He...he had a will. You're in it. Come by Bucky's office in Atlanta on Monday. Nine o'clock. Can you be up and sober that early?"

The last part stung, not that I'd been up as early as nine a.m. in years. Shit, I didn't even own an alarm clock. The closest thing was the couple in the apartment downstairs, the occasional shriek of their arguments welcoming me back to the world after another night passed out alone on a futon.

"I'll be there," I told her. "Lord willin' and the creek don't rise."

What else could I say? Like there was a choice. Even in death, the old man had a pull I couldn't resist.

I HAD a long time to think about the last will and testament of Joe Varga as I drove into the city. I drove slowly, seeing Atlanta for the first time as a visitor might: the skyline, the streets, the ballparks, the squalor, the elegant roads, the neighborhoods, the kudzu. The kudzu was everywhere, and I found myself thinking of it as a metaphor for Atlanta, for Georgia, and for wrestling most of all, creeping over everything that mattered until nothing else could breathe.

It was probably one final rib, Joe having me come all the way into the city just for some lawyer to read a piece of paper that said "Fuck you, Jacobs" while the room snickered.

Joe was a ribber. He was good at it, like he was everything else associated with this godforsaken business. His favorite was to grab a guy in a wrist lock and threaten to hurt him real bad unless he sucked Joe's dick.

It was the look in their eyes when they dropped to their knees, the shame and fear, that he loved. He told me that one night after a couple of beers. He never made them do it. But he liked to remind them that he could have, building spots into his matches where he'd make a heel get on his knees and beg.

Nice guy, Joe.

Bucky Walters had an office in Tommy Thompson's skyscraper in downtown Atlanta, home to the Global News Network and FantasticVision. A long way up in the world from when I knew him in the '70s, dim lighting, wood, and dark leather making it feel almost like the kind of steak house where you'd get asparagus instead of fries on the side.

Peach State Wrestling had come a long way, too, certainly from the days running hick towns in Georgia every week, once a month slinking into Atlanta hoping we could draw a house in the Omni. I'd played a part in that for sure, whether he'd liked it or not.

Now the show went out over cable everywhere. We got it on channel 13 in Alabama and it had been on channel 13 in Texas and even in California. Channel fucking thirteen. The damn thing was nationwide now, and Bucky was slowly starting to dip his toes into other people's water, running a show here and there, always careful not to step too hard on any other promoter's toes. In wrestling, television had been nothing but a big advertisement to get people out to see the shows. That made channel 13 an ad millions were watching without the hope of buying anything. Bucky meant to change that, I reckon, assuming he didn't get himself shot by one of the other promoters first.

Me, I couldn't really bring myself to watch. Too many memories. There are times in your life when you forget, and then there are the times you remember. Channel 13? It rarely left my mind.

Bucky was always there, for one, the soundtrack for a generation of fans who knew you said "suplay" instead of "suplex," no matter what the other reprobates called it. The word was French, you see, and we were civilized men.

At least some of us. Like Rod, tan and lean and wearing his success like a sheen that never washed off. Thoughts of Rod didn't lead anywhere good, his big house and big car and perfect family a sad contrast to my own shambles of a life, a funhouse mirror reflection of what could have been, if I hadn't been such an impossible fuckup.

So, no, I wasn't much for channel 13, thanks very much.

"Bobby."

"Buck."

No smile, no hug. He just looked at my extended hand before I eventually plopped down across from him. The old man may have forgiven me, but "the Voice" sure hadn't. I'd known him before he had a fucking bookcase in his fancy office, before he had a goddamn computer on his desk, for God's sake. Before he started wearing that stupid cowboy hat.

Maybe he didn't like that, someone knowing him from back when he was a man and not a myth. But it didn't really matter what he fucking liked, did it?

"I suppose you heard about Joe?"

"I did."

"He was a hell of a man. Hell of a man."

"He was surely something to behold. That's for damn sure."

Silence lingered after that, as we both looked everywhere but at each other, neither wanting to show weakness, not wanting the other to see tears well up. We sat in silence and thought about death, hoping death wasn't sitting somewhere thinking about us.

"You'd be surprised how often I think about you," he finally said.

"Really, why's that?"

"Even though people might say we did the right thing, I feel like I failed. And I hate myself for that. I know Joe did, too."

"I didn't deserve it, Buck," I said, trying hard not to cry in the man's office, afraid I might fail even at that. "I messed up. But who in this business hasn't?"

"You gave me your word, Bobby. And you broke it. Man who can't stand on his word is no man at all."

"I can't change the past. All I can do is live with it."

Lana came breezing in just then, timing always impeccable, tits perky in her business costume, if that's not crass to point out, her hair highlighted and shiny in a way that you only get at a beauty salon that charges more an hour than I make in a week. A nod for Bucky, a quick hug for me, and then it was straight to business. She was a lawyer now, I'd heard, one of Big Tommy's right hands here in the big building. Rod and I had competed to see who was going to be the bigger star, make the most money, who would rule the world. Turns out the shiniest star was the one in the bleachers watching us pretend to fight.

"Bobby, thanks for making time in your schedule to come down."

I couldn't tell if she was taking a tone with me, but I let it pass, even though she paused to see if I'd take the bait. In some way you never stop being married, I guess.

"Daddy's funeral is Wednesday. I hope you'll come. But before that, I just wanted to run a little business by you. As you probably remember, Dad owned twenty percent of Peach State Wrestling."

It was a reminder of something I was trying hard not to think about. Old Joe was dead and not just to me. She'd lost her father, and even if she was no-selling it big time, I knew it had to hurt. Grief is not predictable. It moves in waves. One moment, you feel like yourself; the next moment, you feel terrible. Everyone grieves differently. There is no right or wrong way to grieve.

"Price I paid to have him come in and drop the belt to old Billy Joules," Bucky added, breaking me free from my inner monologue. "Got him to work the Omni at a discount that way, too. Worked out for everybody."

"Here's the thing, Bobby," Lana said, taking the conversation back. "Daddy didn't leave his share to me. And he didn't leave it to Rod."

I waited. Which seemed to piss her off. I was always good at pissing her off. I wasn't stalling as much as lost. It's funny how easily a beautiful woman can empty a man's mind. Luckily Bucky stepped into the moment, cutting off a staring contest that might have lasted until the sun burned its way down to an ember.

"Son...he left it to you. The booby prize, we thought, stuck in at the end of the will. Usually a joke. This time the joke was on us."

Goddamn, it was a moment. I imagine my chin about hit the floor, knocked cattywampus by the news. I did some quick math on all the towns they were running, all the ads on the TV for local car lots and Coca-Cola and all. I wasn't much on math, though, and those zeroes were starting to loom large and pile up quick. You know?

More than that...he hadn't ever quit on me. I'd quit on him, and on myself, and on everything. But he didn't quit on me. Just the idea of it, someone believing in me. In those few seconds there, processing it all, I wanted to be worthy of it. Wanted to be someone other than me, the version of me he'd seen.

"Now, obviously this hat's a little too big for your head, son," Bucky said, breaking me out of the trance I'd been in, reminding me there were other people in the room. "So we're going to make you an offer to take it right off your hands. Change your life and keep this train moving right along. What we call a win-win."

I'd like to say I had a witty retort, that I bargained hard, that I became a ruthless business guy in the blink of an eye, and not a guy who was actively praying that they were going to validate my parking after this meeting because I didn't have the five bucks for it. But, if I'm being truthful, I just sat there, looking at a grip-and-grin photo of Buck with Tommy Thompson and thinking about why they were them, in their fancy suits and cars with leather seats, and I was living in a one-bedroom apartment with a broken garbage disposal and a drug dealer permanently positioned in the parking lot.

"Fifty thousand dollars," Buck was saying, putting a number on my life's work. And I ain't gonna lie. That fifty would have looked mighty nice. Fifty would have kept them from shutting off my phone. That fifty would have meant my answering machine wouldn't be filled with messages from people I owed. That fifty might have even let me buy a car made this decade.

It should have been an easy call. Ten minutes earlier, I'd had nothing. Fifty was a big improvement on that, surely. But, at the same time, every territory owner I'd ever met drove a shiny new Cadillac, you know?

Suddenly there was a piece of paper on Buck's big desk. If I signed it, I could put it all behind me. Joe, Lana, Buck, Rod, wrestling. The lot of them.

All I had to do was sign. If I signed, I could make all this go away.

Buck handed me a pen, waited as I just sat there. Reckon I might have sat there all day, had they let me.

"Have you ever read the fine print on one of these contracts?"

"No," I said.

"Then don't start now," Buck said.

Lana must have sensed my hesitation, my confusion, the sheer shock of the moment, and swooped in.

"Don't worry," she said. "It's standard language."

"Standard language," I said. "What the hell does that mean?"

"It means," she said, her eyes saying *bless his heart*, "that whatever is wrong with your car, you can fix it. It means food to eat, a decent place to live, a fresh start."

Still, the pen sat, waiting for me. Something was stopping me in my tracks, stopping me from walking out with more money than I'd earned in a calendar year in over a decade. I'd cursed this place so many times over the years. But that was from the outside. On the inside, looking at all this leather, the smell of money, it looked a little bit different. You know?

WE DECIDED to go for a walk, descending the escalator from Buck's office, all the way out of the building, to the park next door. I felt out of place. In my day, the company had been housed in a tiny office out on Peachtree Industrial Boulevard, out where all the Chinese were moving now, the signs on the road a mix of English and the indecipherable, grocery stores selling turtles in their shells for a people as far from home as I felt, watching men in suits and women in pantsuits walk by, each a master of the universe.

I wasn't supposed to be scared by nothing, tough guy like me. I could have taken any of those men and tossed them to the ground, watching the fear bloom in their eyes, knowing there was nothing they could do to stop me. But this isn't a working man's world. Money ruled everything, and the buildings disappearing in the clouds all around were a reminder that my kind of power was less than nothing, all things considered.

Skyscrapers loom, no matter how we try to ignore them. They intimidate. Downtown is where money and power and prestige live, not in a gym — and definitely not in a damn wrestling ring. Skyscrapers were, like it or not, the physical embodiment of a world that wasn't mine.

Strike one against sticking around.

Lana and I strolled past a fountain, through a small urban park in the center of the complex that hadn't existed when I worked here. It wasn't much to look at: a few trees, some daffodils, a plaque, and a monument. Surprised, based on what I know of ole Tommy Thompson, that it wasn't to himself. Of course, considering where I'd come from that morning, it was a paradise.

My apartment complex was a dump, yard littered with rusty cans, old tires, plastic buckets and other debris. Mine was on the third floor, which my gimpy knees didn't really appreciate after a night in the ring. The landing was littered with more junk — a bucket of cigarette ashes, a pile of old newspapers and magazines, the detritus of lives hardly worth living.

Strike two against sticking around. I *needed* that money.

We walked around the building, talking of old times. And that's when she made her mistake, the Omni coming into view, proud as a church, a temple to the thing I loved and hated most in the world. I had been feeling out of place, like a hooker in church.

But here? Here I belonged.

It's here that I'd won the world title, 16,000 fans losing their minds, 16,000 voices becoming one, a single voice that celebrated me, the youngest champion in history. Thousands of people, each with their own lives and problems coming together, more or less in unison, stomping, clapping, shrieking, waving their arms, shouts I couldn't quite make out ringing through the building, the words a blur but the joy clear as crystal.

Old Hugo Schwartz, still getting mileage from a Nazi gimmick 25 years after the great war, had taken most of the match. I'd looked weak, even helpless, only winning the belt with a fluke rollup. It was a change Schwartz had suggested, saying it would pop the crowd big. And it did. But it was at my expense and to his benefit, even if I didn't realize it at the time. I was a kid being put into a tough position with the fans, a kid who didn't need to be starting his reign with a fluke win. Back then I was too mesmerized by the shiny gold to care.

Joe was there in the ring with me, and I thought he'd be proud, beaming. It was a moment few men could relate to, but Joe had done it three times. He was wearing a pale gray suit, a white shirt, and a blue tie with narrow diagonal stripes, looking every bit the dignitary, the champion. And very briefly, I was too.

But it was like the tears in my eyes infuriated him. He looked me up and down as I looked out at the crowd, eyes narrowing as though he had caught me in something. I saw Joe's face get tighter, his muscles getting tenser, never taking his eyes off me. I knew something was up. When he spoke to me, it was little more than a whisper.

"Never forget," he said, his voice low, almost angry, barely competing with the crowd still buzzing over having witnessed history. "Anything they give you, they can take away. None of this is real. None of it."

And then the moment that would define me until the end of my days was over. It all happened so quickly. One minute, we were in the middle of the ring and the crowd was chanting my name, and the next we were in the locker room.

"What was that all about?" I asked.

"I thought you knew," Joe said, his face and voice still hard. He walked over to the corner as I got dressed.

"What? Knew what?"

"You have to know. Every minute in this business is a fight, not just the part in the ring," Joe said, his voice falling to a whisper.

"Every man here, every one of the boys in every locker room around the country, they want what you've got. Hold onto it.

Hold onto *you*," he said, poking me hard in the chest. "This business will try to turn you into somebody else. You're going to be on the road. I won't always be there to protect you. You're going to have to be strong. It's not a story, a goddamn movie. This life, these people, they will try to ruin you if you let them."

Joe was Joe, which meant he was always looking for the next fight. He had fought so many, and beaten so many, that he couldn't imagine not fighting. I had never known anything but success in pro wrestling, everything coming so soon, so easily. So it didn't really make sense to me, his warning. I've tortured myself during a lot of sleepless nights since, knowing that I had the power to stop what was to come, to hold it off. But I didn't.

Because he was right of course. Except there was no *they* crushing my dreams to dust. *He* took it away. And it was very real.

I thought about the money then. Thinking wasn't something I did a lot of when I was younger, but every man becomes a philosopher in time. We bargain, we scheme, we resolve, we speculate, we regret, we fantasize.

Fifty thousand. *Fifty thousand.*

Money is a collective fiction, but it's a fiction that will pay the electric bill, you know? Some folks would tell you money is, in fact, power. But power is relative. On my block fifty grand is rich. For Tommy Thompson, it's a rounding error.

"You think I should take it?" I finally asked.

"I don't see why not," she said.

"It's only money," I said, pretty blasé for a guy who'd tried to pawn a set of steak knives just a month earlier.

"And you can't use it?" she asked, a smile almost creeping through, reading me like a book. The kind with pictures. "You don't need it?"

"Maybe I do," I said. "But Lana...what was this about? Is this what he wanted? Why give me this lifeline, only for me to toss it right back?"

The smile faded completely then and she put on her business face.

"I'm not supposed to tell you this," she said. "But we're prepared to do better."

"How much?" I said, just to say something.

"A hundred," she said.

I whistled.

"Yeah," she said.

Strike three?

But Joe hadn't given me this gift with the idea of pushing me out of the business. It was his way of drawing me back in. Fifty thousand, even a hundred, wasn't worth a hill of beans if it didn't bring happiness with it. It was a delaying tactic at best.

We took a seat on a park bench, painted red for the hometown Hawks. The seat was slatted, paint peeling. Three young men in leather jackets were hanging out, smoking. They had their backs against the wall of the arena as they talked and laughed. But we didn't have laughter in our hearts, Lana and I.

It's amazing what you remember from a moment when it's one that upends your life.

"Can I bum one from you?" she asked one of the men, hand trembling a little as he handed her the cancer stick, unnerved by a woman almost twice his age. Lana could unsettle a man, any man.

She sat with me, silence far from comfortable, smoke disappearing into the air. Lana and the cigarette, both tools of sin, both dangerous in their own way.

"I don't know, Lana," I eventually said. "It's a lot to think about."

"I'm not going to tell you what to do, Bobby. That never worked for me, not a single time," she said. "It's up to you, hon."

"But you could help," I said. "You could tell me what you think I should do."

"I can't, Bobby," she said. "I mean, I could. But I won't."

"Okay," I said. "I understand."

"Do you?" she said.

I didn't.

"Do you?" she asked again. "I'm not trying to be ugly. But nobody can make this decision for you."

I looked into her blue eyes, unable, as ever, to read what she was trying to tell me. She wanted me to sign, to walk away again, this time with no dangling cord. Didn't she?

The fear was overwhelming, paralyzing. It was funny...I hadn't felt it in so long, that tingling tightness in your gut. When you don't care, what is there to fear?

I had spent so long refusing to engage the world, I'd forgotten how it felt, having skin in the game. And it felt damn good. The word selfish has such a bad smell, but when we boil it down, I think selfishness is at the heart of being human.

At some point, we all have to start making decisions for ourselves, standing up for ourselves. We gotta be responsible for our decisions, for our lives, for who we are, for what we will become.

I didn't think I was worth saving. But Joe disagreed.

I didn't know how to say any of that of course, being a dumb hick from the sticks. Instead I leaned back, quickly snatching the cigarette from her startled hand and taking a big drag, the poison giving me the confidence I needed to start living again.

"You know what, darlin'? I think I'm gonna stick around a bit."

To be continued in The Territories: Volume 2

IBLIS, COME TO ME

NICK MAMATAS

TERRITORY:
Sunshine State Championship Wrestling
(*Florida*)
Winter 1982-Spring 1983

Paul Crenshaw found himself in a state of hysterical ecstasy, his very marrow boiling with joy, "slain in the spirit" as his mother called it, exactly twice in his life, both times with his bottom on a hot aluminum folding chair. The first was when he was twelve, during a Wednesday night revival meeting at the Upper Room Pentecostal Tabernacle Church, when Pastor Ricker boomed that it was Jesus who was alive this very day, not Mohammed, not Moses, not Buddha, not Hare Hare Krishna, but Jesus, and that if you, yes you, stand up and open your arms high to the sky and invite the Lord in, He will enter. And Paul, who was with his mother and two cousins, all three of whom enthusiastically took to their feet, stayed seated but, thanks to shame and curiosity, raised up his arms, and yes, the Lord did enter him, and he convulsed and shook and said *abluelabuebcvarlalvabil-lagulfahasshamenaleah* and fell to the floor.

The second time was two years later, with his father at the Wrestletorium in Tampa, on the day after Christmas, 1982. Paul was a fan of the Sunshine State Championship Wrestling *Hour of Power* TV show and had even perfected the twinkle-toe strut of the tubby Poppy Rose. Paul would dance around when he wanted to get a laugh but not in front of mother. But father, who brought Paul to his first ever live show, was mostly just interested in pointing out when the matches slipped into performance. He laughed when Japanese warrior Akira Osaka sprayed his devilish red mist into the middle of the ring and awkward, gangly, second-generation wrestler Kenneth O'Malley had to throw himself into the cloud after missing his initial mark. Or when tiny Caribbean champion Tyson Justice threw one of his patented dropkicks at Demian Rex, missed by two feet, and Rex fell anyway. A moment later, they repeated the spot with a variation — Rex stopped short and made Justice miss and, this time somehow landing on the mat, "hurt" Justice. He rolled around a bit anyway, one palm on his back, while Rex kicked him lightly in the head.

"Don't wreck each other or nothin'," said Paul's father, distract-edly. He was looking at the program guide. Jimmy Redmond, the promoter of Sunshine State Championship Wrestling, also sold used cars, and the creampuffs on his lot were listed in the back pages every single month.

It was the next match that did something to Paul, something much like accepting Jesus Christ into his heart. It was an intriguing match-up for the Southeastern Heavyweight Title: former National Wrestling Council World Champ and college standout Jason Cumberland was challenging big Lenny Loomis, himself an accom-plished Greco-Roman wrestler, albeit one with a temper and a tendency to cheat when frustrated.

It was a fascinating match: Cumberland knew how to attack the legs and use submission holds to pin his opponent by getting him rolling to escape the pain. Loomis knew how to throw hard and reverse almost any pinning predicament. He also had an amazing finishing move: the inescapable rat trap full nelson! And it was applied on the ground, where Cumberland supposedly had the advantage.

Really, the belt was superfluous, at least to Paul. The crowd cheered the sleek, tawny Cumberland and booed Loomis, despite his American flag singlet with a white star on each buttock. Paul whooped at every move, every reversal, and booed when either would resort to mere fists or high knees. The match was long, an exchange of holds — Cumberland on his belly picking at Loomis's ankle, then tying up the leg. Loomis rolling free only to be snagged again, until he fought his way back to his feet with unsportsmanlike but legal chops and forearm shivers. Then they were both up. Loomis whipped Cumberland into the ropes, got him in a bear hug, then hit a beautiful belly-to-belly suplex. They scrambled, Loomis got a chinlock, and the wrestlers sat there, stalemated. Some other kid who had better seats than Paul and his dad bellowed "Boo-riiing" and a few of the grown-ups joined in, making it a chant.

The show was "rated PG," as Paul's mother might have said disapprovingly. Loomis released the chinlock, throwing Cumberland to the ground. He stormed up to the ropes, leaned over them heavily, and cursed the child, spit at him, made a not quite obscene gesture with both arms, and —

"Watch this," said Paul's father.

Cumberland, still on his back, scooted across the ring, put one of his long arms between Loomis's legs and crotched him. Loomis fell backward and landed on his shoulders, and Cumberland scrambled atop him.

"Classic schoolboy roll-up," said Paul's father. "There's a little moral lesson in all these matches, son. Y'see —"

As the ref slapped the mat a second time, Loomis crossed his ankles, caught Cumberland in a body-scissors hold, and turned him over. Cumberland kicked free and sat out, but Loomis grabbed his wrists to keep him from spinning. He got to his feet, planted a big knee between Cumberland's shoulder blades, let go of the wrists, and then sunk in the full nelson.

Paul's father put the program on his lap. The crowd rose to their collective feet, roaring, cheering, screaming for Cumberland, for Loomis. Paul had to jump onto his chair to see anything over the heads of the grown-ups. He was too late to see Cumberland submit. The ref was up, waving his arms. The timekeeper was slamming his hammer against the bell. Loomis kept the rat trap cinched tight. There was a story to this, too — either a bunch of other wrestlers run out from the locker room to save the day, or the referee reverses the decision and maybe even grants Cumberland the belt in light of egregious cheating.

But no. Loomis released the hold. Cumberland slipped to the mat, his limbs and neck like wet pasta. The ref was hesitant, but Loomis proffered his arm, and the referee raised it. Loomis didn't hit the ref or yank his arm back; he simply stood there against a solid wave of boos from the crowd.

And Paul Crenshaw fell from his chair, slain in the spirit once again. It was real, it was real, as real as Christ Himself. He twitched and hugged himself and babbled that it was *realrealreal* until his father picked him up, gave him a shake and the tiniest sip of beer to perk him up, and they both agreed to never ever discuss professional wrestling or what had just happened with mother.

———

LENNY LOOMIS HELD onto the title for a few months longer and displayed the belt, proudly tucked into the crook of his elbow like a football, every Sunday afternoon. Every Sunday during church hours. Paul's mother had a VHS player, though of course Paul wasn't allowed to watch very many films. Paul's mother enjoyed her Julia Child tapes, though, and various recorded sermons from the *Old Time Gospel Hour*, sold for only $49.99. Paul knew the secret of unlocking a pre-recorded VHS tape, though, and managed to record

SSCW programs over the same strip of tape, week after week, without his mother finding out. Thank the Lord she didn't care very much about Child's *Soups, Salads, and Bread.*

Paul was always the last one out of the house on Sunday mornings — "I just can't ever get the danged knot in my tie right, Mama," he'd say, and his mother would blame his shiftless, estranged father — and the first one inside when they arrived back home. "Just have to use the washroom, sorry Mama!" he'd say. His mother had barred the word "bathroom" as being overly suggestive, now that there were just the two of them at home. Paul would retrieve the tape, turn off the VCR, and wait ten excruciating Sabbath hours before his mother would take her pill and retire to bed. He'd wait for it to work in his room, she in hers. Then he'd go back to the living room and watch, the volume dial turned nearly all the way down, his nose practically caressing the screen. Lenny Loomis was a dazzling spectacle of rainbow sprinkles, glowing red, blue and green, even when Loomis finally lost the championship to Blacksmith O'Malley in a brass-knuckle brawl that had kept Loomis from using his grip strength and scientific moves. Myron Lunae's cigarette-and-coffee-voiced play-by-play the gentlest thunder this side of Heaven.

But when Lunae said on one particular late Sunday night, "And now, we have something a little different. The next segment came to us, on a U-Matic tape, along with a check from one Demian Rex. I cannot tell you what is on this tape, as I have not seen it, but Mr. Rex has legitimately purchased commercial airtime on this program. The following is not sanctioned by Sunshine State Championship Wrestling nor its board of directors, nor Redmond Promotions LLC, nor the National Wrestling Council. And now, ladies and gentlemen, Mister Demian Rex."

It was hell.

Rex had always been a weird one, with his Popeye arms and round belly and balding mullet. He'd been the Beantown Brawler, complete with an accent that sounded to Paul as though Rex had been kicked in the head once too often. But now, he was something

entirely different. The camera lens was fogged up from his exhala-
tions, and when Rex's pudgy palm wiped away the moisture, it
revealed a face covered in white corpse paint, with fiery red streaks
covering his eyes. Rex's teeth were red too, and his hairdo obscured
by a thick gray hood.

"I am the Dungeon Master!" he growled, and Paul threw himself
backward onto his butt. Paul had heard all about the game *Dungeons
& Dragons* from his youth minister. It had sounded almost fun, but
since playing involved real black magic, and brainwashing, and has
resulted in at least one murder and a whole nursery school full of
abused children, Paul knew better than to touch the occult — but
now it had invaded his favorite wrestling show. He wanted to turn off
the TV, pull the tape from the player, and smash it with one of the
thick crosses on the wall, but that would be sacrilegious and noisy,
and besides, it wasn't as though the SSCW had sanctioned any of
this.

"And I have journeyed deep into the underworld," Demian said,
his mouth still just three inches or so from the camera lens. "I have
raised my fist against the gates of hell and smashed it into rubble!"
Now the camera pulled back. Rex was in a dark place, maybe a cave.
"And who have I freed from the abyss?" he asked the camera. He
reached down off screen and pulled up, his fist in her hair, a young
girl hardly out of high school, whose cleavage was spilling out over
the top of her flame-red bustier. She growled at Rex, then licked his
cheek. Paul had never seen anything like this! "The Succubus!"
declared Rex.

"And with her at my side, we will dominate Sunshine State
Championship Wrestling! But when the demons and the imps saw
me claim her, they begged, they pleaded, 'Dungeon Master, take us
with you!' and I laughed. I told them, 'Fight amongst yourselves, and
only the strongest, only the sole survivor will attend me. And I sat on
the basalt throne of the Horned One and watched them tear one
another apart, blood and guts, grue and bile! And then, I saw him,
and I howled, 'Iblis, come to me!'"

The camera panned to the left and there he was—Iblis! He looked almost deformed: eyes different colors, black veins across his face, head shaved in random patches like a dog with mange. Rex grabbed one of Iblis's nipples and Iblis growled.

And from the floor of his mother's living room, his sweaty arms sticking to the linoleum, Paul realized that Iblis's voice sounded familiar. It was Lenny Loomis! He had somehow been given over to the devil, claimed by the Dungeon Master Demian Rex, and damned for all eternity. Paul couldn't peel himself off the floor; he was transfixed. Blessedly the commercial ended after a promise to capture the tag belts from the Fantastic Rockers and some cackling from the demonic trio, and the next ad was just for Redmond's used cars. Paul could hear his mother snoring. He could finish watching. He didn't want to, but he also didn't want to climb back into bed, close his eyes, and see Demian Rex and Lenny Loomis in hell, chains and whips in their hands.

Then everything got worse. The next match was Brett Lebowitz, a preliminary wrestler who had a few good moves and even gave a good fight but who never managed to win, against the entire Dungeon. It seemed like all three of them, anyway. Rex entered the ring first and dropped to his knees and raised his hands to the roof of the studio and barked at the lights and pounded the mat and, yes, he spoke in a perverse travesty of tongues. The Succubus prowled about the apron, waggling her bottom for the camera, licking the top rope, crooking a finger at Brett, bidding him to come closer. Outside the ring, loping about like the monster from the Saturday morning Creature Feature Paul could only watch at his father's house, was Iblis. He was Loomis, no doubt, though his singlet was gone, his mop of curls gone, and even the way he lived inside his body was entirely gone. Iblis wasn't an athlete; he was a beast from the pit.

Brett planted himself in his corner, gaze darting back and forth between Rex and Succubus. The referee was pleading with Rex, who had taken to rolling back and forth across the mat, half-seizure, half-tantrum, all demonic possession. The bell rang, and there was Iblis by the turnbuckle. He sneak-attacked Brett, grabbing him by his tight curls and pounding his head against the steel post. Lunae explained, "Yes, the match as listed on tonight's card is Mr. Loomis versus Mr. Lebowitz. He hasn't even entered the ring, hasn't been checked for foreign objects by the referee, and you can all see, ladies and gentleman, Mr. Lenny Loomis, Greco-Roman national champion and former Southeastern champion, has transformed himself, or has been transformed, and he is all over Brett Lebowitz."

But Loomis wasn't all over Lebowitz; Iblis was. Loomis would wrestle a man down, ride him, then just hoist him up with a suplex, or *soo-play* as Lunae always called it. Iblis was a brawler, all thudding forearms across Brett's backs, whips into the ropes, and high knees. As Brett writhed on the mat, Iblis wandered to his corner to get advice from Rex and Succubus. Brett made it to his feet and rushed Iblis. Succubus screamed and pointed. Iblis turned just in time and jammed his thumb into Brett's throat. With his left hand he grabbed Brett by the hair and flung him down, then followed, still spiking Brett's throat. The ref started a count and abandoned it — Brett was twitching, first one shoulder then the other rising off the mat. Iblis thrust with his arm and Brett passed out. The ref lifted Brett's arm twice, and it fell, lifelessly, to the mat. He signaled for the bell.

Even the inescapable rat trap, the finishing hold that had shown Paul that wrestling was real, had been forsaken, and for what? Three minutes of pounding on a smaller, defenseless man. Satan was real.

LEONARD COULDN'T TOUCH his toes anymore, but the boys didn't need to know that. He held the book, the Redmonds loved his ass, and he and Poppy even tolerated one another. But Florida was full of karate guys and bodybuilders and swamp-mad crazies who wrestled gators, so the booker needed to be a shooter. That was Redmond's unofficial policy. Even a year ago, Leonard could have turned anyone into a pretzel, but not now, not with his vertebrae grinding one another into dust.

But he had the book, so he made it work. A bit of brawling, tagging out to Rex, and he didn't have to talk anymore. No more lies about getting a medal in '68 instead of coming in seventh place. The only real problem was the fan mail, all of it for Rex.

Not quite fan mail at that, though it all was tossed in the same big box with the kids' crayon drawings and naked Polaroids from ring rats. Letters of complaint from old ladies who never bought a ticket to a show in their lives. Petitions for Redmond to remove Rex, or at least Succubus, from TV, but with names copied out of the phone book and written in one person's hand. A seventh Bible, and tons of tracts and pamphlets. Vials filled with what Loomis hoped was holy water. Rex never dealt with any of this garbage himself; he was busy trying on new Speedos and railing Succubus. "She's legal, and she has her GED!" Rex liked to say, unbidden.

And today, in the midst of the pile, a letter for Loomis himself. The office, a double-wide trailer in the back of the used car lot, wasn't air-conditioned. The rotating fan made the paper rustle in his hands. The text made his back ache.

Some kid, a local — religious mother, boozy father. Broken home, only child. Didn't seem like an athlete — what kind of sportsman would sit down and write a plaintive letter to a local TV wrestler? The kid expressed his fan bona fides via some complaints: why did Loomis used to always let opponents out of hammerlock rides instead of just cranking the arm till he got a submission? *Because we're just takin' a rest, kid, and nobody on the roster can pull off a convincing escape!* Loomis answered in his imagination.

On page three — three! — of the four-page letter, the kid finally got to Jesus. He didn't blame Loomis for falling into the clutches of Satan, but Rex. He invited Loomis to attend a service at his church and recommended that he wear a hat if we wanted to attend, as his haircut might upset the ladies. Loomis wasn't a huge fan of the 'do, either. His wife had to remind him to apply sunscreen to the side of his head every morning.

Kid seemed pleasant enough and had even included a self-addressed stamped envelope, in case "either Mr. Loomis or 'Iblis' would like to write back." For a second, Loomis considered getting a red Sharpie and writing *AaarRRrrGghhHh!* or something similar on a piece of toilet paper and sending that back, but the poor kid would probably shit himself to death. Instead, he walked over to the file cabinet, found the accordion folder full of tickets to their studio shows, and dropped a couple into the SASE sent by Paul Crenshaw.

PAUL'S MISTAKE was using his mother's address instead of his father's. It had just seemed like the best thing to do. Paul's father liked to ask Paul about wrestling and, if he betrayed any enthusiasm at all, sneer and say, "You know it's for dumb little kids, right? Or do you just like getting an eyeful of sweaty men in panties rolling around together? Is that it, Paulie boy?" Sure, they'd attended that amazing card together, but Paul's dad had ended up buying a lemon from Redmond, a Ford Maverick so bad it was totaled after one tiny accident after just a few beers, so now wrestling was a sideshow for imbeciles and homosexuals.

But Paul wasn't expecting anything other than what he had prayed for: Loomis admitting that Paul's letter had saved him, and that he would return to his previous persona as a proud American wrestler who, for sure, took the very occasional shortcut to win a match.

He did not expect to receive two free tickets to a studio taping at the Wrestletorium. He did not expect to see them in his mother's hand. She was using them to fan herself. Another sultry Tampa afternoon, right before the daily spring rain. The envelope, the address on it written in Paul's guilty hand, was neatly torn open and preserved on the coffee cable for Paul's mother to almost imperceptibly gesture at.

"So, you sent away for something, did you, Paul?" his mother said. "Tickets to a rasslin' show. One that takes place before a live television audience, when you're meant to be at church. I see you purchased a pair of tickets. Is this what you've been saving your lawn-mowing money for? Is this outing meant to be an early birthday present for me? If I'm honest, I'd prefer a nice bouquet of flowers."

"I..." Paul said. "I didn't buy those tickets." It was true, of course, but it was like the blood in his body had just doubled in volume — all the more for Succubus to drink! — so it sounded almost entirely like a nervous lie.

"Your father, then? He thinks I'll let you skip a day of church, and that he can get an extra day beyond that granted him by our...divorce decree" — his mother hated being a divorcée — "with these?"

"No...uhm, he doesn't like wrestling anymore, either. That Ford, you know," Paul said.

"Oh yes, the Ford." She swallowed a chuckle, not wanting to be seen experiencing a scintilla of joy over another's misfortune, but it was obvious to Paul that she was tickled and human nature depraved.

"I won the tickets," Paul said, and maybe that was true too. Maybe they picked his letter out of a hopper and decided to give him tickets, or maybe Christ had been listening to Paul's prayers and moved in that mysterious way He was known to, and the tickets simply came to Paul. "It's just one Sunday."

"Just one Sunday," his mother repeated. "The Lord has given you so much: your body, the air you breathe, the birds singing, Paul. And you begrudge him one morning a week?"

"We go to revival on Wednesday," Paul said. His mother glared.

"I'll volunteer to be a youth minister when I turn sixteen," Paul said.

His mother smiled and nodded once, a deep southern nod.

Paul's mistake was using his mother's address instead of his father's. Not only would Paul have to attend a studio taping with his mother sitting next to him, and not only would Paul have to volunteer to be a youth minister, but since he wouldn't be at his father's house on Saturday night, he wouldn't be able to take his father's gun. He would have to use a kitchen knife.

SEVERAL NERVOUS AND prayerful days and nights followed. Paul knew that demonic possession was real and could come from a comic book, a record album, or an R-rated horror film, but other than that, his religious education was lacking. He dared not ask his mother, and it was summer and school was out. The family, now split, couldn't afford Bible camp, which was just as well. The truth was that exorcisms and demon-fighting seemed to be the exclusive precinct of the Catholics, who were practically devils themselves. Paul's preacher had cast out demons during services now and again, but they were the demons of gambling, of pornography, of anti-Americanism. Those were metaphors. It was obvious, since Jerry McIntyre still gambled, Lurlene Davidson still voted for the Democrats, and Paul himself still stared at the Playboy Channel's scrambled signal in the hope of spotting a nipple when spending the night on his father's couch during his biweekly visitation.

Paul was struggling against metaphors, sure, but also against a real demon.

He liberated the stiff boning knife from his mother's kitchen. She didn't miss it. It was too hot to cook anything that needed to be separated from the bone that week. Chicken salad sandwiches and cans of tomato soup saw them through.

When Sunday came, his mother dressed for church in a lilac dress with matching purse, and Paul wore his khaki slacks and a neatly pressed, button-down, navy blue shirt.

"You're wearing that for television," his mother said.

"Uh...I heard that you shouldn't wear white on TV," Paul said.

"It's too bright with the lights and all." Navy wouldn't show blood stains so obviously, if it came to that, as well.

"Have you heard anything about periwinkle?" she asked. Paul had a better eye for colors than just about anyone. It was lilac, but it wouldn't do to argue.

"It's one of the best colors for television, if I recall correctly, Mama," Paul said. That was sufficient.

Paul's mother found a sermon on the AM radio. It was a good one, about King David, the apple of God's eye, but who was ultimately forbidden from building the Temple as he had "shed much blood on the Earth" — just as the Lord had commanded him to do. The radio preacher quickly explained that wars could be good and just and that the Lord called many to be His soldiers. The point is that even when the Lord turns you down, we must be like David and continue to praise and worship Him. David provided the land for the temple and designed its plans, but it was left to Solomon to raise it. Of all the Bible stories one could possibly hear about, the Lord chose this one to share with Paul and his mother via the miracle of car radio. It even resolved an issue for Paul; he knew now that the Lord wanted him to deal with the Dungeon Master and save Lenny Loomis before the program began, not after it.

Paul's mother was a big believer in arriving thirty minutes before the stated time on any invitation. This had made parent-teacher conferences and childhood birthday parties embarrassing, and medical appointments even more tedious than they would be otherwise, but it paid off today. The boning knife was poking Paul in his thigh, so he was pleased to be out of the car, though the humid air hit like a wave. A knot of fans had gathered on the wrong end of the TV studio building, but most stood in line by the proper entrance. "Mama," Paul said, carefully and casually as he could muster. "Would you wait in line with the tickets while I go get an autograph from my favorite wrestler?"

"You have a favorite wrestler, do you? Who is he? Perhaps I should meet him as well," his mother said.

Lord, Lord, help...Paul had two choices: name some violent ruffian, and perhaps his mother would change her mind about joining him at the wrestler entrance — but she might also change her mind about seeing the card at all and drive them both right back home. Or he could mention some heroic exemplar of good sportsmanship, but that would just encourage his mother to meet with and maybe even witness to such a fine example of athleticism and manhood.

And lo, the Lord did provide. Without thinking, Paul opened his mouth and found himself saying, "His name is Brett Lebowitz. He's always the show-opener, and mama, he always loses his match. He tries really hard, though, and I just want to let him know that I'll be sitting on the bleachers this afternoon, rooting for him and praying for his safety."

"Lebowitz," Paul's mother said, as if the surname were the black jelly bean she'd accidentally placed upon her tongue instead of one of any other color. "I'll hold our spots, son. Don't dawdle." She laughed a bit. "People will think I'm a candidate for the lunatic asylum if I'm just standing in line for the wrestling show by myself!"

"Thank you, Mama," Paul said, and he kissed her on the cheek. He couldn't run with the knife in his pocket, but he sauntered over just in time to see Poppy Rose dance out of his disappointing 1982 Cadillac Coupe DeVille and do some hand jive for the fans. The O'Malleys showed up together, but only oldest son Michael, who was a fan favorite, stopped and pressed the flesh.

"Anyone see Brett Lebowitz?" Paul asked, just in case the sound carried over to the main entrance.

A girl standing behind him laughed. "Haw, jobbers are on ring crew. He's been inside for hours." She sounded like one of those tough chicks from the movies. All that was missing was the crack of bubblegum to punctuate her sentences.

Paul turned to look at her and was about to ask if she used to work at the Orange Julius, when she realized that she was The Succubus, without any makeup and with a lot more clothes. She looked like a high school track star, not a temptress with a whip.

"Oh!" Paul said, and she pushed past him, and then some big man pushed past him, too, and that was Demian Rex, in a tracksuit, pulling behind him a wheeled suitcase. Paul's skin turned to ice. Where was Loomis?

He was wearing a hat, like he would had he been attending church, and he walked slowly, actually limping a bit. His face was clean of the black tendrils, but his expression was twisted, as if he had just been worked over by the leather strap of the Succubus.

Rex turned and smiled. "Iblis! Come to me!" he shouted to the whoops and cheers of the fans. Paul reached for the boning knife and almost stabbed himself. Iblis plucked the hat from his head and threw out his arms and let out a roar. The fans were laughing, laughing!

That's how Satan works. Make it seem harmless, a big joke. Put Satan in music, on TV, on the labels of hot sauce bottles and kiddie candies. Laugh at Satan, go along with the joke, and the next thing you know, you've been possessed, have been enslaved.

Paul got the knife out and ran up to Rex, who smiled at him and held up a palm, then noticed the point of the blade.

"Kid! Take it easy, you're gonna hurt somebody with that." He grabbed Succubus by the arm and pulled her in front of himself. Paul was grimly happy with that. More proof! Not a jury on Earth, much less Tampa, would convict.

"Gary, what the fuck!" Succubus barked as she thrashed about.

"Let him go! I command you in the name of the Lord!" Paul said, brandishing the knife. A couple flashbulbs went off behind him, but he dared not blink. He hoped his mother wasn't coming over to see what was happening.

"Him? Who the hell are you talking about?"

"Iblis!"

Rex loosened his grip on Succubus, and held up both his arms, the victim of a stick-up on a cop show. "Kid, kid, you gotta understand..."

"Holy shit," said Succubus. "Are you touched in the head or something? You know it's fake, dontcha?"

"It's like a movie," said Rex. "Don't you watch movies, kid? Frankenstein? Dracula? Darth Vader, even?"

"I don't watch movies like those," said Paul. "Now release Mr. Loomis from your control. I'm not afraid to use this," he said, waving the knife.

"Lenny!" Rex called out, and Paul's whole hand disappeared in the grip of a much bigger one. He tried to pull away, and Iblis almost let him but then somehow got an angle and swung Paul bodily in a semicircle.

"Drop it," said Iblis.

"No!"

The line in front of the Wrestletorium was rushing in, Paul's mother among them. She called his name, called upon the Lord.

Paul was not going to drop the knife. He reached up with his left to slap at Iblis, to try to get an eye. Iblis's thick arm snaked around his shoulder. He grunted and Paul felt what could have been a boulder slam into his spine. The knife flew out of his hand; he heard Demian Rex groan as the blade hit him, and then Iblis cinched in the full nelson, the inescapable rat trap.

And *Oh God!* Paul thought as he heard something in his neck crack. *It's real! I did it!*

FAT RAT IN YOUNG MANHOOD

DAN BROOKS

TERRITORY:
Grassland Championship Wrestling
(*Kansas, Iowa, Missouri*)
Summer, 1985

In Merle Hay Mall they had a shop called Canton where you could buy an authentic replica samurai sword. It was illegal to sharpen them, is what I heard, but if you did? A real samurai sword! Imagine what you could do with it. I expected people was exaggerating, and they had a store that sold rubber samurai swords or bamboo or something like that. But then, in 1985, I caught the pig that changed my life.

On July 28th the summer after I graduated high school, I captured and subdued a market-weight barrow in 22.8 seconds at the Mahaska County Fair. At the time it was the record for a fenced enclosure. Outside that fenced enclosure, sitting on the steel bleachers like he was just regular people, was Mr. Robbie Geiser —

that's the original Mr. Geiser, not Bob Junior. He wore a yellow banlon shirt with his business card in the front pocket. When I hoisted that barrow over my shoulder, and them dudes started hooting like I canceled Christmas, Mr. Geiser said — and he told me this directly, after the fact — "That boy is a showman."

It's true I was aware of the record. It had stood for 22 years, and some of them dudes had taken odds on whether I would beat it. There is always someone to say you cannot do a thing, and many of them have money. The money was nothing to me, though, when I had that barrow up in the air. All I could see was them dudes hollering and kicking over their spitters, and I was lording it over them. It impressed Mr. Geiser to where he give me his card, and that's how I come to Des Moines and seen that Canton was real, and they did have a samurai sword there, and it cost $235.

I had $300 in my pocket.

"Is that a wrapped handle, or is that fabricated?" Greenwood Gordy Hayes asked.

"That is wrapped," the owner of Canton said. He was a Chinese guy, Filipino maybe, wearing those leather gloves without the fingers on them. He lifted the sword off its stand with both hands and held it out to me. I pulled it out of the scabbard just about an inch or so. I never held a real samurai sword before, but I knew enough to do that. The handle was rough but soft, kind of, like you could feel the raised parts where the ribbon had been folded over and wrapped around. Here is why you bring an experienced fellow like Greenwood Gordy with you to the sword shop, I thought. A young man is not going to know everything right off the bat. I pulled the sword out of the scabbard and held it over my shoulder like I was standing at home plate.

"Straight up," Greenwood Gordy said. I held the blade straight up, in front of me, and squinted across the mall to where some kids were hanging out in front of the arcade. "There you go," Greenwood Gordy said. "Like a real goddamn samurai." The Canton guy nodded.

"That's authentic," he said.

Long story short I bought the sword. The Canton guy didn't charge me any sales tax, out of respect for Gordy, so I had $65 left, which was enough to get me through to the show if I managed it wisely. Gordy treated us to Mr. Mistys at the Dairy Queen, and then we drove down Douglas Avenue in his IROC-Z with the top down, bugs slamming off the windshield, and that samurai sword sticking up in the seat next to me, and god damn, I felt like I was going somewhere. *This is it*, I thought. Them dudes were down in Oskie still detasseling or working at Pamida, and I was in Des Moines, a real professional wrestler with a place of my own or at least a place at Gordy's place. It was a short hop to Kansas City from there. That's what I was thinking when we stopped into the Hy-Vee so Gordy could get a couple pounds of hamburger and a case of beer.

Obviously you can't leave an authentic samurai sword in an open-topped car in the parking lot of Hy-Vee in Des Moines. There's criminals. So I brought it in with me, tied around my waist with the red sash that come with it. I had to suck in a little to get it to tie off nice, but Gordy said it looked good, and I walked through the automatic doors with my hand resting on the butt end, taking it all in. Of course I had been to Hy-Vee before, but I never felt like anybody. It was different when you had a sword.

Gordy got his hamburger and his beer, and then we had to wait in line behind some old boy who had coupons for another store. He was convinced they were good, and the checker had a hard time talking him out of it. Behind us was a kid with Down Syndrome and his mother. She was distracted by the magazines, and I could see him checking out the sword. He reminded me of Morris, who I missed pretty good by that point, so I put one hand on the scabbard and the other on the handle and gave him my steely samurai gaze. The boy was not impressed. He made a noise like you do when somebody does something stupid, a kind of "duh" sound that everybody knows, I think, but that a special kid makes pretty loud. His mother looked up from the magazines.

"Are you making fun of my son?" she said.

Gordy turned around, and so did the checker. A rangy fellow in glasses looked over from the next aisle. I tried to explain that it was a misunderstanding, and the boy had made that noise at me and not the other way around, but his mother would not hear it. It did not help that the boy set up crying as soon as his mother and me had words. I thought maybe he was not so upset and was just being wily. Morris gets the same way. Anyway the argument went poorly for me. The more I explained myself the worse I looked, and the fellow in the glasses, who was pert near tall as me, come over and started talking like he would stand up for them both. There was a crowd by then, with some of the sackers drifting over to see what was going on. The man with the glasses got between the lady and me, like I might take after her or something, which of course I would not.

"Tough guy when you've got a sword," he said.

At this point Gordy put his hand on my shoulder. We left the Hy-Vee with a crowd of people behind us and the glasses guy, who had puffed up now he understood that he would not have to cash any checks, hollering personal remarks. My hands was twitching. I pushed through the door, and it was like opening an oven. The parking lot was yellow and close, with the sun going down and the locusts droning, which always sounded like heat to me. That's how I remember it now, anyway. At the time I wasn't thinking about it; I was so het up. I opened the door of Gordy's IROC, and then I spent a long time fiddling with the knot in the red sash, trying to get that sword off my waist. It felt like a long time, anyway.

"That was just a misunderstanding," Gordy said when we turned onto his street in Beaverdale. Beaverdale was a part of Des Moines — not its own city but a name for part of it, like maybe it used to be a city and then it got absorbed. We had been quiet to that point. As we pulled into the driveway Gordy said not to worry about it. You can't control what people think of you, he said. Then, as he was stepping onto the front porch, he stopped and said actually, controlling what people think of you is probably the most important thing in professional wrestling, but you learn it. That didn't sound so good, and by the time we got to the kitchen he was kind of frowning, like he had something to say and didn't know what. It was kind of funny to see the shape of his mustache, which I recognized from Saturday noon TV, except he wasn't suplexing El Pantera or holding a microphone or what have you. He was just in his kitchen. He put the beers in the fridge and then tore open the case and handed one to me. He turned on the light, and I could hear it buzzing right over my head.

"You all right, kid?" he asked.

I said I was just hot. "You want me to make those hamburgers for Lola and you?" I said. "I'm good at hamburgers."

"Lola will not be joining us," he said.

"Girls' night out?" I said.

"She is an independent woman," Gordy said. He took two more beers from the case in the fridge and tucked them under his arm. With his free hand he opened the sliding glass door and went out to the back porch, where there was a lawn chair. He sat out there until the lightning bugs come out, at least. That's when I went down to the basement. It was cool down there, and I took a hot shower in the open stall they had set up in the corner. I thought about going up for another beer but also thought that might be rude, but finally I went up to the kitchen again. The hamburger was still in the fridge. I don't know what became of it, but the beers was gone by Sunday night.

I GUESS that lady at the Hy-Vee was a realtor or something, because on Monday the whole thing was in the *Register*. The boy went to a camp in the summertime, and the director of that camp told the reporter that it saddened him what a bully would do. The paper gussied it up considerable. I don't know if somebody told them I had signed on with Mr. Geiser's promotion or if they recognized Gordy, but Grassland Championship Wrestling was in there, too.

"That is a problem," Mr. Geiser said on Monday morning. We were in his office at the gym, which was Bob Junior's office when Mr.

Geiser was not in town. Mr. Geiser was in town, though, setting in a folding chair with his hands on top of his cane while Bob Junior set behind the desk.

"I'm trying to build something here," Bob Junior said. "I'm trying to get something going. I can't have some kid —"

"He is eighteen years of age," Mr. Geiser said.

"I can't have some hayseed, some young ad-ult up from Oskaloosa, come in and wreck my whole operation."

"I don't think he wrecked it, Bob," Greenwood Gordy said.

Bob Junior snapped open the newspaper like it was a bag of snakes. He read aloud: "*Witnesses said that Nicholson, 18, carried a Japanese sword and spoke abusively to the boy and his mother. Nicholson was in the company of Gordon 'Greenwood Gordy' Hayes, a performer with Grassland Championship Wrestling.*"

"That's inaccurate," I said.

"Which part?" Bob Junior said. "Gordy wasn't there? Is that not your sword?" He pointed at it, there against my chair between me and Gordy. I had put my hair up in a bun, too; it was a little scruffy, but I figured it would grow out over the next couple months. My idea was this: The White Samurai. I would not use the sword in the ring, of course, but it would complement my imposing physique.

"I didn't abuse anybody. It was a mis—"

"Of all the people," Bob Junior said. "Of all the people to go out and abuse, you pick a —"

"Robert," Mr. Geiser said. Bob Junior folded up the newspaper and wiped his mouth with the palm of his hand. Then he used a word that I do not care to repeat, so I will substitute a different word. "Not all wrestling fans are bananas," he said. "But all bananas are wrestling fans. They get it."

It turns out that camp sent about a hundred kids to the Labor Day show every year. They had a standing deal. On top of that was the regular attendance from members of the community and their families, plus the public relations. The public relations was what vexed him, Bob Junior said. Something like that in the newspaper could kill a promising local promotion, which depended on the good-will of the community and the reputation for professionalism that fans throughout the lower Midwest associated with the Geiser name. That's about how he put it, anyway. I cannot quote him directly, because midway through it occurred to me I was getting fired, and the whole room got kind of quiet and far away. Bob Junior worked himself to what they call a fever pitch. He went on about the damage I had caused the organization, with my various behaviors, until Mr. Geiser cleared his throat.

"What we got here is a story," he said, reaching toward the desk. When Bob Junior did not respond, Mr. Geiser snapped his fingers and held out his hand. Bob Junior passed him the paper.

"A story," Mr. Gesier said, holding up the *Register*. "However many people read this story in the newspaper, they got an idea of you now. And that idea is: he's a villain. He is what in the wrestling busi-ness we call a heel. You understand?" He looked around the office at all three of us. We nodded. He put the newspaper under his cane and sat back in his chair.

"Greenwood Gordy Hayes," Bob Junior said, "has fallen under the spell of the evil Fat Rat. That is you." He pointed at me.

"I was thinking I could be The White Samurai," I said. "I got the sword, and I could wear like a robe over my trunks, and I come in all stern like I —"

I broke off on account of Bob Junior was staring at me with his mouth open. I thought somebody had come in behind me and done something crazy. But there wasn't anybody back there. Bob Junior was looking that way at me.

"Are you bananas, son?" he asked.

"I would rather you did not use that word," I said. "My brother —"

"Greenwood Gordy has fallen under the spell of Fat Rat, a dubious character who wears tie-dyed shirts and lives in a van," Bob Junior said. "Ever since he took up with Fat Rat, Gordy seems confused. He lacks motivation. He has stopped standing for the values we all share, and he has become a damned hippie. Fat Rat has got him so twisted up he can't even wrestle for six to eight weeks, starting August 17th."

August 17th was the day of Gordy's knee surgery.

"It is possible — although we would never say as much," Bob Junior continued — "that Greenwood Gordy Hayes is under the influence of marijuana. Marijuana that he gets from you, Fat Rat, the heel everyone hates. That's what happened down to the Hy-Vee this weekend."

"Why would Fat Rat have a sword?" I asked.

"He doesn't have a sword!" Bob Junior rared up out of his seat like he was about to spit. He was not a tall man, but his delts were like softballs under his shirt. "Do what you want with that sword, but it won't go with you to my arena. It could go home with you to Oskaloosa. It could go right up your ass."

"Come on, Junior," Gordy said. Bob Junior turned on him.

"What'd I say to you about Mr. Nicholson?"

"Keep him out of trouble," Gordy said.

"And what did you do?"

"It was a misunderstanding," Gordy said, but Bob Junior was not interested. Mr. Geiser was not interested. We had our marching orders, and we marched out of that office, Gordy and me, with Bob Junior scowling across the desk and Mr. Geiser jiggling his leg like he had all the problems in the world to worry about. Which I don't blame him, since he didn't know me, and he did not know what I could do.

The idea was this: Greenwood Gordy Hayes, the Young American, now 38 but still the ace of Bob Junior's River City branch of Grassland Championship Wrestling, was slated to wrestle Big Wallace Russell, out of Kansas City. Gordy and Wallace was both faces, which normally you wouldn't see in a A-show, but Mr. Geiser had cooked up a feud.

Greenwood Gordy and Big Wallace had both fallen in love with the fabulous Ms. Sheila Bernhard, no young American herself but still a handsome woman who could — and I seen it — throw a grown man through a trestle table using some kind of judo. She had been a champion down to the junior college. Anyway, Greenwood Gordy and Big Wallace had once been the best of friends, but now they was at odds over this woman, a story as old as time.

They was supposed to have it out in the headline match of the Labor Day show at Veterans Memorial Auditorium, but then some old boy at Mercy told Gordy that if he didn't get his knee scraped out or sewn together or something he might never wrestle again. So the plan was he goes out there to wrestle Big Wallace, but I don't want him to, and I hit him with a chair. Then Ms. Sheila throws me through a trestle table. Bonzo gonzo, the match is a no-contest, and they reschedule it for two weeks later in Waterloo, where a kid they call the Rhinestone Cowboy hits Big Wallace with a chair. Then they do it for real as the headliner of the Halloween show at Veterans, and me and the Rhinestone Cowboy duke it out on the undercard in our debut appearances.

I didn't know who this Rhinestone Cowboy was. He wrestled at the college in Iowa City, and he was supposed to be flamboyant. Anyway the thinking was I hit the hometown boy in Des Moines, and the Cowboy hits Big Wallace in Waterloo, where the crowd is mostly black, and then people in both cities watch the match on channel 17 because they hate us so much.

"You ever hit somebody with a chair?" Greenwood Gordy asked.

I said only recreationally. I was smarting off, on account of I didn't come to Des Moines to get thrown through a table and booed for selling imaginary drugs. I came to wrestle. That's what I told Gordy when I got in the ring with him and he started explaining the parts of a folding chair to me. Gordy looked at me for a long time.

"Do you like me?" he asked.

"Sure, Gordy."

"Why do you like me?" Gordy asked. I thought about it for a piece and said because he was an older fellow who knew what he was doing, and it seemed like he was looking out for me.

"That's right," Gordy said. "I am looking out for you. Now before you pick up the chair, you got to step on it, like this." He lay the chair face-down on the canvas and put his foot on the bottom of the top part, the backrest part. "It's got a lip, and if you hit me with it and you forgot to flatten that lip, it's going to give me a concussion. You don't want to give me a concussion, do you, Russ?"

"No," I said.

"Okay, so step on it," he said, pointing at the chair. I stepped on it. The lip flattened out.

"You got to do it casual," Gordy said. "You can't walk over to the chair, look at it, step on it, and then pick it up. It's not natural."

"Okay," I said. He showed me how to take a step like I was going to grab him and then look back at the crowd before I picked up the chair. It worked two ways: it gave me a chance to flatten that lip, and it made sure the crowd was watching, because they knew I was up to something.

"And it shows you're afraid to just grab me," he said. He turned his back and told me to try it.

"Okay, but how about this?" I said. "You got your back to me, and I come up behind you with the sword. And just as I'm pulling it out, you turn around and push it back into the sheath. And then it's like we're struggling."

Gordy turned around.

"That ain't what Bob Junior said to do, is it?" he said.

"No," I said carefully. "But Bob Junior didn't hire me."

"And you think Mr. Geiser is going to like your idea so much he tells Bob Junior to fuck himself."

"Well," I said.

"Come with me," Gordy said. "There's something I want to show you."

He led me back to the office, which was empty now except for the smell of onions coming from the waste basket. There was a big mirror with a sheet over it in the corner next to the desk, and Gordy walked me over to it and took his shirt off. Then he told me to take my shirt off. It was not what you would call comfortable, but Gordy was my trusted advisor, so I skinned out.

"Okay," Gordy said, and he whipped the sheet off the mirror. "What do you see?"

There was Gordy, kind of loose in the middle but still broad across the shoulders and tan as the back of your hand. His hair was long and straight, mostly blond and some places blonder. I had seen it tied back and knew that it was moving up his forehead, but hanging loose you couldn't tell. He looked like an old rascal, or maybe a young man going to seed. You wouldn't like to see him driving your sister around, but you wouldn't try to run him off, either. He looked soft in the eyes and hard in the mouth.

"That's a wrestler," I said. "Uh, a veteran...wrestler. Wily. Lot of experience."

"Old?" Gordy said. "That all means old."

"Yeah okay," I said. "Older wrestler. Uh, blond."

"That's right," Gordy said. "The Young American, huh? I been the Young American for ten years. Before that, down in Kansas, I was The Hand, which was a farmer theme where we both wore overalls and whatnot. In Peoria me and this boy Martin was the French Connection."

He said Martin like "Mar-teen." They wore striped shirts and mustaches, Gordy said, but Martin couldn't really grow a mustache, and it never looked right. They got booed in Bettendorf. After that Martin went to work at a body shop his girlfriend's dad owned in St. Charles, Missouri.

"You ever been to St. Charles?" Gordy asked. When I said no, he said they had a body shop down there with a guy in it who looked kind of French but mostly sad. The point was that everybody has a type. The crowd sees it. The promoters see it. If I wanted to wrestle, Gordy said, I had to see it myself. He pointed to the mirror again.

"Who is that guy?" he asked, meaning me.

"Um," I said. "Young guy. Tall guy. He's a strong...guy."

"That's a heavy," Gordy said.

"Does that mean fat?" I said, a little heated.

"Well," Gordy said. "You ain't French."

He slapped me on the shoulder and went out of the office to the changing room. I stood in front of the mirror for a while, looking at the posters on the wall instead of at myself. They had promotional materials from Grasslands shows going all the way back to 1971 — shows in Lawrence, Topeka, Columbia, Lincoln, Cedar Rapids, the Quad Cities. The later ones was in full color. There was also some flyers, just black on peach sheets advertising shows in Mason City, Waterloo, even Ottumwa. I looked for one from Oskaloosa, but I couldn't find any. There was an old-timey picture of Harry Houdini behind the desk. He looked lean. Finally I looked at myself in the mirror, and there I was again, so to speak, with my hair up and my titties out. I thought about picking up that mirror and throwing it across the office. It probably weighed 200 pounds, but I could have done it no problem. The slim man gets the attention, but it is the heavy man who is strong. I picked my shirt up off the floor and went out of there wiping my face with it.

That night me and some of the younger guys went to the Ingersoll Tap, and Tremendous Tyler Vogel was bitching about how Bob Junior sent him out to buy a satin bedsheet at 3:30 in the afternoon and then spent half an hour telling him how to drape it over a mirror. I liked to knock his teeth out. Thirty minutes! Anyone could see he was exaggerating. Bob Junior had Tyler as a face, but his eyes were too close together and there was something about him I did not like. I sucked on my beer and laughed at his story like everybody else. I was thinking.

I hit the gym pretty hard after that. There was three weeks before the Labor Day show, and I already knew how to whack Gordy with the chair. It was simple enough if you did it right. My thinking was I could lose four pounds a week and then cut five, maybe even ten pounds of water weight before the show, and then I'd come into Mr. Geiser's office twenty pounds leaner and show him my White Samurai act. Bob Junior, too, if he was in there. Once they seen it I figured they had to know how good it was. So in the mornings I ran laps around Gray's Lake and then went down to the Southside Y and pushed weight, and in the afternoons I practiced with the sword in Gordy's back yard. There was a heavy bag back there, hanging from the maple tree on a chain, and I practiced chopping at it and turning the blade to hit it with the flat. I found a pair of sandals in the basement that Lola said I could have, and I took short little steps with the same front foot and whacked that bag to who laid the rail. I did that routine for about four days. Then my knees started hurting, and I figured I'd better take a day off running, although I still did my sword work and the weights, and by the last week of August I weighed 268 pounds. That was four pounds more than I started. I thought maybe Gordy's scale was off, but he couldn't tell me much about that, having not recently calibrated it or compared it to another.

I was feeling discouraged. I had planned to go in and give Bob Junior and Mr. Geiser my White Samurai routine on Friday, August 29th, before the Labor Day show, but when that morning come around I wasn't so sure. I waited outside Mr. Geiser's office with my sword and my hair tied up while Big Wallace Russell had some kind of conversation pertaining to automobile mileage. It was hard to follow through the door, but it sounded pretty heated at first, although it settled down eventually. When Wallace come out he looked cool and satisfied, in his signature purple satin jacket with a pick stuck in his hair. People thought that pick was part of his gimmick, but he wore it all the time. I seen him wear it to bed.

"How's the old man?" I said when he came out. Wallace stopped and shut the door behind him. Up close he was a lot bigger than he looked on the TV. He might have been taller than me, although I believe I was heavier. He got a pair of sunglasses out of his jacket pocket and spent a long time unfolding them.

"What is your name?" he said.

"Russ Nicholson," I said. I almost added *The White Samurai*, but then I didn't.

"The old man is not here, Russ Nicholson," Wallace said. "He's in Kansas City, where he lives."

"Oh," I said.

"He is going to come up for the show tomorrow," Wallace said, "like he always do." He studied me for a while. He did not seem in any kind of hurry.

"What you got in your hair?" he asked. I said it was chopsticks, and he pursed his lips.

"That won't work in the ring," he said. "What you want to do is short on the sides and long in the back." He laughed and added, "Like a sophisticate." Then he walked off, drifting past the ring where the Cosmonauts were working on a piledriver, not even looking at them, moving through the warehouse like it was a dream he was waiting to wake up from. I reached for the door to the office just as Bob Junior opened it from the inside.

"What do you need, Mr. Nicholson?" he said.

"Nothing," I said. "It just looked like the doorknob was crooked."

Bob Junior said if it wasn't one thing it was another.

THAT NIGHT I called my mother. She and Morris was supposed to come up for the show the next day, but the car broke down. Mama said the radiator was cracked, although it could have been anything. The bus cost $36 — apiece — and Morris was not suited to it.

"So that's a non-starter," Mama said. She laughed. *The Fall Guy* was on in the background, and I heard Morris telling him to watch out. "You get this samurai deal figured out?" she asked.

"Not yet," I said. "They want me to be somebody called Fat Rat."

"That Rat?"

"Fat Rat," I said. There was static on the cordless, and I had to say it again.

"Well," she said.

"Well what?" I said. I could hear that I was angry, but I couldn't stop. "Well I'm fat?"

"Well," Mama said. "I expect Slim Rat's job is secure."

WHAT A LOT of people don't know about Mr. Geiser's operation is how professional he ran it. We all had to be to the auditorium by four o'clock, even though the show didn't start until seven. There was a sheet on the door to the locker room area — the call sheet — and it said when the matches were and what times you had to be where, and when you got to the auditorium you had to sign it and put the time next to your signature. So nobody would cheat, they had Bob Junior's daughter Lindsey set up by the door at a card table with a watch on it. She was nineteen years old, but she looked about fourteen.

"Is Bob Junior here yet?" I said as I signed in.

"Not my turn to look after him," Lindsey said. She smelled like an ashtray, and she was wearing a t-shirt that said "Easy Livin'" above a picture of a car.

I had my sword and the sandals and a size XXXL karate outfit in a duffel bag. They call it a gi. I got it from Gordy's friend who ran a Taekwondo place out in West Des Moines. Gordy said that old boy could chop through a cinder block with his hand, but when I went over there to get the gi he didn't have any. I didn't see any broken ones around, either.

It was a long hallway to the locker room, and I wished it was a little longer. Honestly, I was nervous. Gordy had dropped me off outside and told me not to worry about signing him in. I guess he had worked some deal with Bob Junior. When I got to the locker room it was Tremendous Tyler telling a long story about a girl in Ankeny while the Cosmonauts was taping up. Big Wallace was over in the corner with his eyes closed and headphones on.

"Good evening, Russell," Tyler said. It wasn't yet four o'clock, but he was full of himself.

"Tyler," I said. There was names on all the lockers, and I found mine. It said "Russell Nicholson" in neat black letters on a card in a little plastic sleeve. Under that it said "Fat Rat." I opened the locker, and there was a tie dyed t-shirt and a pair of coveralls. Tyler said they give me a wardrobe and laughed like that was a joke. The Cosmonauts laughed, too, on account of they were polite. I heard they had been Mennonites before they run off.

"That ain't mine," I said. I got the gi and the sandals and the sword out of my bag and put them in the locker. The sword got Tyler's attention. I could tell he wanted to get a close look at it, but I wouldn't let him. I turned my back to him and arranged it real careful in the locker, which amounted to leaning it against the back corner. Tyler was too proud to ask. He had a hand mirror he brought with him, a pink one looked like he stole it from his kid sister, and he started moussing his hair up. He was always particular about his hair. I asked if anybody had seen Bob Junior, and Mikhail — that's the younger Cosmonaut, the one who got in that wreck down to Keokuk — said he thought he had seen him around concessions. I didn't know where that was, but neither did I want to listen to Tyler talk about his date for two hours, so I went looking. I walked down the long hallway out of the locker room back to the time sheet, and there was Mr. Geiser sitting at the card table.

"Good afternoon," he said.

"You taking over for Lindsey?"

"She went out to buy a pack of gum," Mr. Geiser said, making a smoking gesture with his fingers. It occurred to me that he might be the only honest man in the whole organization. Everybody else was putting on a show, except maybe Gordy, but even he thought I was a kid. Mr. Geiser and I understood each other. He had taken me on in the first place. It was a waste of time trying to put an idea in Bob Junior's head, when Mr. Geiser ran the show and had the artistic vision. I took a deep breath and laid it all out. I explained what I wanted to do that night, with the sword and my struggle with Gordy, and my whole idea of the White Samurai. When I finished he took a pack of Juicy Fruit from his shirt pocket and offered me a stick. I thanked him, and then he unwrapped a second stick for himself, real methodical like an older man will do.

"You came up with this idea by yourself, or did somebody help you?" he asked.

"By myself, mostly," I said. "Gordy helped with the outfit."

"That's a lot of thinking for a young man," he said.

"I just want to contribute, sir."

Mr. Geiser chewed his gum and looked at the head of his cane. He drew himself up in his little folding chair, and when he started to speak it was like he was looking down at me, even though he was sitting down and I was standing up.

"Son, I took you on because I saw something in you. We've got a lot of shows to do this year, and I'm going to need you," he said, "to either quit my employment or never speak on this subject again."

I went back to the locker room. Tyler was talking about some particular thing this girl from Ankeny could do, some kind of thing with her joints, and I told him to shut up. He didn't like it, but I did not care.

One by one the other wrestlers come into the locker room: Jim Dandy and the Outlaw Jason Rose, the Scorpion twins, The Summoner, Major Brawn and O'Shaughnessy, who was a little person doing a leprechaun gimmick. Years later, just before he had a heart attack, he wrote a letter to the paper saying he shouldn't have done that and apologizing to little people everywhere, but it looked like he was having fun at the time. The room got pretty loud, and I was quiet. Gordy had his own dressing room, and Big Wallace got up to go talk something through with him in there, nodding at me as he went out. I ate a sandwich I brought with me. It wasn't much, but I wasn't hungry, either.

Bob Junior come in to call places for Tyler and The Summoner at 7:15. Wrestlers was coming in and out for the next hour and a half, leaving the locker room bouncing on their toes and coming back sweaty and cursing. Ronnie Scorpion twisted his ankle in an Irish whip, of all things. When he come back, limping, I had my locker open and was just sort of looking at the two outfits in there. I felt like whichever one I put on I was going to be wearing for the rest of my life. That wasn't true, but I had built it up too much in my mind.

I don't want to draw it out for you like I did myself. Long story short I put on that tie-dye t-shirt. I put on the overalls. I left the sword in the locker. When Bob Junior called me for places he looked me up and down, kind of smugly, and I almost went back and got the sword just to spite him. But I left it. When I closed the locker my palms were wet and greasy on the cold steel.

Leaving the locker room I saw Tyler's mirror on the bench, and I took it with me.

As soon as I stepped out of the tunnel they started booing. You never heard such a noise in your life. There was hippie music on the sound system, and a whole section of kids was screaming over it. There must have been a hundred fifty of them. When I pulled that mirror out of my back pocket and held it up to look into it, preening my hair and kind of smiling at myself like Tyler had done, they went ape. The kid from Hy-Vee was in the third row, and he stood up and pointed at me.

"He's not even handsome!" he shouted.

I blew him a kiss and blessed his heart. I expect it's what your 18th-century Tokugawa samurai felt like, when he finally got his shit together.

TAKE NOTES, MEATLOAF

RICHARD FIFIELD

TERRITORY:
West Coast Classic Wrestling
(*Los Angeles, California*)
April 29, 1992

One— 10:00 AM, 2664 S. Redondo Blvd

His grandmother used a hot glue gun, but she had delicate and accurate hands, could apply a steady bead, a neat thin line. He hated his grandmother, and he hated her stupid birdhouses. It was the only time she let him sit at the dining room table. He felt an urge to call her, still remembered the phone number, one more thing he couldn't shake from his past. They didn't have a phone in the apartment on Redondo. Couldn't afford it. If they did, he would have dialed her number, hope she hadn't died. If she answered, he had it planned out in his head.

"You never had a single bird. All those years, not even a crow. And crows are stupid fuckers."

These hands were new things. Within a month, the injections had tailored a new suit for his body. An inch, maybe two inches, he poked at his skin and watched his fingertip disappear in flesh. Supposed to be muscle. His finger should bounce off and cry about it. Now he could barely hold a glue gun, but Ace wanted him to take even more. Ace knew the answers to everything, so Blaine would do what he was told. More drugs. Less staring.

Last week, Ace cut rehearsal, called him over to the ropes. "Goddammit, kid. Flashing red light. That's where you look. Stop looking at me." Blaine didn't even know he was doing it. "I'm not going anywhere, Blaine." He gestured for Blaine to come closer, but Ace was incapable of whispering. All the other wrestlers heard it. "Twenty years, and I've never said this before. You scare me. You got a look in your eyes. I always think somebody's standing behind me."

"Okay," said Blaine.

"It's all right, kid. On camera, it's a moneymaker."

He asked Labelle, his girlfriend. "Do people think I'm a monster?"

She plucked an ice cube out of her tumbler of Crystal Light, and he thought she was going to throw it at him, but she preferred a different kind of ammunition. "Most people think you're a giant imbecile. The woman below us thought I was your fucking nurse."

He burned himself again and ripped the cord from the outlet. KTLA still broadcasting from the courthouse. Just like everybody in L.A. Talking too loud and never saying anything. He kicked pieces of stereo components as he rushed to the television set, took a deep breath, just like in training, saw it for what it was, he had control, glared at the reporter in the burgundy blazer and reached for the volume knob. Enough. Fuck. He went too far. Not the answer. The knob rested inside his meaty palm, the plastic broken. The reporter moved his mouth, but silently. Good enough.

He turned around and realized he had stepped through the decks of a Sanyo and a GBX. No glue gun could fix that.

He looked at the digital alarm clock. 10:15. He needed more stereos.

Blaine hated driving in Los Angeles, no such thing as shortcuts or back streets when you can't understand all those maps. Ace told him to take the 10. Everything is off the 10. Wednesdays, he waited to leave until rush hour was over, drove the same circuit, always to Long Beach, Temecula, Anaheim. Ace had leased the car in his own name. Blaine had no license, but Ace had the answers to everything.

Blinker, turn on to Redondo, and then the fucking 10. Never west. Santa Monica was the closest city, nine miles away, but Blaine knew he would have another freak out. He had nearly wrecked the car the first and last time he saw the ocean. He lost his breath, felt his heart skip around in his chest, scraped the corner of the car on the side of the low wall at the first exit, pulled over and vomited. He wondered if he was dying. For fifteen minutes, homeless men sold oranges around his car, pissed off at where he parked but scared of his size. Blaine knew how they felt. The ocean was the biggest thing he'd ever seen. He could not fight back.

Tomorrow was his audition. Ace always came through, and now he had the chance to be in a movie. Unfortunately, the movie was called *Jellyfish! 3-D!* Too many exclamation marks and way too much ocean. Ace's assistant underlined them with a pink highlighter. He told her Blaine had a learning disability.

People talked to themselves in their cars all the time. He needed a distraction. He recited his lines.

"Wait, Veronica!"

"Beat!"

"I've spent my life adrift, and it's time I put down an anchor."

No "Beat!" in the script, but the assistant had suggested he say it out loud, to remember that Veronica had a line, and that he should pause and pretend to listen to her. Just like at home. Nod, be a good boyfriend. Pretend to listen and always give her the money for the utility bills.

In Long Beach, the pawn shop owner seemed to be waiting for

him. This was his favorite pawn shop; the black cashier asked for his autograph and framed it behind the cash register, and every Wednesday, he had boomboxes ready. Cheap or broken. Didn't matter. Blaine gave him five bucks for two Sonys and a yellow Memorex. The owner gave him change and also a handgun. Blaine stared at it, resting on the glass counter. This morning, the owner had pointed at the tinted glass door. Blaine hadn't noticed the wooden pallets or the drill when he entered, but now they glowed pink with the neon sign. "I'm boarding up as soon as you leave," said the owner. "I figured you'd be coming in. You're lucky I didn't stay home."

"I appreciate it," said Blaine. He didn't understand, assumed it was hurricanes.

"Shit's going down this afternoon," said the owner. "A buddy of mine said they were gonna wait until the stores had a chance to barricade."

"Wow," said Blaine. "We don't have hurricanes in Montana. Is there something I should be doing?"

"Jesus," said the pawn shop owner. "You heard of Rodney King?"

"Of course," said Blaine, which was true. The other performers talked about it.

The pawn shop owner reached beneath the register, slid a pistol across the glass counter. "Don't take offense, but you're the whitest person I have ever seen in my whole life, and I've been to Disneyland three times."

"I just want the stereos," said Blaine. "I can take care of myself."

"I'm sure Rodney King thought he was pretty tough," said the pawn shop owner.

"I could take down four cops," said Blaine. "I'd beat them with their own batons."

"Fifty-three times," said the owner. "Go home and lock your door. This city's gonna explode. Not gonna matter how big you are. Turn on the TV until they tell you it's safe."

Blaine had refused the gun, carried his stereos outside. Thought maybe he looked like a looter. Fuck. Threw them in the back of the rental car, got back on the 10. He needed a distraction from the shiny rockets hurtling past him, but the usually filthy shock jock didn't have strippers, or the spinning wheel sex toy game, or three Metallica songs in a row. Grim, warned his white audience to lock their doors, told his black audience to keep their shit together.

Traffic was light on the way back to Redondo, and as he drove into his neighborhood, he couldn't help but notice every black person on the street. He realized that he must look like the monster. Six foot five, coming up on 275, hair frosted and glowing like a 40-watt bulb. The new muscle, the new girth, made him walk differently, like he was unthawing or something. Blaine wasn't a racist. The black wrestlers were the kindest to him, but on the street, Blaine would probably run away from himself. One million hurts. MHz. Don't ask him about the frequency of radio transmissions. He doesn't know. He will sign anything you put in front of him, grateful for MHz, just three letters and you're welcome.

As he tried to leave the pawn shop in Long Beach, the owner had shouted after him. "The gun is free!" Blaine leaned against the door, arms full of crappy electronics. A last offer. "You're a good customer! Dead guys can't buy ghetto blasters!"

He parked the car and craned his neck to check every direction, just in case. Blaine had picked up the vibe of the people in southern California. Everybody he met carried doom around with them, like they knew they would die by earthquake, freeway, or serial killer. Yet everybody had fake names, and the police were lazy, and that was a bad combination. Even his girlfriend. Labelle was a stupid name, but she didn't choose it. It happened to him, too. Los Angeles was like that. So many things he swore he'd never be, things he'd never do. In Montana, it was easy to see the line and not step across it. In Los Angeles, you just snorted the line, because everybody else was doing it.

TWO — **12:30 PM**

Taking the boom boxes apart no longer required concentration. Routine. Gutting a fish, really. Toss the guts into the bushes and grab the next trout. In the apartment, he didn't have to worry about the blood, just threw the entrails of portable stereos next to the couch. Sometimes batteries, D cells that he could put in a sock and beat somebody to death with. The wires and the amplifiers and the housings barely weighed a pound. They were taught to put on a good show. Entertain. Whatever it takes. If he left the batteries inside the boom box, he would kill his opponent. Guilty. His mind went weird places sometimes, but the TV in the corner mumbled KTLA; the sound was turned down, but he figured he'd know trouble was coming from the faces of the court reporters. Where he came from, nobody had a video camera, and when trouble came nobody was ready.

This whole city was ready to fight. The reporters were safe, forty-nine miles away in Simi Valley, moved so the cops could get a fair trial. Blaine was used to the geography of Montana, empty miles and empty roads. In Los Angeles, a mile could mean a half hour, or two hours; they had their own math. According to Labelle, they also had their own justice, and for once, don't root for the hero. The uniform was another costume, but the batons were real, and a million people felt the blow. A million hurts. Mega Hertz. He hated math, but he knew the population was almost 2.5 million, easy to remember, a good story Ace forced him to tell at cocktail parties, exactly a thousand times bigger than his hometown. More than a million hurts today. Probably fifty thousand fake ones. Goddamn actors.

It wasn't unfair to call his girlfriend a drama queen, because she actually went to school for it. Not even a school, because they studied some made up crap called The Gizzard Method, and not in a classroom, but in The Quarry — the rock garden of some old fucking vampire actor. Labelle's eyes glazed over when she talked about it, which was constantly. A cult. A weird chicken stomach cult. Believed real actors trained a fake muscle in the stomach, digesting unspeakable truths, indigestible truths, grinding all that goddamn truth just like a chicken shitting out grit and rocks. Two grand a month, if you were chosen. It took Labelle a year and a half, $300 for a Saturday learning how to demolish the stone inside her, break it up into authentic moments. When she told him about those Saturdays, he knew she was crazy. New students screamed out dialogue in the blazing sun, swinging hammers at landscaping boulders, the yard pierced by ringing sounds as five chicks with fake boobs made contact, frustrated and sweaty and dodging sparks and sometimes chips of shrapnel. Labelle assured him they signed a waiver, showed him a scar on her shin from a flying chunk of shale.

"Like a chain gang?"

"Don't be racist." That was all she said, which was rare for Labelle, so he knew something was weird until he noticed the outline of a claw hammer in her white leather purse. He thought she had graduated from all that, gave her the two grand a month for advanced acting school. Every actor he met was a creep. Ace forced him to go to "industry" parties, Hollywood parties, and there was Labelle, but he didn't know her name, even though she had unzipped his pants and given him a blowjob without asking.

Ace thought it was great, watched the whole thing, shook the hairy shoulder of some stranger, proud of his purchase. "Hung like a horse!" Fuck. People clapped. Labelle went home with him and never left, but he was too scared to tell her no. He was also too scared to ask why she was carrying a hammer again; he got held back in the fifth grade, so he could understand the shame. He started checking her hands for blisters, but she said nothing, just kept going to every open call and audition. She only got one part. Maybe her gizzard wasn't strong enough. Maybe she needed some blisters.

The thought reminded him of the glue gun in his hand, could feel the warmth, knew he was squeezing it without thinking. A pistol for America's next action hero. He still had time before Labelle came home from the mine. Nobody was there, nobody was watching, nothing to fear.

"It's too late to turn back!"

He deepened his voice. Tried again.

"It's too late to turn back!"

Better. An echo around the empty living room, he continued.

"You took an oath to save lives, Veronica!"

"Beat!" In the script, Veronica was described as an exotic beauty, and he didn't know what that even meant, so he just imagined a Native American woman in a lab coat.

"We may have lost the mayor and the city council and the dogcatcher, but if I turn the boat around, their deaths will be meaningless!"

A long piece of dialogue, but he nailed it.

"Beat!"

Chiropractors are basically doctors.

"Beat!"

"No, Veronica! You're not useless!"

In the script, he was supposed to grab her by the shoulders, so he dropped the glue gun, and held out his arms. The assistant had said the trick to acting was remembering to use your five senses. He closed his eyes, but all he could conjure up was the smell of fish. He was supposed to be madly in love with her. Sincere. Sound sincere.

"Your love is the real motor of this boat. And you can crack my back as soon as we defeat this..." Fuck. He could never remember the word. He always said "lesbian," and it was close. He took another deep breath, and the moment he relaxed, the word flew from his mouth.

"Leviathan! And you can crack my back as soon as we defeat this leviathan!"

Victorious, he leaned back on the couch and swung out a massive forearm, and as if it were hinged, it folded at the elbow and froze, hit a perfect lock. It was a good day. He dropped his arm, rose from the sagging couch, and froze once more. Unplanned. He had every intention of practicing, but froze again, but not in a top-rock or up-rock. The volume on the television was so low that he had to lean his entire body across the coffee table, studying the new reporter, a woman who kept touching an earpiece hidden in giant wings of fake blonde hair. No panic on her face. No breaking news. Still no verdict.

At least Rodney King got a jury.

Labelle had a hammer.

She called him a meatloaf. Jealous. Aerobics every day to take weight off, while he swelled. Two twenty-five. Two forty. At 260, she stopped touching him. "It's gross," she said. "I can't even hug you. I can't even reach around you. I'm just going to pat your back, okay? You know that I love you, but I didn't date a pot roast. A giant piece of meat. Worse than a pot roast. A cheap meatloaf."

"There's no such thing as an expensive meatloaf," he said. "I don't care. Sex takes away my edge."

If anything, Blaine was all edge. Training was sharpening the knife. Memorizing his lines was part of his job. Nobody knows, except for Ace. He knows everything.

"For you, I will give up my first love. The ocean was a cruel and unforgiving lover."

The reporter disappeared, replaced by the grainy videotape. Wished they would stop showing it so much. He was used to it, didn't react to it anymore, and the cops and the man on the ground were just actors now.

"Beat!"

"You are predictable and easy to navigate. If I'm with you, I won't even notice that I'm wearing pants."

The only person Blaine trusted in the entire world tucked in his shirt. Where Blaine came from, a tucked in shirt was fishy. Gay. He remembered the way Ace had looked him up and down. "You don't look like a caveman."

"No, sir." Blaine had good manners.

"Handsome kid," said Ace. He had looked Blaine up and down one more time, but not like the queens on Redondo Boulevard, more like the livestock at the county fair. Cocked an eyebrow. "You need to get a whole hell of a lot bigger. But not meaty in the face. That face is gonna make me rich."

"I chop wood every day," said Blaine. "I'm not allowed to go to the high school gym. Drink lots of milk."

Ace grimaced. "The farm boy thing isn't gonna work. We already tried one of those. But he didn't look like you. Milk is bad for your skin."

"Yes, sir."

"I'm going to put you on a regimen," said Ace. "You're gonna bulk up, but from the neck down. We live next to goddamn Hollywood, but all my wrestlers look like mongoloids."

After three months of the injections, Labelle lost interest in his crotch. His dick slowly sunk into a new mound of flesh, but he trusted Ace, didn't have to fuck Labelle, didn't look like a mongoloid. Everybody wins.

Memorex on his lap, no batteries. Pliers to the springs, wire cutters to dislodge the amplifier. On the TV, no amplifier, the reporter moved his mouth but didn't look panicked, so Blaine returned to disemboweling the cheap machine. Should he be worried about Labelle? Could she survive a race war? Did he care?

THREE — 2:00

He swore as he pressed the casing of the bright yellow Logitech together — too much glue, and he had to let it burn his finger, take the pain, take the pain, take the pain. If he didn't squeeze the plastic together with his fist, the seal would be loose. After the GBX had fallen apart in his hands on live television, he learned his lesson. Just like wrestling. Take the pain. See it for what it is. A cheap hot glue gun. The pain went away, and he knew the glue had dried. Five bouts a week, seven stereos, just in case. The Logitech joined the others on the coffee table, and he only had the Memorex to scoop out, his least favorite brand; the tabs always broke off, and he had to use a black magic marker to disguise the damage. He glanced at the television, saw the same goddamn clip, real life beating, and because some idiot happened to catch it with his camera, they were all in danger. He looked at his watch, and Labelle wouldn't be home for an hour, time enough to finish the Memorex and clean up all the mess. He didn't want to hear it.

The hustle of it all. He could sprint and never catch up. He ran because Ace told him to. No mystery. Ace knew everything.

Last week, Ace had shooed the booking agent away. He was the type of man that could dismiss a person with a tiny motion. "Go put on another track suit. One that doesn't smell."

"They all smell."

"Who the fuck is doing your laundry, kid?"

"I am."

Ace sighed. "Fine. We've got an appointment." Blaine never argued, followed Ace to his Ferrari, the passenger seat so small that he had to stick his shoulder and head out the window like a dog. Ace shouted at him as they hit the freeway, which he was also used to. "Just be yourself, kid." A few seconds later: "I take that back. Don't be yourself. Do you know Dolph Lundgren?"

Blaine nodded, but it was a foreign language, and the Ferrari picked up speed as other drivers honked. Maybe they were worried about the blond kid flying out of the car, but more likely because Ace drove how he lived. He swerved around any vehicle less expensive, cut them off without a thought.

Silence until they drove into Burbank, and Ace consulted his watch. "Fuck. We're late. At least you don't smell so bad. It all blew off you. You ever think about acting?"

Blaine was accustomed to Ace's motormouth, so he just nodded, as Ace squealed into a parking space in front of a low-slung office building. Ace reached into the backseat for his briefcase, and Blaine followed him across the pavement. Ace was still talking. "I don't think you're gonna have to fight a jellyfish today, but be ready for anything. These Hollywood types are perverts."

"What?" Blaine stopped, but Ace kept walking. He chased after him.

"We need a star, dumbass. Outside of the ring. You've got the face. And you're young and white. That's all that matters. Acting is no big deal. Hell, I was on *Starsky And Hutch*."

"My girlfriend is an actress," said Blaine. "Is this an audition? She always comes home crying after auditions."

"Easy, tiger. If you cry, I'll fucking dock your pay. Unless they want you to cry."

Blaine's stomach turned as they walked into the lobby, and Ace put his briefcase on top of the secretary's appointment book. He looked at her, tapped his watch. Blaine rarely spoke out of turn, trusted Ace to always have the answers. But he had to say it. "My girlfriend said that auditions are usually blowjobs."

"She's right," said Ace. "Good thing you like milk."

ON THE TELEVISION, a live shot of the courthouse. The blonde reporter moved her lips, and all of that stiff hair no longer filled the shot, camera pulled back to show darker faces, bright white poster board taped to yardsticks, streaks of magic marker he could not read. The reporter's hand traveled to her hair and remained there, blood red fingernails disappearing into the fake blonde, like there was an invisible wind. Blaine could see the change in her expression. Things were serious. Somebody might try to steal her hair.

In the silent apartment, he heard Labelle on the stairs. Early. She was never early. He hated the sound of it, the echoes of heels, rapid fire clicks as she ran up all three flights. Every single fucking day. She trained harder than he did.

Sound of the key in the lock, and she barely looked at him, breathless. She nodded as she opened the refrigerator, drank the bottom of a pitcher of Crystal Light. And she dared call him a hillbilly.

He bent down and scooped up the stereo parts and thought about the future. Maybe he might even wear a suit tomorrow, or a tie or some shit like that, but he forgot that he no longer fit in anything besides specially tailored track suits. He would wear deodorant.

"The audition is tomorrow," she said.

"Not if there's a race war," he said.

"Whatever," she said.

"We aren't leaving this apartment. The blacks and the Koreans know more than we do. It's not safe. We're just some dumb white kids. The first to die."

"You would be a target," she said. "You could have a piece of hay sticking out of your teeth. I pay good money for this tan."

It was true. She didn't even have a bikini line. "I wonder if black people can tell it's fake."

"Jesus, Blaine. I wasn't planning on leaving. Everybody in class was talking about it. That's why we got out early."

"Do you think we should barricade the doors?"

"I think you should barricade yourself in another goddamn room."

"We only have two rooms," he said.

They both flinched when the doorbell rang, and Blaine dropped the Memorex, thinking it came from inside. No batteries. A ghost. Jesus. Everybody was a mess today.

The FedEx man was impatient, until he looked up from his clipboard.

"Holy shit. You're Mega Hertz!"

"Only when I'm at work," he said. The FedEx man just continued to stare, until Blaine snatched the ballpoint pen out of his hands. He forgot his size sometimes; it was still a new suit, and when the FedEx man flinched and stumbled backwards, he flashed the smile he had been taught. "Now you have my autograph," he said and carried the purple and red envelope into the apartment, pushing the door shut with his foot. He didn't want the FedEx man to see the stereos.

Labelle snatched the stack of paper away from him, and the pink Post-It notes on the new pages fluttered in her bitter little hands. "Another revision. Jesus, Blaine. This is a piece of shit. You know it; I know it, but they think it's a masterpiece."

"I'm probably not going to get it," he said. "They want Jason Priestley."

"He's a megastar," said Labelle. "You need to read the trades. This is a B movie. I bet you don't even know what that means."

"No."

"Do you know how lucky you are? For once in your life, take something seriously, meatloaf. Did you memorize your lines?"

"Yes."

"Are you ready to fight a fake jellyfish?"

"I was born to do it."

She was not amused. Instead, she inspected the television set. "Goddammit, Blaine. How are we supposed to know when it's safe? You broke the television. We need a radio or something." She looked around the floor at all of the stereo components and shells of boom-boxes. "Broken," she said and finally laughed. "I bet they didn't teach you about irony at Hillbilly High."

"I've been watching their faces. I'll know when it's okay to leave."

"There's one good thing about you."

"One?"

"I've always appreciated the fact that you stay out of my art. Just like I stay out of yours."

"I don't have an art."

She snatched the script from the table. "This. Revisions. Sending you goddamn new lines the day before the audition. Typical."

He tried to look over her shoulder to count the Post-It notes.

"I don't think you know what it's like to be me," she said. "Now I walk into a casting, and they all know I'm dating somebody famous."

"Doesn't that help?"

"Yes. I suppose I should probably do something nice in return."

Blaine didn't know what to say. Instead, he craned to look out the inch of window. Palm trees were a disappointment from the neck down. Scaly, peeling, messy, like a burn victim or something. "You've already read the script," he said. "That was nice enough."

"Teachers show up when you least expect it," she said. "A guru comes along when you need it most." He thought of Ace. He didn't think of her. Until she shook the script in front of his face. "I'm going to help you get ready."

"That's okay," he said. "The verdict could come any second."

"This is like my job and stuff. How often do you get stuck in a room with an actress?"

Actually, it had happened once before. The first week he was in Los Angeles, a present from Ace. All actresses are prostitutes; don't take the 10; chew with your mouth closed. All good advice. Nobody knows, until they are told. "Never," he said. "Okay. Guru me."

She cleared her throat and straightened her back. Maybe this was actor posture.

"Take notes, meatloaf."

ACE HAD PROMISED many things and always came through. In the ring, Blaine was Mega Hertz. At home, he was The Meatloaf. At the offices of West Coast Classic Wrestling, he was The Face. They tried to explain demographics to him, Nielsen ratings, *Beverly Hills 90210*, Vanilla Ice, hip hop, tracksuits, gold chains. It was all a costume. At least he got to be a good guy. Probably because he was blond. Take the pain. When the choreographer showed up to the gym to teach him how to pop and lock, they were both embarrassed. A gay white guy showing a redneck white guy how to copy black people. It was a niche that needed to be filled, and the fan mail proved it. In Montana, he was hillbilly handsome but radioactive. In Los Angeles, the stylist frosted his hair and shaved lines in his eyebrows, and every Thursday, she came back for Sideburn Maintenance. He didn't mind the track suits, but they had to buy bigger sizes every week. Eventually, Ace had to pay a tailor to make special track-suits, happy to shell out cash as long as Blaine didn't get puffy face. Puffy face was Ace's biggest fear. On Tuesdays and Thursdays, a Korean woman came to the gym to push and pull Blaine's face, and then a half hour of hot towels, a steaming pile on a gleaming silver tray. He knew the other wrestlers talked about him behind his back. Sony offered free stereos, product placement, but Ace turned them down. Ancient ghetto blasters gave Blaine street cred. He took the pain, paid for the gas, and drove around every Wednesday morning, piling the back of the rental car with prop stereos.

"Save your receipts," said Labelle. "You can write those off as a business expense." Blaine nodded. She did know some things.

They rented a VCR to watch her only movie, *The Michelles Go To Hell*. She peppered him with questions when it was over, and he reminded her that he didn't grow up with television, and he never thought he would be in love with a real movie star. Flatly, she explained how it was supposed to be camp, and he had no frame of reference, one more thing that went over his head. Honestly, he only paid attention when they showed her old tits. Many times.

Now she was his teacher.

FOUR — **3:30**

"An armada of invertebrates will soon arrive at Seaside Village!"

"Beat!"

"Blaine, I'm Victoria. You need to get in a natural place, or you are going to say 'Beat!' tomorrow, and I will be mortified."

"Okay."

Labelle cleared her throat. "Slade, it's too late."

"No, Victoria! We are the last hope before every street..."

"Stop," she said. "I know the title has too many exclamation marks, but in the script, pay attention. Make it literally an exclamation. Try again."

"No, Victoria! We are the last hope before every street is littered with the bodies of our friends and family!" He waited for Labelle to stop him. She was silent. "Maybe not the streets. They don't have legs. Damn these creatures! So mysterious! You're the chiropractor. Can a jellyfish chase somebody?" He exhaled. It was a long stretch of words.

Labelle shook her head and dug inside her giant white leather purse. "This script is a piece of shit." She removed a silver box, threw it at his chest. He snatched it out of the air before it made contact. He expected her to praise his reflexes. Instead, she tapped the back of the cardboard box. "Read this carefully." He squinted. "This sucks, and if we're stuck here, you're going to frost my hair. If we die in a race riot, I want to be blonder than you."

"Okay."

"We'll keep doing your crappy lines," she said. "But at least it won't be a waste. Don't fuck it up. I bought the expensive stuff."

Thankful for the break, he watched her stir the powder into the plastic container, her face wrinkling as she opened the tiny bottle of chemicals. When she returned, she sat on the floor in front of him, and he tucked his legs back on the couch, focused on getting the tiny hook into the perforations on the plastic cap. His eyes watered, but this was the kind of pain she was used to. He hooked another strand of hair, and she reached for the script. She was accustomed to the smell; she would survive a nuclear war. She would dance in the blast and come away with a better tan.

She raised her hand, folded it into a tiny fist. Blaine assumed it was dramatic, knew for sure when she delivered the line. "I can't lose you, Slade! Please don't fight the jellyfish!"

He blinked through tears and knew he sounded congested. He knew better than to complain. "I'm not afraid anymore. Your love has given me a Mexican."

"What the fuck?"

"Oh, man. I'm sorry. I'm starving."

"For Mexican food?"

"I don't think we have that in the cupboard," he said. "I'm almost done. Three more rows. Then I'll make some sandwiches."

He couldn't see her face, didn't know if she was pouting. He pulled the last strand through, and she stomped off to the bathroom.

HE TOOK HIS TIME. Anything to delay class with Labelle. She returned from the bathroom with a towel wrapped around her head, just as he smashed the last of the sandwiches together. She made retching sounds from the couch. The liverwurst and mayonnaise sandwiches horrified her. So did watching him eat over the sink. His grandma never let him use plates, unless it was spaghetti. Always paper towels over the sink. Ace had taken him to The Ivy, to show him off, but Blaine was more interested in the waiter, all of those plates and bowls, the smooth way they appeared before him. Ace assumed Blaine was embarrassed. "It's okay, kid. Everybody is staring, but that's a good thing. Be proud. A hero needs to be proud." Blaine looked around, and sure enough, he was on display. Ace did this stuff on purpose. Blaine expected to be led around the dining room, be forced to expose his gums and teeth, show his haunches and hooves, like an exhibition at the fair.

Labelle no longer commented on his meals, called them poor people food. She made another pitcher of Crystal Light as he drank a pint of half & half and a tower of generic Oreos. Maybe this was luxury. If his grandma had her way, she would have thrown his food in the yard like she did for the chickens.

BACK TO WORK.

"There are some things worth dying for, Veronica. I'm not afraid anymore. Your love has given me a second chance."

"I don't believe one word you just said." Labelle adjusted the towel on her head, and Blaine looked over at the television, hoping for the verdict, some way out of this. Behind him, a tiny gust of wind from the strange rectangle of a window above the couch, covered with a piece of pebbled plastic. The window only opened inward and was attached to small metal arms, not a real window, no sill, just cut into the wall randomly. Sloppy, really. A third of the way up the stucco wall. No way to use it to escape a fire. From outside, it was decorative, not framed with a fire escape or even a landing. A portal in a submarine. Just another useless part of Los Angeles, like an appendix. A gizzard.

"What do you want me to do?"

"Acting isn't supposed to be capital A. A verb, not a noun."

"C'mon, Labelle. You know I don't know that kind of shit. Are you going to teach me grammar?"

"I'm trying to teach you how to be real."

"Pinch me," he said. "I'm real."

"Wrestling is acting with a capital A. The audience is a bunch of fucking hillbillies, so they make it simple. Good. Bad. You ever watch a silent movie?"

"I already said sorry about the volume knob. Jesus. I have a glue gun. I'll fix it."

"Say it again," she said. "This time, pretend you're talking to me."

"There are some things worth dying for, Veronica. I'm not afraid anymore. Your love has given me a second chance."

"Jesus, Blaine. That was even worse. I should break up with you."

"I tried to sound real."

"That's the story of your life," she said. They were silent for a moment, and he thought that maybe he really was a monster. He considered this, weighed it in his mind, and decided that it was okay. Monsters made things happen.

"Wrestling is soap opera," she said. "Just with ugly people. Exaggerated, obvious. Not acting. If I can see you acting, then I don't see Mega Hertz. I see Blaine."

"Labelle, it's a movie where I gotta fight a fucking jellyfish. People aren't going to care about the love story."

"I care about the love story," she said.

"Call Jason Priestley. I won't even bother showing up tomorrow."

Labelle stood, the bright white towel a crown against her tan forehead. The queen. Here comes the speech. Blaine sighed. "Let me ask you one question, Blaine."

"No," he said, and meant it.

"Are you the jellyfish?"

"What?"

"Stop being spineless. Invertebrate."

Fuck. He didn't know that word. Watched as she stomped off again, this time returning with a hair dryer. Unfortunately, she pointed it at him like a gun. "Say your goddamn lines."

"There are some things worth dying for, Veronica. I'm not afraid anymore. Your love has given me a second chance."

Labelle waved the hair dryer, looked him dead in the eye. "Third chance, Slade. The town already gave you a second chance."

"Rehab doesn't count. If I die, just make sure they all know that I returned from exile to rescue the ungrateful town that shunned me."

"Better," said Labelle. "You're good at being a martyr. You won't die, Slade. And if you do, I will make sure the town knows all that you risked. Jellyfish are complicated."

Blaine exhaled. End of scene. Labelle blew him a kiss but then switched on the hair dryer. He watched as the dark wet hair became brilliant, sparkling. Maybe she wasn't so bad.

Silence. She had turned the hair dryer off. She had something to say. "More Mega Hertz, less Blaine. Nobody wants Blaine." He changed his mind. She was that bad.

"We are the same people, dumbass."

Once more, she aimed the hair dryer at him. "You suck at being Blaine. Sorry to be the one to tell you."

"There's nothing wrong with Blaine."

"Because he doesn't exist," she said. "Even the name sounds fake."

"Blaine?"

"It sounds like a preppy rapist."

"Fuck you," he said. "How much did you pay for your tits?"

She shook her head. "I don't know how to get through to you. I want something real. Tomorrow, they're going to want something real. If it makes you uncomfortable, that's a good thing. That's fucking real."

He had no response, just sat on the couch until he heard the hair dryer in the bathroom.

She was made of plastic and fake hair and teeth, painted and cheap. A bird house. Nothing could live inside her.

Now he was uncomfortable.

———

HE NEVER STOOD A CHANCE. Too young to know he was supposed to be looking for an answer. He tried to avoid her, live like a ghost, but he was terrible at it, enormous and clumsy and breaking things. His grandma should have been thankful he was so strong, chopping all that wood and pushing her out of snowbanks. She should have. Just like the wrestling coach should have taken him aside as a fifth grader, told him that he was going to be a champion someday, told him to skip Little Guy Wrestling and go straight to high school. Instead, his grandmother had to sign a ten-page waiver for liability, and he showed up the first day and everybody treated him like a sharp knife. Too big, too reckless, the only person who grappled with him was a linebacker they brought in during the off season.

Nobody knows. When you are a monster, they don't even think you have feelings. The linebacker taught him rudimentary moves, as he wasn't a wrestler, and when he ran out of those, he taught Blaine something he learned in football. Take the pain. Take it. If it hurts, it's real, and it's good.

The Little Guy coaches knew none of this. Nobody knew. Freshman year, he left the hard basketball courts of the junior high and finally stepped onto the mat. His first mat. He felt spring loaded, light for the first time in his life. The answer. He took the pain. The high school coaches saw the crazy in his eyes, and they taught him real holds. He couldn't compete against rival schools without following the rules. They demonstrated the motions but spared the kids, and Blaine wrestled with a tackling dummy for the first month. Luck, something new to him, as other schools had at least one giant on their squad. He defeated them easily, quickly, and a few schools were frightened by his intensity, told his coaches he wasn't welcome. Freshman year, he won the state championship. The hold that was easiest for him was the hammer lock, and also the quickest. Most kids just surrendered as soon as they saw the look in his eye, flopped like fish. Sophomore, junior, he moved through high school with none of the swagger of a star athlete destined for a full-ride scholarship. He was a knife.

His grandmother only signed one more piece of paper in his lifetime, and that was permission to commit to the University of Washington. The state championship was just another match to him, until he saw the assistant coach from UW in the bleachers. The answer. And Blaine did what he was known for, the hammer lock, but the excitement of an answer made him forget to stop, and ignored the ref slapping the mat, and he pulled the kid's arm after the match had been called, kept pulling until it sounded like a lake cracking open, sharp echo through an entire silent gymnasium, and the kid was white with shock, something sticking out of his collarbone.

Splinter of bone, proof at last. Am I a monster?

An answer.

FIVE — **5:30**

Labelle returned with dry hair and the folding mirror with the small light bulb. She examined her pores and talked about Shakespeare.

"I never really got into that guy," said Blaine.

"Every man in his plays is flawed. Haunted. Bloodthirsty. Maybe we could start there."

"That's okay," he said. "I think I need to focus on what I'm going to wear. I don't have a suit that fits. And I can't go out and get one."

"Priorities," she clucked, and with perfect aim, ripped out a tiny errant eyebrow hair.

"Tomorrow isn't Shakespeare," he said. "Tomorrow is me fighting a giant sea creature and fucking some scientist on a boat."

"Perfect," she said, and he assumed she was talking about her eyebrow. "Let's start there. What's the line on the boat? After you screw her on the tarp?"

"I've spent my life adrift, and it's time I put down an anchor."

"Take this seriously! Make her believe you mean it. You just banged her on a tarp! No woman would like that!"

Blaine didn't care. In his mind, serious things. Real things. Every time he took a hard corner and bled from his head, he hoped Montana would leak out. Last week, he saw a guy get hit with a folding chair, and even though it had been rehearsed for weeks, he missed his mark and took it full in the face. The cut across his forehead was the biggest Blaine had ever seen, and now he was hungry for it, for a great rattling of his skull. It wasn't simple. The answer kept changing. Once, he found it in the ring, good guys and bad guys, and nothing in between. Now he knew it was bad acting.

"I think I'm done," he said.

"Not until I say so. Stop. Breathe. Think about what it means to love something. Those puffy pig pieces. You get so excited when you find them."

"Pork rinds?"

"Exactly."

"They remind me of home."

"There!" This was Labelle's enthusiastic voice. After months of living with her, he knew all the voices. He stared at her, and she began applauding, which only made it worse. He wanted to punch her right in the fake tits. "I just saw it on your face! Do the line again, and forget about Victoria. She's a pork rind."

"I've spent my life adrift, and it's time I put down an anchor."

"Better!"

"This is dumb," he said.

"This is acting," she said, dropping the cheerleader voice, reaching for the acid. "This is my craft. Do you think you're better than me?"

"Probably at some things," he said. "Moving heavy stuff, for sure."

"Real actors don't make money. They do it because they would die without it."

"Die?" He laughed, fully aware that it was bad acting; the fakest laugh would hurt her the most. "So dramatic! Oh, wait! That's your whole thing."

"I'd like to see Blaine in 3-D. You have no fucking depth." Her tan flushed, and the combination was kind of orange, like a traffic cone. "No dimensions. Not in real life. Not in the ring. Not in this relationship."

"My name is on the lease. You and your gizzard can get the fuck out."

IT WAS weird when he felt it. As soon as he said the words, they belonged to someone else. Like a video. Caught on tape. Captured without knowledge, some stranger traps you inside some fucking machine from Japan, maybe when you are getting your ass kicked by cops or maybe when you are pinning a kid from Three Forks to a cheap blue mat. You are inside the Sony, but not the story; maybe you mouthed off to the cops, maybe the kid from Three Forks begged you to stop in a quiet voice. You get famous, a victim of racist cops or a high school senior who secretly enjoys breaking bones, beats off and thinks about the snap. Ten seconds and you are a hero, when maybe you're really a villain; you can't even do the math to subtract ten from all the other seconds of the day when you are at your worst. If you keep your mouth shut, you become a god; everybody wishes that Superman was real, and you have the power to set your massive city on fire, the power to erase your tiny hometown and the first years of your life. If you keep your mouth shut, they might march on the streets on a Saturday night, or they might just sink into their recliners waiting for you to beat a fake African warrior with a bone through his nose.

He could speak the words, and he could walk away from them.

"You're a scientist, Veronica. You know that nature is impossible to control."

"Beat."

"You didn't take a single science class?"

"Beat."

"Well, you wash your hands in between every client. That's the kind of expertise I need on this boat."

BLAINE ALWAYS THOUGHT he would have a short story, couldn't imagine living much longer than his parents. He lost the scholarship, and his grandma knew before he even got home from Billings on a mostly silent wrestling bus. He didn't have a car, so she showed a tiny bit of grace, knowing the only way he could get a GED was in the next county. Graduation was two months away, and he was allowed to stay, with the understanding he was on his own the second he walked across that stage.

He chopped wood, he kept his head down, he didn't read the newspapers. In a small town, infamy brings shame to every citizen. When asked, he was sure they shook their heads at the mention of his name, nobody knows, nobody knows. For ten years, he was a monster, and now he had gone and done something monstrous. They were right all along. Nobody knows, so he chopped wood after school, trying to make it up to his grandmother, nearly twenty cords stacked up in the barn. His hands had callused years ago, but the axe shot out slivers that stuck to him like a porcupine, and he took the pain. In May, he cleaved a piece of cedar that exploded, so old, and the piece came toward his face in slow motion, not a sliver, more like a piece of kindling. He ducked and it sailed past, and then he thought maybe it did hit him, because his head filled with an unfamiliar sound. He tried to shake it off, and then realized a car was parked twenty feet away, at the bottom of the driveway, and somebody was laying on the horn.

It was a year ago, but when the ice breaks you never expect it, and never to break your way. He just remembered that Ace looked him up and down.

"Stats?"

"Two-forty, six feet and change."

"At least a roll of quarters."

"Huh?"

"Take me to your leader," he said, and Blaine remembered that the car was clearly a rental from the airport. White, Hertz, he drove from Billings. In the living room, he remembered Ace motor mouthing Grandma, but then realized she wasn't a rube, so he switched to charm. Yes, she did make all the macrame. Yes, she made that afghan. No, she didn't know that those things were worth money in big cities. Blaine's jaw was open, trying to chew everything taking place. Finally, somebody knew.

Ace brushed imaginary dust from the arm of the couch. The next time he opened his mouth, he didn't stop. He saw the film, he saw the face, he liked the story, he needed a hero type, and he had big plans, and they started now.

"He's no hero," said his grandma.

"With the right makeup, anybody can be a goddamn hero," said Ace. "I beg your pardon."

"I won't miss much," said Grandma. "Maybe the checks."

"Jesus," said Ace. He looked at Blaine. "Does she want money?"

"Dunno," said Blaine. "She signs all the forms and stuff. It's the rule."

"You eighteen, kid?"

"Yep. In April."

"She don't need to sign a goddamn thing." Ace jumped up from the couch, again brushed imaginary dirt off his pants. "I'm gonna go wait in the car. We've got a flight tomorrow morning. Pack up your shit and try not to rip your grandma's arm out of the socket."

Five minutes later, Blaine walked toward the idling rental car, a duffle bag that drooped, nearly empty.

He threw it in the back of the car.

"That's all you got?"

"Yes, sir."

Ace began to back out of the driveway, but Blaine found some sort of courage to stop him. "Wait. I guess I did forget something." He leapt out of the passenger door and sprinted a circle around the house, returning with his massive arms full of cheap birdhouses. Ace didn't say a word. When they drove through town, Blaine pitched a birdhouse with full force at each stop sign, each fire hydrant and, finally, nailed the sign that announced that they were leaving city limits. Number One In Friendly!

SIX — **7:00**

"You need to hear something." Another of Labelle's voices, Labelle in love, Labelle apologizing to the pizza man for not having money for a tip. She tilted her head toward him, frowned sadly. At the same time, she wrestled with ice cube trays, wrenching them free, a downpour into the pitcher, a clatter.

"No," he said. "I don't." It was true. His head was filled with a giant cracking sound, something enormous breaking, something about to be revealed. He wanted to listen for it.

"Remember that night at the Bellagio?"

He sighed. Go away. Go away. "No," he said, and honestly, he didn't. All those fancy names blurred together.

"The place in Las Vegas? With the jets of water and the laser lights?"

"Right." He remembered the water. How could he forget?

"Do you remember eating at the buffet?"

What was she doing? What was happening? "Everybody clapped," he said.

"And then you shit your pants."

Crack. Whatever was underneath was rising. "I'm not proud of it."

"You went back to the room because you didn't have any other clothes. You told me to go out and enjoy myself."

"I must not be that awful."

"I went to Ace's room. I fucked Ace that night. And I liked it."

HE WAS NOT RODNEY KING. Blaine took the pain because it was sports. Take the pain, take the pain, take it. It's being given to you. It's going to be the only thing given to you.

The crack, and this time he recognized it. A frozen lake, water flexing muscle, not a hero, not a villain. Enormous things can hold the questions and the answers.

NOBODY KNOWS. How did it happen? When did it happen? Why did it happen? Cops, the social worker, even the guy who dove down and attached the chains to the car. His first Christmas without them, presents still wrapped and waiting, just in case. Nobody knows. His first birthday without them, turned five in April, no presents at all, six months and grandma couldn't stand to look at him.

The lake cracked that night, the thaw his present; the fishermen moved off the ice and it had been there the whole time. The knock on the door an answer for his grandma, but it wasn't a relief, because it still didn't make any goddamn sense. A husband, a daughter, and an idiot son-in-law. The kids at school pretended they knew, and maybe they did. Now they spoke at him, cornered him, offered him ghoulish stories like candy. Decomposition. Unclear who was driving, the bodies rose, tangled, rotted, trapped forever by the burgundy roof. He remembered that color, so it must be true. A thousand minnows, perch hatched in the stomach of his father, his grandfather still clutching a can of Pabst Blue Ribbon. Bet your mom was driving; women get lost and can't read a map and they end up at the bottom of a lake. To Blaine, it sounded true, and now he could picture them, stuck there, his mother's hand on the dome light. Missing persons were impossible to imagine in a world so big, and he had never been further than Billings. He would not join the other six-year-olds in the summer for swimming lessons. Sure it was a different lake, but in the depth, in the dark, nobody knows.

The next five years, his grandmother made it clear he was not an answer to anything, not to her loneliness or her anger or her grief. He heard her say it out loud. Not a fair trade. God got all the good cards, and she was ready to fold. She rarely spoke to him, but she had words for anyone willing to offer solace. Always those two words. Nobody. Knows.

IN THE LIVING ROOM, he saw Labelle from a distance, and she was small. He felt sorry for her. She didn't know when to stop, just like him. They both pulled at anything within reach, desperate for something real, but always pulled too hard.

"I'm leaving," he said. "I can't be around you right now."

"Run," she said. "Go find another Ace."

"If you don't shut the fuck up, I'm going to take that hammer out of your purse and beat your face in."

She showed no fear. They were the same. Wait. Why is she smiling? "Yes!" She screamed, and rushed toward him. He pushed her away. "I saw it! I saw it in your face!"

He grabbed the keys from the coffee table as she continued, and now she was crying, which he was used to, but happy crying, which confused the hell out of him. "Whatever," he said and tried to move past her.

She reached for him, and he slapped her hand away. She refused to stop. "Blaine! This is the real you! I found him!"

"You lost him," he said. "I'm sure I'll see you in porn someday."

She opened her mouth, maybe to beg him to stay, maybe to say something cruel, but for once, there was nothing. Her jaw moved, and he wished that he could have given her the line. Nobody knows.

Nobody.

That's the line.

Keys in hand, he descended the stairs slowly, concentrating on his breathing, take the pain, and at the landing on the second floor, he stopped. For the first time in a long time, he knew the right thing to do, didn't have to be told. Take the pain, take the 10 to Santa Monica, take his shoes off and wait for the ocean.

Outside, he stepped into the flames.

THE JOB

JASON S. RIDLER

TERRITORY:

Northern Lights Wrestling Federation

(British Columbia, Alaska)

Spring, 1986

Northern Lights Wrestling Federation was an island of misfit monsters. The territory stretched from Victoria, B.C. to Juno, Alaska, but its heart was in the feathering lights and perpetual spring that is Vancouver, B.C. Long-haired teenagers with paisley shirts vied with geriatric Hatpin Marys to scream and chant for retired former National Wrestling Council heavyweight champ Bronc Snyder's butcher show. In the ring, bikers chopped meat with Korean sumo rejects, college linebackers with wrecked ACLs were tossed into the stands by anabolic strongmen, and bouncers clotheslined construc-tion workers of ever-shifting ethnicities. Six months back, Bronc had put the strap on his new boy, "Satan's Choice" Chuck Pitts, an actual chapter member of the Devil's Brigade biker gang. Former powerlifter Pitts was built like a dump truck that loved denim. Greasy long hair and acne scars finished his look. He could headlock, wristlock, and power slam, but the rest was just chops, elbows, forearms and clotheslines until his opponent was a broken mess. He wrestled so stiff some of the boys hit back with receipts until the bell rang. Dirt Sheets claimed Pitts was wanted for the murder of a young girl in Portland, but the mark press had said zip.

For all his costs, Pitts had the only gift a wrestler needs: he filled the shows with drunk skids and patched bikers who bought enough beer and Pink Elephant popcorn to warrant cleaning up their puke and roaches. Their arm candy came dolled up like parade queens, but closer inspection suggested they'd turned eighteen a day before the match. Bronc had banned Pitts' crew from TV tapings, no arguments. Pitt wasn't so bulletproof he could threaten Bronc's new contract with CHAN TV. Those videos were keyed into other territories' TV time, which built revenue to keep the lights on.

Fans gawked on camera as local athletes and tough guys took serious beatings from the boys. The matches were rigged, but the fractures were real. And while the boys came off like gods, few jobbers lasted more than a month. Enter Rueben Shafir, a.k.a Ruby Shakes. He was the little Jew going up against the Goliaths, paid never to use his sling. To the boys, he was Jobby, the best loser in the business.

Ruby had the casual happiness of a newsboy shoved in a gaunt twenty-five-year-old man. No biker or gym rat, Ruby dressed in red Puma running shorts and concert tees slapped on a cut and blade-thin physique of lean, hard muscle. His clothes and shoes never lasted a month, vanishing as he ran through the city, Stanley Park, straight into work and off again. His hair was either wild or shaved and impossible to predict, unlike his stink. His B.O. was so caustic and hazy Bronc ordered the boys to put soap in his pockets to ensure the death of his toxic fume.

The boys never saw him at the bar, the peelers, or the gym. He never loitered after the show for a ring rat's number, and when they showed up in the back or the parking lot he never dropped his character, the valiant hero who never won but always tried. "It is very nice to meet you, Samantha. I hope you enjoy the show and get home safe. After all, it's a school night!"

No one knew where he lived, but Pitts swore he was a homeless hippie, living out of a rusted Cutlass Supreme near the beach. Ruby would arrive at house shows or TV tapings on his own, drenched in sweat, shower with soap for the first time in days, and reveal his catalog of face scrapes, plum-dark bruises etched in his back, welts and bandaged cuts that would mutate into something permanent.

But the scar down his neck was memorable. Grunt Tomasko of the Rocky Mountain Wrecking Crew had tossed Ruby into a corner missing a turnbuckle (cheap rings and drunk ring crew: not part of the show). Ruby took the brunt on his back, but he finished the spot they had planned by sliding down in the corner to set up Tomasko's Ninja Knee-Strike. One of the hooked end fittings was bent and dented, creating an edge like a razor. It cut his descending neck and peeled open his skin like a scalpel. When the stitches came off it was replaced by a purple zipper made of scabby flesh. And soon, Ruby was up and running. The boys welcomed him back and treated him like a mascot.

Before every card, the booker would talk to Ruby and his opponent. They'd work out the match, the set-ups, and finishes, and throughout, Ruby made friendly suggestions like "or you can backdrop me onto the edge of the ring, and I'll fall on the concrete shaking like you crushed a vertebra." Every suggestion transformed the brutes and thugs into supervillains, and the fans went wild to watch them paintbrush and ragdoll all 150 taut pounds of him. Beyond that, Ruby never said a word besides pleasantries and a fistful of heroic advice to the crowd. "Drink your milk and stay in school, and you can do anything!" Then he was on the run.

After a few months, gratitude soured. Mack Titan went to Bronc and asked if "Jobby" could take a powder for a month. "He's going to die in there, boss, the way he takes bumps. And one of us will hang for his murder." Next thing the boys saw was meat-hook fingers dragging Titan by the throat before tossing him onto a card table, where Judo Sumo and Kicker Karstoff were playing cribbage.

"Saying this once." Bronc's voice was bitter cold. "Any one of you comes to me about Ruby again, and you're outlawed. I will bury your career quicker than you can spit. That little Jew is the only one making you look good on TV. And ya know why? You idiots are stiffer than a dead man's cock. I don't give a shit what you do to each other on the road or on TV, but most of you can't work a thirty-minute show. You ain't working angles, just routine spots. You're getting fat and lazy. So we need the jobbers to pick up your shit. Problem is, none are staying longer than a week because you're sending too many of them to the emergency room.

"Except Ruby. You can go hard-way until his face is a crimson mask, splash him in the crowd, shoot in the ring until he's stretched and pissing blood — and he'll sell it. He'll sell all of it and make you look mint before you ram each other like drunk pachyderms. Anyone lays hands or talks shit about Ruby better pack their boots first. Hear me?"

They did. But Pitts played deaf.

The champ had never worked with Ruby, having been fast-forwarded to the front of the line because of his stellar run in Portland (murder accusations notwithstanding). Jobbers were beneath his rank, and outside of giving a swirly or two so they brought him two-fours of Heritage House or a carton of Players or a ring rat just shy of jailbait, he wouldn't piss on them if they were a flaming Buddhist. But after Bronc's warning, Pitt's crass nature flickered.

The barrage was verbal. Idiot, homo, skid, but none of the names registered. Ruby just smiled, nodded, and ran. He'd use his soap only to hear Pitt laughing that he'd already tested it with his asshole. Ruby lathered so hard the shower was a bubble bath before he used the bar on his body, smiling. But when Pitts bragged about how he was getting everyone a "teen scream queen" for his next birthday because

"I'm tired of sloppy second seniors," he saw Ruby's grin retreat behind everybody's cheers.

Next day at a house show in Cloverdale, Pitts and his crony Father Padre were emptying cans and playing gin rummy as Ruby toweled off. "Worst ring rat?" Padre said, his bull neck speckled with red sores with frosted tips. "One of those Crofton House girls. Virgin bitches are the fucking worst."

"Because you're a weak lay. Last night I picked up this strange, so eager and horny, and a screamer, but brother, she was so young and fresh, so clean, I swear she was turning thirteen." They laughed and grabbed fresh cans. The boys read books, did curls, and laced boots. Devil's Brigade could party, but they also killed anyone who crossed their own. Big or small.

Padre cracked a frothing cold one. "Why do you get all the good ones? Mine was crying for her daddy."

"But you finished."

"Fuck yeah, after all that noise, I earned it."

Ruby stood at the table, each man on one side of him. Hands at his sides, a towel knotted around his waist, Ruby's chest and torso were a gnarled landscape of dense muscle and agony. "Gentleman you can't talk like that. Not about girls. Not as a shoot. Not back here."

Pitts howled and clapped three times. "Finally, Bumpy Jew speaks his mind. But I know I didn't hear you telling me what to do, Bumpy. I know you're not that stupid." His grin was crusted, and his lips were peeling. "You know Rueben here has a rap sheet as long as my cock? Drunk and disorderly, assault, boy knows how to fight, just not win." He cackled, then grinned with sarcastic delight. "Oh, I'm sorry. You hiding a sister we don't know about?" The grin curled.

Faster than a hiccup, two fingers stretched in a V thrust inside Pitt's eyes. He crumpled on the floor, hands over his face, screaming. Padre rose but two fingers hard as ice jammed his eye sockets until something gushed. Padre fell beside Pitt, both screaming for a medic as if they were dying in the muck of Khe Sanh. Ruby gripped his towel knot, hurdled over the bodies, and sprinted out of the room. The boys were slow to rise, though none aided the champ.

Weeks later, Pitt stood in Bronc's office with the belt on his shoulder and a patch over his right eye, left one still red. "I want him. I'll either do it here and make you money, and maybe he goes home in a body brace, or I'll find him outside, and you lose your whipping boy. Hear me?"

Bronc leaned back in his chair, put up his oxblood loafers on his magazine-strewn desk. "Seems you're in the wrong place."

"What?"

"Does this look like the unemployment line?" He tossed Pitt a crumpled check. "Drop the belt. Take the check. Leave."

Livid, Pitt spoke slow. "I am the only thing keeping this idiot league from drowning. I am not going anywhere."

Bronc cracked the knuckles, and Pitt winced. "Right. Your take over. Turn my promotion into a drug front. That's gone, too. I see your scab friends near my territory again, and they'll find it hard to ride a bike with two broke legs."

Pitt hissed. "You're dead, fat boy."

"Not according to your local chapter." Bronc breathed in deep, exhaled slow. "You think I didn't talk to your president when I hired you?" Fear flickered in Pitt's one good eye. "Told him I'd keep him informed if you were trying to start an outlaw outfit."

Pitts snarled, but there was no gas in his tank. "You're full of shit."

Bronc's big hand shoved his phone to the end of the desk. "Call him." Bronc slowly rose to his full height, as if a bear was lecturing a fire hydrant. "Or take your shot, rube. Either way, once you leave, your little sister Amanda in Placerville will be told she'll never find your carcass."

Next Sunday night, fans tuned to CHAN TV to watch Sunday Night Wrestling Stars. When the title zoomed out of focus, they saw former World Champion and CEO of NLWF Bronc Snyder in the ring with announcer Karl Edwards, the heavyweight title in his mitt.

"Ladies and gentlemen and wrestling fans all across the world, I am here under unfortunate circumstances." His words were stiff as a rusty Underwood. "I regret to inform the fans that Chuck Pitts has vacated his title due to a family emergency in Portland, Oregon. So tonight, we have the first-ever Northern Lights Wrestling Federation Heavyweight Championship tournament!" Teens stood and clapped while the Hatpins screamed murder. "So, without further ado, let's see our first contender!"

The collective gasp held until the curtain was shoved, and from the darkness emerged the massive figure of Father Padre, blessing the crowd while the recycled beer-fueled screams and Century Sam cigar smoke thickened the air into a mist. Father Padre took to the ring, eye patch so big the chant of "Pirate" swarmed the arena. Bronc cleared his throat. "And his opponent. From Parts Unknown . . ." One hundred and fifty pounds of dynamite ran toward the ring to wild applause. "Ruby Shakes!"

Ruby climbed the corner ropes and glared at the crowd — he'd changed his look by a sliver. Across his chest was an R and S in very bright red. "Drink your milk! Stay in school! You can become what you want to be!" And the rings beneath his eyes had darkened, giving him the countenance of a happy skull.

Bronc lifted the belt as the two wrestlers faced each other, the mic now out of the ring.

He shook Ruby's hand. "Change in plans, kid."

He shook Father Padre's hand and held it in a bone crusher vice. "You're jobbing. Ruby goes over." Father Padre gasped as Bronc let go, then turned to Ruby. "If you even smell him making this a shoot you have my permission to take his last eye."

Bronc left. Ruby smiled, a snarl in a corner of his mouth. "Today, I take you to school."

Then the bell rang.

THE REBIRTH OF THE BRICK WALL

RYAN DILBERT

TERRITORY:
Texas Wrestling Alliance
(*Texas*)
1985

Ronnie "Brick Wall" Brooks used to pound a man's face until it swelled and bled and grew misshapen. He did it to make a living as much as for the euphoria that came with it. "Whiskey is nice," he used to say, "but it ain't nothing like breaking a man's will."

In that dusky honky tonk bar, he didn't want any reminders of that time in his life. He had come to down a beer and sit somewhere quiet. This Tuesday night prelim bout between two rookie welterweights on the TV above the bar was not that. Just hearing the sounds of the fight in the background gave him the empty-on-the-inside feeling he'd been running from. Ronnie didn't need to be thinking about how his torn Achilles left him too slow and cumbersome to box anymore. He didn't need to be thinking about how aimless he was now, a bloodhound no longer fit for the hunt.

"You mind turning that off?" he said, pointing the neck of his beer at the TV.

"I'm watching that, buddy," a bearded man with deep-set blue eyes grumbled.

"Two 0-2 fighters nobody's ever heard of? Yeah right."

The man, a rig driver with more than a six-pack in him, shot up from his stool and marched toward Ronnie, who just kept on drinking. As the guy asked, "You scared?" in his ear, Ronnie knocked back the last of his beer. He signaled to the barkeep to get him another.

"I'm talking to you," the truck driver said.

"I know that, and I'm not listening."

"You get your black ass off that stool and face me. You don't get to mouth off in here without something happening."

Ronnie snapped his head back to evade the punch that came his way. That defensive fighting instinct remained sharp even after nearly two years away from the ring.

"You don't want this fight," the boxer warned.

Drunk and outweighed by a good sixty pounds, the truck driver came charging anyway. Ronnie sidestepped him and landed a right hook that crumpled him.

From the far corner of the bar, Texas Wrestling Alliance head Hugo Schwartz paused mid-puff on his cigar as he eyed the commotion. His informal meeting had ended more than an hour ago, but he'd stayed in the bar alone. That's where he came up with a good chunk of his best booking ideas — buzzed, staring at the wall, country music as white noise.

Hugo hadn't caught the punch Ronnie threw, but he sure saw him now, a wide-bodied tank of a man towering over a lifeless heap of flesh.

Ronnie, thinking the moment was done, slid back onto his seat. Two of the rig driver's buddies rushed him, though.

"You're dead," one of them barked.

A bar fight swept across the place. Ronnie stood at the center of the storm. He ducked, blocked, pushed these men away. But they kept coming, stubborn and beer brave. Ronnie lifted a man by the collar and flung him through a table. Broken glass clinked underneath him as the would-be attacker groaned on the floor.

Hugo had instinctively moved closer to the action. His cigar lay tilted downward in his ashtray, abandoned, as the old man shuffled mindlessly toward the brawl.

All he could think of was how perfect Ronnie would look in his ring. What a sight! What a physique! His long, thick arms shone under the bar lights. His fists hung at the end of them as big as war maces. Hugo was used to seeing sleek bodybuilders come through town looking to get trained, but rarely did he see a man who looked so convincingly like he could put another man through hell.

Hugo walked up to him.

"You want some, too, old man?" Ronnie sniped.

Hugo shook his head and waved his hand.

"You and I are going to make big money," he told Ronnie, smiling wide enough to reveal every one of his missing teeth.

———

IN A RING SET up inside a rusty barn, trainees took turns slamming each other. They scooped each other up with the same fluid motion, and each man made the same thud when their backs hit the mat. The early morning sun cut through the holes in the old building, making a spotlight of sorts on it all.

Ronnie stood at ringside with his arms crossed. Hugo slid next to him, taking a long drink of his coffee before putting his hand on the boxer's big shoulder.

"You about ready to give it a go?" Hugo asked.

"I don't know about this," Ronnie said. "They're really wrecking each other in there."

"Pain can't be nothing new for you. All those years getting hit in the jaw."

Hugo scratched his graying stubble as he spoke about how much easier everything got. Adrenaline carries you, he promised. The crowd noise fills the air. The match flows. Everything else is lost. He was a convincing man with a voice thick as corn syrup. He talked so much that you didn't have time to push back, to question. The words came steady like rain on a rooftop.

"Y'all take a breather," he called out.

Once the shirtless, sweaty prospects rolled out of the ring, Hugo pulled Ronnie in there with him. He positioned their bodies to face each other.

"Come grab me," the booker said as he guided Ronnie's arm into a side headlock.

Ronnie's thick, muscular arm hung too loosely around Hugo's head. It was more of a brotherly embrace than a wrestling hold. Hugo barked at him to tighten it. Even when he had the headlock clamped on to Hugo's liking, Ronnie felt off.

Once he noticed trainees had gathered around to watch, Ronnie stiffened up even more. He flubbed every move Hugo tried to teach him. He tripped on himself at one point and didn't dare look up at the reaction from the onlookers. Maybe this wasn't for him, Ronnie thought. Maybe he'd be better off trying to sell cars at his brother's dealership. Maybe he'd already gotten all the mileage he was going to get from his body.

But Hugo kept buzzing in his ear, telling him about all the success coming his way.

"You got a body like a statue," he told Ronnie. "You're handsome. Your name has weight. You're strong as a dang bull."

It was enough to keep him training, even if it wasn't enough to push the doubts all the way out of his head. For weeks, Ronnie practiced rolling, falling on his back, curling a man's arm behind his back with a hammerlock. He was too slow and too soft. He was driving a car unsure of how much pressure to put on the pedal.

"Come on, Brick Wall," Hugo would say. "You can give me more than that."

One afternoon, Hugo's sons, all wrestlers, all tanned, all with dreamboat smiles, leaned on the ring apron to see Ronnie in action. Kelly's golden curly hair fell atop his bulging shoulders. Kyle, the youngest, wore a tight polo over his wiry frame. Connor, who had abs that looked carved out with a chisel, stood between them.

The Schwartz boys slapped their hands on the ring edge, chanting "Brick Wall! Brick Wall!" but Ronnie could barely hear it. A haze filled his head. His thoughts tumbled around. He felt as if he was lying to himself somehow. I'm playacting, he told himself. I'm doing the steps, but I'm no dancer.

Hugo motioned for Connor to step in the ring. Connor nodded, tossed his robe over a chair, and soon stood inches from Ronnie, his face squeezed in an intentional snarl. He didn't have the fanbase or the charisma that Kelly did, but he was the best wrestler of the bunch. His father often threw him into training sessions like this one.

"My boy will help you with something new," Hugo said. "This will suit you. It's called a lariat. Just swing your arm like a club. Hit them across the chest. Connor's going to fall and sell the hell out of it."

After twice demonstrating the move, surprising Ronnie with how well he still moved around, Hugo stepped back and tucked in a corner to watch.

Ronnie sighed. This just felt like a new way to fail. What's the point of learning a new word in a language you don't understand? He charged at Connor as he'd been instructed, banging his arm against the kid's sternum. Connor flopped backwards. The ring shook a bit.

"Not bad," Hugo said.

On the second try, Ronnie ran faster and hit with more force. Connor grunted. The boxer repeated it all, four, five times. He lost count. The move got crisper and more violent, and Ronnie began to land it perfectly. He stopped thinking about it. The act whisked him away to that zone he used to get into when he had a foe trapped in a corner and he'd lay a three-punch combo on him.

Ronnie didn't notice the Schwartz boys' applause or Hugo's yellow-toothed grin. He was busy pulsing with the thrill of success. He felt as if he had slid into place, a key in its rightful keyhole.

HUGO HAD JUST WRESTLED a six-man tag with Connor and Kelly and now sat shirtless in his office, his hairy chest shiny with sweat. He motioned for Ronnie to sit down. The TWA boss pulled a longneck from his mini-fridge and offered Ronnie one.

After they clinked beers and each took a big swig, Hugo laid out his plans for his new star-to-be. Tonight, Ronnie had just watched from the crowd, taking in the atmosphere, the rhythm of matches, the facial expressions of the boys in there. His own turn was coming.

"My youngest, Kyle, he's going to make you look like a beast," Hugo started. "The fans pull for him. They love him. You beat him good in your debut, and you'll get their attention. I move you up the ladder. Win, win, win. We start talking title shot at some point. People will eat it up."

Ronnie didn't know how to react. He should have been excited, but he felt more numbness than anything. It still didn't feel real. Never mind that he hadn't put on boxing gloves in years. Never mind that he spent hours and hours training as a wrestler. Never mind that Hugo got a seamstress to stitch him up some gear with RB on his boots. Never mind that his face was on a poster next to guys like The Demolisher and Sweet Feet Billy Lane. He was still a boxer in his head. Shaking off that identity to make room for another was proving hard to do.

Of course, he didn't tell Hugo that. He didn't tell anyone much of anyone that was going on in his head.

The night of his debut, he didn't have room in his brain for these doubts. Nervousness took up most of the space in there. His stomach swirled as he tightened the laces on his boots. When Kyle saw him backstage and wished him luck, his heart thumped so hard that it rang in his ears.

The fans were a blur around Ronnie as he walked down the aisle and into the ring. Try to walk naturally, he told himself as he felt his gait grow stiff. Caught up in the thoughts flooding his head, the boxer didn't hear the ring announcer call his name or every teenage girl in the building squeal in delight as Kyle trotted out with his fist raised high and his blond bangs bouncing on his brow.

Once the bell rang, he and Kyle tied up in the center of the ring. The youngest Schwartz boy did as his father promised — made Ronnie look good. Everything Ronnie hit him with sent him tumbling. He howled when Ronnie punched him in the midsection. He clutched his back like it was broken after a body slam.

The match sped by. The crowd seemed engaged. Ronnie hadn't tripped, injured himself, or thrown up in the ring, as he thought he might. "I'm doing decent," he said to himself. It wasn't nearly as good as those matches Hugo had made him watch on VHS, but he wasn't embarrassing himself, and that was enough for now.

"Tornado punch," Kyle whispered to him.

This was going to be one of Ronnie's signature moves. Hugo thought it best for a former boxer to bring over his punching power to the wrestling world. He'd told Ronnie during training to make the spinning big and just glance with the punch itself.

Ronnie whirled with his fist ready and struck Kyle. His momentum, his muscle memory, it all had him swinging harder than he meant. He could feel the cartilage crunch under his knuckles when the shot landed. Kyle's blood sprayed from his face like the juice from a grapefruit.

As Kyle fell to his knees, Ronnie's fist remained cocked, his hand stuck in the air, a statue aglow with sweat. Blood dripped down Kyle's chin, darkening the mat.

A collective gasp from the crowd came first. Then an eruption. Fans cursed, spat, pushed against the metal barricade around the ring. The referee pulled Ronnie out of the ring and guided him back-stage, knowing worse was coming. On the hurried trip up the ramp, someone tossed a cup of beer at Ronnie's head, and people pelted garbage at his back. Ronnie had been told that Texas fans were forever protective of the Schwartz boys, their handsome heroes, but he didn't understand what that meant until this moment.

Before he ducked behind the curtains to safety, Ronnie looked back at the bedlam in the building, surprising himself with a prideful grin. He was the tide that created this wave, the man behind this unraveling. He laughed to himself. He would never have imagined this would be where he ended up — in tights, in a sawdust-covered arena, stinking of beer, a wanted man, a wrestler.

LAKE EFFECT

CARRIE LABEN

TERRITORY:
Rock City Wrestling
(Michigan, Ohio, Western Pennsylvania)
Winter, 1983

First they had to kidnap Jeremy. They said that as a joke, but Danielle wasn't entirely joking; she was three months over eighteen, and Jeremy was two months past his seventeenth birthday, so taking him any place his parents didn't want him to go was a felony, she was pretty sure. Especially since they were crossing state lines. You went from Ohio into Michigan, the roadside didn't look any different, the frozen brown grass, the distant lights in the houses, but there was an imaginary line in the world, and suddenly hanging out with your boyfriend meant you could go to jail.

But only if you get caught, she told herself. Which they had perfected not doing over the six months they'd been dating. She'd parked two blocks down from Jeremy's house and made Rob run out in the cold to stand just out of the streetlight circle and flick a lighter where Jeremy could see. Jeremy's mom didn't like Rob either, him being Danielle's brother and also a bad influence in his own right, but he was younger and didn't set off the Brazen Hussy Alarm that the old lady apparently had like a particularly mean kind of ESP, like the police scanner that crackled all night in her kitchen.

It took Rob long enough for Danielle to get anxious and irritable. She felt weird anyway. There was a sense of bad mojo about the night. The clouds were down low and gray, and if they had to drive back in the snow, she was going to have to stay mostly sober. And she hadn't told Jeremy about how she was going to be dressed. Baggy t-shirt, baggy jeans, two sports bras layered to smash down her tits. No makeup, hair tucked up under a knit cap, even though it was lumpy and itched like hell. Honestly, she liked it — people hissed *lezzie* behind her back anyway, even people who knew about Jeremy, and being a dude at one of these shows seemed like it would be way less hassle. She wasn't sure how Jeremy would take it, though.

Anyway, there they were, Rob linebacker-big since his latest growth spurt but somehow still less awkward than Jeremy, who was reedy and slouched, unsure what to do with his height. They were trotting, eager to get out of the cold and on their way, probably, but it didn't look like they were running away from anything.

Jesus Christ, I am on edge, she thought. *Running from what? Mrs. Hall is gonna lift her fat ass off the sofa and chase them down the street like Godzilla? I need a beer. One beer, a couple-three should be fine, if it doesn't snow.*

She turned the lights back on, the heat all the way up, and put it in gear as soon as she heard the solid clunk of both doors. Jeremy, riding shotgun, barely even glanced at her before he sighed and slumped further. She didn't think that she looked that bad, not with her coat still on.

Rob, sitting behind her, was considerably more enthused. "Alright, we're on the road! Onwards, Danny!" And they were; it didn't take long to get clear of Jeremy's neighborhood, where there was always a risk, however small, that the car might be recognized and Mrs. Hall might get a tip to wait up all night.

As she navigated toward the 280, Rob scooched over so that he could lean between the two front seats and talk. "Do you think tonight's the night that Larry L'Amour takes the belt off the Maharajah?"

"More likely it's the night that the Maharajah takes Larry's nose clean off his face," Danny said. "Larry's overconfident."

"He beat 'Big' Wallace Russell pretty good."

"Wallace was having an off night," she said. He had been, too; it was obvious even through the fuzz that plagued TV reception from Detroit when the clouds were low. He'd looked like he was favoring his right leg before the match even started.

"I swear, sometimes you want the bad guys to win."

"I'm just a realist."

"What do you think, Jer?" From the corner of her eye Danielle saw Jeremy turn away from the dark window at last. She was never sure whether Rob didn't sense the tension of Jeremy's bad moods or didn't care. "Is Larry gonna take it?"

Sometimes Rob's bull-in-a-china-shop approach snapped Jeremy out of it; sometimes, like right now, not so much. "Dunno," he muttered, and clammed up again.

"I mean, true." Rob laughed. "That's why we watch the matches, right? Because anything could happen." He paused. Jeremy said nothing.

"God, you're both on the rag tonight. Turn on some music or something."

If he'd said it a moment earlier, she'd have leaned forward and reached for the radio, and then she wouldn't have seen the Mustang coming up on their ass until it was too late. As it was she barely got over, and the car blew by at what must have been ninety, a hundred miles an hour. But the weirdest part was that in the middle of December, well after dark, it had its top down.

"Jesus Christ," Jeremy said, in a completely different tone than before — less petulant, almost dazed. Almost awed. Almost in tears. "It was them."

"Them?" It was nice when Rob took point on being confused, because Danny hated to admit that she didn't know what was going on.

"My dad was saying at dinner that he arrested Larry L'Amour this morning for crashing his car, driving fucked up. And he said that 'Big' Wallace Russell came and bailed him out. He said that it proved wrestling is fake bullshit, and that I'm an idiot for caring about it."

"He was probably lying just to mess with you," Rob said. It was, in fact, probable. Jeremy's dad was an asshole even by cop standards.

"But the weird thing was, he said Wallace Russell was driving a Mustang Cobra with the top down in the snow."

THEY WEREN'T GOING to make it back to Detroit if they died. Or maybe they would. Maybe the Cobo Arena was Hell, and he'd have to serve his whole sentence there. He'd earned it, the good Lord knew. But Eugene Lawrence Larson, professionally known as Larry L'Amour, or occasionally The Lonesome Cowboy or Kid Larry, understood that Wally was doing him a favor. Backseat driving would be rude.

Still, they'd just about clipped that Cutlass. He'd seen a kid's face staring from the passenger seat, pale and shocked. Life wasn't great, but moments like that told Larry he really didn't want to die.

On the other hand, the faster they drove the sooner they'd be out of the cold. Wally had been pretty proud of the deal he'd gotten on the car — a Cobra for a song, and he knew a guy who knew everything about fixing them up. Except that guy was down in the Florida panhandle, where Wally grew up, and this car was here in Michigan, and the top got stuck the first time Wally put it down. Wally's solution for that was to keep a hat and gloves on while driving, and keep it moving at a good clip. He swore that if he went fast enough he could move between the snowflakes.

Larry stuck his own gloved hands under his armpits and huddled down. It wasn't like he'd never been cold before. He'd grown up in North Dakota, done two pointless years at a naval base in Alaska. But it had been a goat rodeo of a day, which increased a man's susceptibility.

Wally seemed to sense that, had been respectful of Larry's need for silence. But it couldn't last forever. As soon as the big man straightened up and took a breath, Larry knew what was coming.

"How'd you even manage to get your shitbox up onto someone's porch and into their living room, anyway?"

"I wasn't in the living room," Larry said, wishing all those bored gossipy cops some real problems to deal with. Wasn't Toledo a city? Didn't they have sex fiends, or gas station robberies? He knew for a fact they had drug dealers. "Dented up the front door pretty good, but it wasn't like I drove inside and gave myself a tour."

"Either way, you must have totaled your car for real if you called for Wally and the Bust-tang in this weather."

"I hit some ice. I'd been driving all day. Exhausted."

Wally's eyes didn't leave the road, but he stiffened a little, and Larry realized the implication of what he'd said. "I went to Corning to check on Maureen and the kids."

"You were trying to make that whole round trip today?"

"It's not like any other day is better. And she needed cash right away, couldn't wait for the mail."

Maureen had insisted. That much was true. And he'd decided he couldn't do New York to Corning to Detroit sober, not when he was already late leaving New York to begin with. And now his car was totaled, and it was just a mercy the cops had let him call Wally to pick him up, and he wasn't sure that some of them hadn't recognized him, and some of them definitely thought they recognized Wally — though they were disappointed when they ran the Bust-tang's plates. But that was a problem to deal with after the problem they faced right now, which was to get to Detroit alive, but also on time, and do their jobs. And the next step after that was to get a bottle of whatever, bourbon if he was lucky, and as many pills as he could find, and some warm company ... when he thought like that, he almost thought everything would be all right, if they just made it to Detroit.

Short-term thinking, Maureen's voice said somewhere behind his ears. *That's always been your problem. You sit there, you big dope, and you only see what's right in front of you.* Wally, who had three ex-wives and seven kids between them, said that Larry would shake Maureen's voice out of his head one day. But the problem was that Maureen was right. Not all the way right — he wasn't going to quit wrestling; he wasn't going to join her in studying this weird computer programming stuff she'd latched onto, or read any of the books about reincarnation she kept trying to give him, which were outright idolatry and also nuts — but right enough. Other guys, they were plotting, planning, building their careers according to a system, not just luck. The boss himself could think out all the outcomes like some kind of supersonic chess guy; he knew what would happen in the future, years from now. Wally knew less than that, but he knew what would happen in a month or six, which Larry did not, and it hurt his head to think about. Larry wasn't dumb, Maureen had said once, but he liked things concrete. The abstract passed him by.

The boss said he liked that about Larry, liked a man who could keep his head in the moment, when the heat was on.

The man in New York said it was a good thing, too.

He wished that he'd passed Corning by, let her wait for the money or sent it by Western Union. But he couldn't figure what the smart thing to do now was, except try to make it through to Detroit and do the job in front of him. Maureen didn't even drink anymore and wouldn't give him a drink when he stopped in, which was bullshit. The pills that had gotten him in trouble were gone now, with nothing but a headache to remember them by.

He could ask Wally's advice, but if he'd judged wrong there was no taking back the fact that he'd been to New York. He'd make an enemy of Wally. He didn't think he could stand that. No matter what anyone said, this black guy who ground his teeth and let his hair grow wild and growled like a dog at the audience was the best friend that Eugene Lawrence Larson from North Dakota had ever known, the one he trusted, whose advice he took. Maureen's advice might be good, but she didn't know the business. The boss's advice might be good, but even Larry L'Amour wasn't shiny-faced innocent enough to trust The Maharajah all the way.

For sure Wally didn't trust the boss all the way either. But how were they supposed to talk about it?

"Oh fuck me," Wally muttered, as the first few flakes of snow began to fall. "These white bitches."

ROB HAD MISSED IT. He hadn't seen what Jeremy thought he'd seen — Larry L'Amour and "Big" Wallace Russell riding in a car together on their way to Detroit — but the whole idea set him on edge. During the last four months, Rob had learned a lot about how professional wrestling worked. How it really worked. But, so far, he was holding those secrets close, keeping them from his sister and his best friend. The idea that they all could be spoiled in one, unlucky instant made him nervous. Still, he told himself to calm down. He knew Danny's eyes had been on the road, that she didn't have time to see, either. They'd all been startled when the Mustang came flying up behind them. But Jeremy remained absolutely sure it had been them.

Rob told himself it didn't matter. What mattered wasn't who Larry L'Amour was. What mattered was who he, Rob Drake, was, and he was still someone who could pull off this plan. He could still be the person he thought Larry L'Amour thought he was. Right? Sure. He could do it if anyone could.

"Can your dad even tell one big black guy from another?" he grunted, getting Jeremy to half-turn in his seat to look at him. "Can he tell one busted-ass car from another? Was he even sober enough to tell what direction they drove off? You tell me."

"Plus," Danny said from under her hat, "he does lie to mess with you. Like, all the time. Remember when he tried to tell us that he'd arrested Rob Halford for public indecency?"

Jeremy frowned, like maybe he was warming up to the argument. Maybe their skepticism was making him think twice about what he'd seen. Maybe he was warming up in general. He'd been waiting for a while out in the cold before Rob and Dannielle had shown up to get him, and sometimes that was all it took to piss Jeremy off. "Who the fuck knows," he said, unsure of himself now. "I don't trust him. Honestly, I don't care. I just want to see the show."

"That's what we're gonna do," Danielle said. She bent forward over the steering wheel like concentrating could get them there faster. The snowflakes were slicing down across the windshield. The signs at the side of the highway rose and faded. They crossed the state line. Rob's mood started to lift again. They were going to make it. He was going to pull it off.

Jeremy's mood didn't seem to change, though. Rob knew that he could be an idiot about these things, but he wasn't completely blind. He knew when Jeremy was pissy. It made more sense to let him get on with it, sometimes. How Danny didn't get that, when she was Jeremy's girlfriend and all, Rob would never know.

Like right now, when she was driving and it was snowing harder by the second, was probably not the greatest time for her to say "So what else is eating you?" to Jeremy with an edge of sarcasm in her voice.

"Like you don't know." Absolutely predictable response from Jeremy. It meant he wanted to be left alone. Which Danny would never, ever do. Rob had been so naïve six months ago. He'd thought that his best friend and his sister dating would make life easier.

"No, I don't. It seems to me that we're about to have a very nice night out, if you don't sulk it up."

"You're dressed like ..." Jeremy trailed off. Rob knew what he was about to say and was really glad Jeremy at least had the sense not to actually say it.

"I'm dressed like I'm not going to get hassled all night like last time."

"You're dressed like if I try to kiss you I'm going to get beat up."

"You don't need to be pawing at me every damn second of our lives; we're paying to see the show, not be the show."

Rob leaned forward between them and turned the radio on himself.

LARRY JUST WANTED to change his shoes. He'd had to walk the last blocks while Wally drove around and approached the stadium from the other side; enough snow had accumulated that his feet were wet and cold. He should be in the locker room anyway, getting dressed and getting straight. But Wally thought it was a good idea to take this bull by the horns, and it was Wally's butt in a sling, too, if things went wrong. He might as well go with The Big Wallace Plan as his own no-plan. All he could do on his own was pray, and it didn't feel right to pray in here. Praying made him picture his mother. The last thing he wanted was his mother taking a good look around this place.

Jesus Lord, how had he ever thought that he was going to pull off even half of this day? He must have been crazy to try it. And it wasn't over yet. He'd nearly forgotten about the kid in all the other mess. He could maybe blow him off, but that didn't sit right either.

Maybe the kid hadn't made it from Toledo in the snow. Maybe his parents were smarter than Larry and nixed the trip. That would be a mercy.

Before he could get his hopes up about that or anything else, Wally emerged from the office. Larry waited for a sign or a gesture. Wally shook his head.

"He says he'll talk to you after the show; ain't got time now."

There was no way that wasn't a brush-off, meant to keep Larry stewing longer. But what could he do? He caught up with Wally, who was already heading down the hallway, in a couple of cold squishy strides.

They were surely out of earshot, but Larry spoke low anyway. "What'd he say? Besides that?"

"He chewed my ass pretty good. But in the end he had to agree that there wasn't much choice. Couldn't leave you in Toledo, could I? And there was no time to call no one else." He shrugged a little. "I didn't make it out all your fault. Leaned hard on the weather, the ice. But it would be easier if you'd come clean about what you were up to, and we got a story straight."

"I went to Corning ..."

"Come on, Larry. You know you're a shit liar. Maybe you went to Corning, but that wasn't what this was all about."

"Fine. I went to New York, too. Stayed the night there. Had to see a guy."

Wally wasn't a man who gave away a moment of fear, public or private, but Larry saw his back stiffen a little. He couldn't go through with it, couldn't tell him the whole thing. "This guy Maureen's been giving all her money to."

"You went to New York City the day before a match this big to warn off a gigolo?" The laugh stung Larry.

"Not like that. He's some kind of cult guy. He's got her all riled up about meditation and eating lentils and being the Queen of Sheba in her past life."

"Damn. Like those crazies out in California who put the rattlesnake in the guy's mail?"

"Don't think it's the same bunch, but he's just as crooked. And he's taking all the money I send for the kids. And I thought I'd make it clear to him what I thought about that."

Wally didn't say anything, and Larry started to worry that that wasn't enough, even though it was true as far as it went. He needed more. "Then in Toledo there was this young guy; he's been writing to me. Convinced that he wants to get in the business, he's been going to Garza's gym, has a whole thing worked out. And he's coming here tonight. But since I was going through anyway, I thought I'd stop and check him out beforehand ..." He realized as he said it that it sounded stupid and overcomplicated. Should've stuck with the truth. Stupid, stupid.

"How did he look? Any good?"

"Oh — I don't know; I didn't see him. Ended up on that porch, and you know the rest of the story."

Wally nodded.

"Maybe we'll find out tonight, if he makes it here in this storm." There. Now if the kid did show, it'd back up his story. That was a good thing. He hadn't thought of that.

"Dunno if anyone's going to make it here. The parking lot looked like a graveyard when I came in."

"Well, that part's in God's hands, not ours."

"I hear you, Preacher Larry. Let's get ready for whoever does show up."

HER JAW ACHED from gritting her teeth for the last thirty miles, watching the clock tick over while they crawled through a snow they never saw except when the wind came from the east. She hadn't had the attention to spare to see if that Mustang had ended up in a ditch along the way, but that seemed like the best-case scenario given how the guys in it had been driving.

That'd be a hell of a way to find out that Jeremy's son-of-a-bitch dad was telling the truth for once, show canceled because Big Wallace and Larry L'Amour were dead, necks broke and slung over a guardrail outside Luna Pier. Especially when Rob had done the good work of getting Jeremy cheered back up. She didn't want to think about that argument any more.

At least it wasn't hard to find parking once they got there. It wasn't totally empty, but there wasn't a wait to get inside. And the line for beer was short enough. People weren't crowding her, brushing against her like they usually did when she was alone. Or even when she was with Jeremy — because no one was afraid of getting in a fight with Jeremy. Now they moved aside and let her walk through without a second glance. She didn't even lose any beer to jostling elbows. She wasn't sure it was all the sparse crowd, either. People weren't eyeing her up the way they did when she dressed like a girl.

I could get used to this, she thought.

Rob and Jeremy took their beers, both smiling now, excited enough that they looked younger — there was a reason only her fake ID would do. If it stayed like this, not too crowded, and she wasn't spending all her money on beer, maybe she could hit the merch table and get a T-shirt. Something big enough to disguise herself even better next time she came to one of these. She almost grabbed Jeremy's hand for a squeeze, seeing him this happy, but he was right that it would have looked damn weird.

After a while the other seats did start to fill in. The first match got started only twenty minutes late, when they were on their second beers. It was quick; Arnie Lundgard squashed Cockroach Jimmy like his namesake. She honestly wondered why they kept a guy called Cockroach Jimmy around, but maybe he was someone's cousin or brother-in-law, needed the job. Or maybe it was to train up new guys on. But she didn't have long to think about it, because Lundgard brought him to the mat like thunder at the very moment Jimmy tried to grab for his neck, and there was a little sad leg-twitching like a real cockroach, and then the three-count. Lundgard barely seemed to care what he had done; he turned his back on the flattened Jimmy and grabbed the mic from the announcer.

"I'm tired of swatting bugs," he roared, fury giving fullness and gravity to his usual Sven-and-Ole accent. "We need to get rid of all the vermin! Rock City needs a real house cleaning; the bad guys think they run this town! Next on my list is the rabid animal Big Wallace Russell!"

The crowd was big enough to roar approval, that was for sure. Danny yelled with everyone else, joy not only for the promise of excitement to come — and that would be a hell of a match — but the excitement of right now, too, the excitement of feeling the excitement, of yelling along, sharing emotion.

Rob knocked over his beer without seeming to notice, slopping the cold liquid on her knee, bringing her down. Jimmy had rolled himself over and was crawling from the ring, forgotten, while Lundgard circled and promised Big Wallace the same fate as Old Yeller. For a moment she couldn't help but feel sorry for the guy, even if he called his own damn self Cockroach.

IT WAS impossible not to lose himself in this, lose track of time and lose track of the different elements of his plan, too. After spilling his beer on Danny, Rob got a lot more careful about checking his watch. He had to keep reminding himself that there even was a plan. He'd thought, *Oh damn, I wish I could be here for that one*, when Lundgard called out Big Wallace, before realizing that if he pulled it off tonight, he would be; he'd be here for all of them, forever. And for a moment he felt dizzy, because that couldn't be real. One day the crowd could be yelling for him, the mic could be in his hand, the lights shining off his hair and his shoulders, his voice ringing. He knew how it felt to win a wrestling match at a school meet, or press a new personal best, but he couldn't even imagine what it must be like to be Arnie Lundgard in that moment.

And then during the tag-team match, with the Bushrangers and the Bolin Brothers vying to go up against the team of Larry L'Amour and Kingbird Curtis for the championship, he forgot and remembered again, forgot in the moments of craning forward to see as the play-by-play man's voice rose in excitement, remembered when he recognized a grip or the broad outlines of a strategy. The Bolin Brothers fought their hearts out. Rob could feel the pull and burn in his own muscles. But it only took one crucial moment for Miss Sheila to distract the ref — half the audience, too, and there were appreciative hoots from the color commentator. Then the boomerangs came out and went low. Boos echoed through the arena, and cups of beer hurtled towards the ring. The ref recalled himself, Sheila jeered and waggled away, but it was too late for Nick Bolin, half-stunned under the weight of Captain Thunderbolt.

So Larry would be going up against these cheating bastards. He was tougher and smarter than the Bolins, good as they were. But those boomerangs looked like they'd hurt.

He checked his watch again, more cautiously this time. The show was going to run late, but then, the fight for the championship would be last, so it's not like Larry would be standing around waiting. Just, Danny would want to get out fast, get Jeremy home before his mom had one of her random midnight wanders and found him gone. He'd thought he'd have time to explain everything, give his reasons, say goodbye.

He lost himself again in the next match, another battle in the years-running war between Carl Schwann and Victor Trementino, this one a long brutal grind that could be won only by submission. It started clean and precise. Arm bar, shift of hip, levered up and out. Leg hooked, rope grabbed, release prompt. But as the match wore on second by second, he could see, almost feel, how they'd begun to lose the first crisp precision of their moves. They shifted to endurance mode, started to slip on each other's sweat and each other's strategies. They hadn't conserved their energy as much as they might have. As much as he would have in a match like this.

He'd already begun to understand from a couple of sessions with the trainer Larry had suggested that this wasn't like high school wrestling. You had to put on a show, exaggerate, make your moves big enough to see from the backmost seats. He got that. Therefore the punches and strikes, therefore the shouting, the dodging. But it still

looked frighteningly out of control at moments, ready to snap ligament and bone, even before Schwann dug his nails into Trementino's
forehead and drew blood.

The crowd had roared for Lundgard, hollered at the Bushrangers,
but now the collective animal tensed and sounded like a dog on a
scent. Rob was in with them all, forgetting again that he was Rob or
that there was a plan or that it could be him up there, except that it
could be him, because it was every man who'd ever been in a
desperate fight. The blood and sweat flowed down in a sheet with
hardly a pause, even for Trementino's bushy eyebrows. A few bright
splashes blotched the canvas. Trementino, the bigger man, knocked
Schwann back into the post and tried to slam his head, only to be
dodged again and again. Schwann slipped under his arm and went
for his knees.

Rob was near-hypnotized by watching the color and the swirl of
the wrestlers, now grabbing and pounding each other with almost no
science, only fury. He no longer had a sense of time or space. He
didn't actually see, only heard the shout when Schwann's manager
tossed brass knuckles into the ring. Danny laughed with glee but only
a single bark.

Swiping blood away with his forearm, Trementino seemed to get
a second wind, alert to a new level of danger. Ducking beneath the
loaded swing, he slipped behind Schwann and got him by the neck.
The knuckles slipped off, and both men fell to their knees grabbing
for them. Trementino had more oxygen and longer arms, so he got
there first.

He didn't even bother to stand up again, just swung from where
he was. A weak move, less leverage, but Schwann's attempt to dodge
put his head right into the swing, and he crumpled from a lithe blond
snake to a laundry bag on the canvas in an instant. Trementino barely
seemed to notice in his rage. Jumping on the inert form, he put him
into a crossface hold and began to crank his neck back.

There was no reaction. Schwann remained limp, his eyes blank.
The crowd noise subsided, row after row leaned forward in their

chairs. "He can't submit if he's dead," someone shouted on the other side of the arena.

The ref leaned close to Schwann's face, touched his wrist, shook his head. Gesturing broadly, he made Trementino release the hold. Schwann once again flopped to the ground without a twitch.

Trementino was clenched with frustration, still desperate to fight. But there was no more fight. The ref called a draw; the match would be continued at a future date. And as soon as the words of final authority left his mouth, Schwann moved behind his back, sat up and smiled.

The rain of thrown cups was thick, and the boos were near-deafening. And now it was intermission.

Danny stood. "Hell of a way to sell beer, pissing everyone off like that." As if to prove her point, she nearly slipped in a puddle maneuvering around Jeremy's knees to the aisle. "I'm going to the merch table, do you want to come with?"

Jeremy almost stood up, even though Rob knew he didn't have a penny on him. But he glanced over as he did, and something in Rob's face must have told him to stay back. Danny didn't seem to care either way.

"Listen," Rob said as soon as she was well away, leaning across the seat she'd vacated. "There's something I didn't tell you, because I wasn't sure it was happening until we made it here. We're not going back."

"What?" Jeremy leaned in too.

"We're. Not. Going back. To Toldeo. With Danny." There was no way she'd hear him over the crowd, not now.

"What the hell do you mean?"

"Ever since I started cutting school in September, I've been spending all my extra time at this gym, training with this guy Rafael Garza who's tight with the Detroit wrestlers, and I've been writing to Larry L'Amour. And he said if I came up here tonight they'd put me up and give me a trial. To be a pro. A full-on professional wrestler!"

"That's ..." Jeremy looked like he'd been hit by a pair of brass knucks himself. "That's amazing. I mean, awesome! You deserve it more than any of those meatheads who are still on the wrestling team getting scholarships and shit. But what do you mean *we?*"

"Dude. Obviously I'm not leaving you behind. I told them I have a manager. That's gonna be you."

"A manager? I don't even know if I can talk in front of all those people, man. I might start to stutter or some shit."

"You've never stuttered a word in your life. Think about it. You'll be able to say whatever you want to to assholes like Carl Schwann. You can pretend he's your dad and really tell him off, and if he wants to smack you around he'll have to get through me, which he won't."

"I mean ... damn. You're serious. Damn."

"Never have to deal with your dad again. Never have to deal with your mom narcing on you to him, either. The assholes at school, all of that, fuck it, forget it."

"Why didn't you tell me before this, though? I coulda packed. I don't even have a toothbrush or a change of pants — what am I going to do, be a hobo manager?"

"I told you I wasn't sure this was going to happen." He hadn't thought about it, to be honest. He had a bag with a couple of his own things in Danny's car, but now he wasn't even sure he was going to be able to go outside and get it. "It's not that hard to buy a toothbrush and some clothes; I can cover that, and once we start getting paid you'll be fine. Say you'll do it."

"I'd be crazy not to!"

"Ok. I wanted to explain everything, but the way things are going, I think it would be best to just give Danny the slip at the end of the show."

———

THE SHIRT MADE her inexplicably happy, even though it smelled like beer and smoke before she'd ever worn it. Maybe she'd dress like a dude all the time from now on. It seemed worlds easier.

Might be a little hard on Jeremy if she did that, but she'd been kind of getting tired of the whole Jeremy thing anyway. Now that she was out of school she didn't have to prove anything, and she was mostly his friend because he was Rob's friend in the first place. It would feel like kicking a puppy, she supposed, but that was just a phrase she'd heard. She'd never kicked a puppy, and she'd never dumped a guy before. It might be fun, for all she knew.

One advantage she could already think of — she wouldn't have to buy him beer anymore. The thought made her feel generous, and she brought beers back for him and for Rob too, and one more for herself. One more wouldn't hurt. She'd been fine to drive on worse.

The gentle buzz made the wrestling even better. Made her more able to stay in the moment, go with the ebbs and crests of the crowd's mood. They'd brought in some kind of martial artist from Japan to fight Kingbird Curtis. Curtis won despite all the strange rolling and flipping — he was as good as his name, light on his feet, always moving, but it never looked like he was running away. He was always on the attack. Despite what Rob said about her rooting for the bad guys, Curtis was maybe her favorite wrestler of all time, and it was his T-shirt she'd bought.

That said, she had a weird respect for "Big" Wallace Russell, too, watching him shriek and bite at his own wrist-guards while his manager Billy MacKenzie boasted about how he'd eat up Arnie Lundgard like the big dumb side of beef he was. He was definitely favoring that right leg, like she'd thought, but he didn't even seem to notice himself. To be in that kind of a state and still get in there and wrestle a guy like Larry L'Amour. To be in that kind of state and do this job at all. She'd never want to meet him, but the man must have a spine of iron under the crazy. And at least some smarts to realize he should take his crazy to the wrestling ring and not end up in jail or shot. There was something in that.

Then on to the main event, the Maharajah himself and Larry L'Amour. She felt Rob, who'd already been like a stalking cat on cocaine all night, sit up straighter and almost rise to his feet to get a better view. Larry was a lone ranger, no manager for him, but the Maharajah had his usual entourage: a pair of beautiful girls in barely any costumes and a short, squat man in a turban with a sword slung at his side. You'd never doubt or forget for a moment that the Maharajah owned Cobo Arena, even though the city of Detroit actually owned it.

She'd been right that the Maharajah kept the belt. He didn't bite Larry's nose off, though, just produced flames in his hand from nowhere and threw them in the cowboy's face. The color guy was yelling that neither scientists, nor chemists, nor researchers could tell you how the Maharajah did that. Larry should have expected it, even if science didn't, but he reeled back half-blinded. He kept fighting, though the Maharajah put him through a table and half-choked him on the ropes, kept fighting and fighting, but ultimately he was pinned when the little man with the sword reached into the ring and grabbed his ankle for a moment, long enough to throw him off balance. Larry probably should have expected that, too.

There was a dark match after that, Steve Kennedy versus a young guy she didn't recognize. Judging by the crowd noise when he came out, and again when he won, he must have been a local favorite. She couldn't pay much attention to that one, because she was realizing that she desperately needed to pee — maybe she should have thrown her beer instead of drinking it after all. Before the cheers died down she was out of her seat and looking for the johns.

She didn't quite have her hand on the door of the women's room when she realized from the dirty looks that she had a conundrum. Only it wasn't a conundrum, there was only one answer. She moved sideways, squinting a little as though she was nearsighted, and pushed into the men's room instead.

She fixed her eyes on an open stall door and beelined for it. The urinals were in her peripheral vision and she couldn't make out detail, but the splashing streams were plenty loud enough to make her acutely aware that they were all full. That was a lot of guys. If she somehow slipped up, if someone figured her out ... but as soon as the stall door was closed behind her she realized this was the optimal situation. If the urinals were all in use, it wasn't weird that she didn't use one. If there were a half-dozen guys in here, it would be riskier for any one of them to call her out, because if he was wrong, how would he look, what would happen to him? *Be calm,* she told herself, *you can think your way through anything.* But the hair on her arms didn't settle until she was halfway back to where she'd left Rob and Jeremy.

They weren't there; only their coats were. She scanned the crowd, realizing afresh how damn near everyone was wearing a black t-shirt. But there was Rob's hat and Jeremy's beside him, not heading to the exit or to the beer stand for one last or anywhere that made sense. Heading down an aisle towards a door marked Personnel. She took off running after them. Goddamn squirrelly kids, were they actually idiots enough to go looking for autographs when they needed to get home in a storm? Probably.

This time, working against the current of the crowd, she was being jostled and impeded at every moment. Or maybe it only felt that way. They were long gone through the door by the time she got there; she had no choice but to follow.

Luckily the hallway was a straight shot, no mystery where they'd gone. In fact they'd stopped by a door and were standing still, conversing in voices she could hear but not quite understand. They both looked up as the door behind her swung shut, thudding into its frame. *Ok, you little jerks. You have entire seconds to come up with a good excuse.*

When she reached them, they both avoided her eyes. Jeremy actually stepped behind Rob a little, as if to hide, which was stupid; she'd feel way less guilty about smacking Rob if it came down to it. She and the beer and the unease she'd felt driving and just now in the men's room were all ready to take this very personally.

Rob, with his lifetime of experience of her, knew better than Jeremy; he came out placating. "It was wrong not to tell you. I didn't plan for it to be like this. But the weather and the show running late and everything ..."

"What are you doing? Explain." Shrieking wouldn't work, so she pitched her voice down to a growl. She had a lifetime of experience with him, too.

"We're staying here in Detroit. Jeremy and I. I'm going to be a pro wrestler; I have an offer already, and ..."

"And you thought, oh, Danny will go home and take the heat for it, two minors running off in the dead of night, dead of winter, she's the last person who saw them. That'll be fine for her. Sure." She paused. "The hell you have a job offer? You're seventeen and still in high school."

"Joe Varga turned pro when he was sixteen."

"Joe Varga's dad isn't going to have me arrested! You halfwit. How do you know you were writing to the real Maharajah and not some goon who wants to rip you off or sell you into, I don't know, white slavery?"

"I wasn't writing to the Maharajah; I was writing to Larry L'Amour," Rob said, like that explained everything. "And, c'mon. White slavery? That's not even a real thing. It's not like I'm a little kid. I've seen some shit; I always make it through."

"You always make it through, do you?" She could feel herself getting louder, but she didn't let her voice go up the scale, not a half-step. She was going to scare this idiot straight; it was her only chance.

THE MAHARAJAH HAD RE-DONNED his ring cloak, though he'd wiped down his face and rinsed off the flash powder and sweat. Larry, at his heels, had to both keep up and avoid stepping on the trailing hem. And at the same time think of what to say. He was really glad now that Wally had made him go over the story beforehand.

"Very gallant," the boss said sarcastically, "to defend your lady-love from a swindler. Fake gurus are a plague on my people." The Maharajah always talked like that. A little too fancy, like a man from a book. Wally said it was another way to keep people off-balance, and then he'd said *especially big dumb white guys* and laughed.

"This was a white guy," Larry said, and immediately wished he'd kept his mouth shut. "Calls himself Friedrich or something."

The Maharajah grunted dismissal. "Either way I think we can all agree it would have been smarter to warn him off over the phone, under the circumstances. But, as I have told you so many times, I don't pay you for your brains."

This time Larry did keep his mouth shut. He glanced over at Wallace, who hadn't exactly been invited to walk with them but hadn't exactly been told not to. What a guy. He didn't seem to have any trouble keeping off of the boss man's cloak.

"As for this new talent you want me to take a look at, I did call Rafael in Toledo last week, as you suggested. And he agrees that there's potential. But you can't go dragging home every stray pup with potential. Especially when it seems you're far too distracted with personal matters to train him yourself."

"He'll learn quick. He already has his own manager, a gimmick worked out ..."

"And we'll no doubt have to get rid of the gimmick and the manager both."

There was a voice down the hallway. Shouting. Unintelligible. Wrong direction for the sounds of the locker room. He looked up and there was the kid Rafael had been training; he could tell even from the back, but he had two other kids with him. One had to be the manager, facing towards them, doing the shouting. Short little fire-plug-shaped kid but absolutely unafraid. The third was lanky and pale and could've vanished for all he was doing. As they got closer, it looked like he wanted to.

The Maharajah turned to the men behind him and held his finger to his lips, smiling.

"... bull through life and expect a smile and blond hair and aw shucks to get you wherever you want to go," the short kid said venomously. "Everyone's always liked you and you know what that's made you? A spoiled baby who thinks of nobody but himself. Honestly, I ought to give you a spanking and send you back to bed!" The kid, pausing for breath, looked up. He clearly recognized the Maharajah. It wasn't like you could mistake him. "And that's what I'd tell Larry L'Amour if he were here right now. That he doesn't even know what being a cowboy is, and it's time for him to admit it. And then you'd take him down."

"Well, Larry," the Maharajah said, laughing, "I don't know about your baby wrestler, but that'll bring the heat all right. Can you imagine a little punk kid talking to you like that in front of a crowd?" And little punk was the right description, too. Boy was lucky if he was sixteen.

Now the other kid, Robert Drake it was, or Richard, maybe, turned to face them. He looked staggered, as though the short kid had even scared him with the intensity of the promo.

"What's your name, boy?" The Maharajah was still more interested in the short kid.

"Danny Drake."

"And do you propose to see this untrained meathead you've brought defeat Larry L'Amour?"

The kid hesitated, but not for as long as Larry would've in his place. "Yes. He will."

"You realize that once he's done that, the only thing he'll have left to achieve is coming for me?"

"I'm not untrained," Rob-or-Richard broke in. "I've been working with Rafael Garza for four months now."

"Four months. Wonderful."

"And I know I'm not going to take down Larry L'Amour right away." He stumbled for a second. "I mean, I didn't come here gunning for Larry L'Amour at all; he really helped me out. Sir," he added, looking directly at Larry for the first time. "But I do plan to be the best. I'm not messing around about that."

"I suppose it's worth seeing what your best is, anyway," the Maharajah said. "You have a room booked for tonight? Good." He brought out a card, and handed it to the short boy. "I want to see both of you at this gym at 7 am tomorrow. So you'd best get some sleep."

They all looked at each other, the short boy and the tall one and the inexplicable silent one, and it was the short one who nodded first and said "Ok. We'll be there."

"Now," the Maharajah said once the kids had scurried away, "this doesn't let you off the hook, Larry. You're on probation. If I hear that you're taking unauthorized jaunts out of town again — and I don't care if your house is on fire and your children all gone, like a ladybug — that's the end of you and Rock City Wrestling."

IF SHE'D THOUGHT that Jeremy was in a crap mood on the drive from Toledo, she hadn't seen anything compared to what he was like now. Normally, she would have been all sympathy, but she hardly thought he deserved it. The best she could do was not dump him tonight on top of everything.

That they hadn't succeeded in screwing her over didn't mean they hadn't planned to do it. In some ways, they had succeeded after all. As soon as she got recognized for what she was, she was as bad off as ever. Plus this was her waitressing job gone, and it would be damn lucky if Mom would even let her move back in. On the other hand, there were waitressing jobs in Detroit, too, and staying the hell out of Toledo for a while might be the smart move. She'd make a long-distance call in the morning. And send Mom a nice postcard with no return address.

"Look, man," Rob was saying earnestly to Jeremy. "It's not the end of the world. I have my foot in the door, so does Danny, we'll get you in too. That's how we do things. Together, man."

"I can't believe this. I mean, are they all blind?"

"I dunno, Danny makes a pretty convincing guy. But you're the one dating her, I get why that'd be a sore spot for you." Rob laughed and slugged Jeremy in the shoulder, and Jeremy laughed back like he was trying hard not to. Pair of assholes. Like she hadn't saved the whole thing by stepping in like that.

"I don't see what you're crying about," she said to Jeremy. "You don't have to get up in the morning. I'm going to sleep." And she did, kicking off only her shoes; she didn't really want to be in skin-contact with the sheets on this bed.

At least I have a clean shirt, she thought as she drifted off. *That smells like beer.*

JOLLY ROGER'S LAST STAND

KEVIN SECCIA

TERRITORY:
NorCal Wrestling Association
(*Northern California*)
1987

If I had to guess, I would say that my biggest mistake was allowing them to saddle me with the pirate gimmick. I think I didn't realize just how much talking like a pirate it would entail. Honestly, that part's probably on me. I had definitely seen pirates before, and I should have put it together.

I wish that I'd pushed back on the idea, but I didn't. I was just happy that Mr. Promoter, the so-called "Professor" Ray St. John, had something for me. And I think I was also relieved to have avoided being the car mechanic guy, which was a character that he had been very excited about. Apparently the idea had come to him outta nowhere, in a bolt of inspiration, shortly after he'd gotten a flat tire out on the 101. Who can say how that stuff works? I'll leave that to the creative types.

The car mechanic gimmick sounded okay at first. You can get a jumpsuit pretty cheap, and maybe you get to swing a big metal wrench around, but from there the pickings get kind of slim. I guess you could wipe some oil stains on your face? That already sounds tiresome. And then what? What can you really do with "auto repair" or "towing" in the ring, to make it sound menacing? How is that a possible finishing move? The winch? The ... carburetor job? No.

At least with a pirate you got a lot of options. Bandannas and giant hats, maybe a sword. You can think about adding a parrot or doing something with a fishing net. Name-wise, maybe you're a captain, or maybe your focus is more on the color of your beard. So many ways to go. So much lingo to explore. You could try to incorporate "walk the plank" or "shiver me timbers" or like "man overboard," which I think is just boats in general, but you could try it and see how it went. Plus the flag! Oh man, that flag. You know the one, with the damn skull and bones on it. It's the coolest flag ever, and it's called the Jolly Roger, which is admittedly less cool, but that's how I got my name.

Yeah, I really felt like I could do something with the pirate thing. Not my first choice, or my second, but way better than the car mechanic. Oh, and my only other option, which was Guy Whose Pants Keep Falling Down, since they had a pair of rigged up old clown pants from the circus that fell down when you pulled on a little string. Even I could see that there was no future in that one.

Actually, I was wrong about that, too, because Joe Delucca took it and turned it into a sex machine gimmick, calling himself Buck Manly, a guy who seemingly dropped his pants at will any time a pretty lady showed up. Then he'd just start winking and waggling his eyebrows into the camera. The crowd went crazy for it. I did, too, the first time I saw it. But by then it was too late to switch with him. I mean, I didn't think that it was, but he did when I asked him about it. And then he'd have these little hilarious messages written on his boxer shorts, like "SEXY" or "HOT STUFF." Just the funniest things you can imagine. To be honest, I'd have never thought to do that ... Okay, I'm getting off-topic here.

I know I might sound bitter now, but I don't care. You slobs can just sit there and listen to it. Oh, and another thing, this damn eye patch! Mr. St. John warned me not to go with the eye patch, but what the hell fun would that be? They all told me about this bullshit thing called depth perception, said that it would mess me up. Well, it turns out that it wasn't bullshit; it's a real thing, and they were all right, but fuck 'em anyway. I stumbled a lot at first. Walked into a lot of chairs on the way to the ring. Sometimes even just making a tag in the corner seemed like a long shot. What I'm saying is, I slapped a lot of tag team partners square in the face. My ex partner Barnacle Bob took it especially hard, and that's why we became exes. Not sure why he was so mad at me; broken eardrums can heal. They do it all the time.

At first, people loved it. I'd come out draped in that Jolly Roger flag, yelling "Arggghhh!!" and waving my sword around. I also didn't have the right sword, which, again, Mr. St. John got mad about. I guess I needed a cutlass, but what I had was a letter opener that looked like a King Arthur sword, which he told me was both histori-cally inaccurate and ridiculous. I said, "Well, how do you know that a pirate didn't steal it from King Arthur?" and then he replied, "Because he was a fictional character, and pirates came much later in history, and the damn thing is six inches long!" so as you can see, there was just no talking to him.

So they gave me a couple of wins, and I felt like stuff was finally starting to happen for me. That lasted a few weeks, and then it's like, all of a sudden, they started treating me like a joke. Just because of the trouble I had from the eye patch, falling down unexpectedly, and then my pants splitting open one time on account of they were not real wrestling pants; they were blue jeans I'd spray-painted black. I guess the paint really stiffens up the denim. Hey, live and learn. People started laughing at me, but how is that any different than what

Buck Manly does on purpose? Maybe I did it on purpose, too. You ever think of that? How do you know I didn't? Okay, sure, my eyes might have welled up a little bit, but that also could've been part of it; the point is nobody knows. That's the beauty of a work.

Suddenly, just 'cause of that, guys are being booked to go over me. And not just the top guys, either. They let that guy who wrestles in basketball sneakers beat me! The one whose uncle owns the concession stands. Shit, I think he's still in high school.

Also, I'm not a trained actor. I can say "Arggh!" and yell "batten down the hatches!" with a snarl, but do you know how hard it is to order a plain chicken breast with egg whites and steamed broccoli in a pirate voice, when you know regular people are listening in? Not sure if you've noticed, but pirates don't say those words a lot. So now I'm out here guessing how they'd do it, and just adding a snarl to the words, and then getting self-conscious because they're all giving me weird looks, and man, I just wanna eat and go back to the hotel room. I guess I panicked and said "sacrebleu!" at one point, and that's not even pirate; it's like French or something. That part really did not help matters. I actually felt bad about that. You ever see the light of pure wonder go out in a kid's eyes? Believe me, you don't ever want to. One minute it's there and then suddenly, nothing. Like they flipped a switch. That shit is heartbreaking.

How about this — think of all the places you'd want to be treated like a pirate. I can think of one: in the ring. Or, okay, maybe on a pirate ship. That's two. Here's where you wouldn't want to be treated like a pirate: at the bar, at the gas station, at the Arby's drive-through, in the back room of the video store — the one through the swinging saloon doors, for adults only, you know the one I'm talking about — and any other damn place you can think of.

One time, on the way into the arena parking lot, a guy yelled at me for driving a car. What am I supposed to drive? A ship on wheels? A ship towed by a car? That's still not accurate. Wouldn't I, the pirate, wonder what was pulling my pirate ship? How does a pirate know what a car is? He don't! And I'll tell you right now, each and every one of you pathetic wretches listening to the sound of my voice: I'm sick of it.

It wasn't supposed to be like this. I was an elite athlete. Well, okay, maybe not elite. I could've been a little bit more muscular, and maybe taller, and my gas tank was, shall we say, not the best. But hey, that's why we have gas stations, AKA rest holds. Gimme a few minutes, let me fill 'er up, and then we can go again. What's the rush, guys? Where's the fire, huh?

Okay, so I had some deficiencies. But I could talk. Boy, could I cut a promo. If you've never heard the term, it means the thing that I say that makes you want to pay to see me beat someone up. I was the guy who did the famous "This ain't over!" promo. I'm sure you remember it. That was the one that let my opponent know "This ain't over!" It was quick and to the point. You should've heard it. Actually, you just did; it was just those three words, like that, but what else do you need?

Some people struggle with the promo, but not me. Another example. Remember my feud with Lou Gatti? I hate that guy. He had interfered in my match, and I'd wanted revenge, so I talked about how I wanted revenge on him. That one was partially inspired by "This ain't over!" Also, I wanted to punch him in the face, so I mentioned that. Then I stated when and where I expected to do this stuff. Great, right? Well, no, not according to Mr. St. John, who apparently needs everything to be perfect. He said it was too plain-sounding and asked me to add some more personal touches to it, to make it more from my specific point of view, using my feelings. Yeah okay, professor. Well, I'm tired of listening to him, and I'm tired of busting my ass for you lousy people! And you're all gonna listen to me for once!

As Mr. St. John and his flunkies have just now realized, I've taken the liberty of using my own titanium padlock on that steel cage door. The best one they had at the hardware store. Yank on it all you want, guys. You could shoot it with a .45 and not even dent it. Ain't nobody getting in here to shut me up. You're all gonna listen to me for once! Shit! Okay, so I said that line already. Big deal.

I see you, Lou Gatti, smirking at me from the barricade, Mr. Tough Guy. Well guess what, buddy? That's right, I'm flipping you off. You look at that finger, and you take that! Cause there ain't a damn thing you can do about it. Mr. Bigtime Shooter. Mr. College Rasslin. Mr. Knows How To Calculate The Tip at the Fancy Restaurant. And, as you all may have guessed by now, this microphone that I've been talking on is hooked up to the speaker under the ring, not the PA system, so they ain't cutting me off.

Okay, nice try, Mr. St. John. I see what you're doing over there. Giving Lou that set of bolt cutters. Go ahead, try and cut through the cage wall. As soon as you get close, I'm gonna stab at you with this broom handle I got, and poke you right in the eye! Just like so! Almost got you, Lou!

Ha, interesting plan. You think with three guys climbing up on different sides of the cage at the same time, that I won't be able to poke all of you off. Well, you got another thing coming — okay, fine. Get up there. Good for you; I don't give a damn. Stay up there all night, for all I care. Not much you can do without the— all right, so I see that Mr. St. John has managed to throw you up the bolt cutters. Big whoop!

Listen up, Lou, you dummy. You think just because you're up on the roof of the cage, out of the range of my broomstick, that you can just cut right through it. Well...it appears that you're right. So, that's one for you. And now you seem to be dropping down into the cage across from me. I admit, I had not anticipated this.

Oh, so you want to fight, huh? Well, I guess we're gonna find out if you are as good as advertised, when it comes to shooting, because I have my doubts. Come at me, you coward! Hope you like the taste of broomstick — oh c'mon!

Why don't they make those things easier to hang on to? Jeez. They should've added a rubber grip on the handle or something. I bet you think you're pretty slick, snapping that broomstick in half like that and tossing it aside. I don't. I could've done that too, if I'd wanted to. I just don't think it's cool to damage other people's property. Okay, here we go. Time to dance…Let me have it, Mr. Tough Gu —

All right, I'm not gonna lie to you, that one hurt a lot more than I expected it to. I do not like the feeling in my abdomen right now, and my legs, well, they've certainly been steadier. Hey, unrelated, I may have been slightly off when I called you a coward earlier. It seems that you're not just a gimmick, and you do know how to punch but…I still see this thing going my way. And I'm about to set this microphone down and teach you a lesson.

Okay, I see that you also know how to kick. Truth be told, that one also got to me a little bit. I'm feeling kind of sick, actually. And now my vision seems to have been compromised — not sure if this is just sweat on my face or, okay, no, it is my own blood. I don't like to bleed, personally; that's just me. To each his own, though. I'm not one to judge.

I guess now I'm wondering if you'd still be interested in talking this all out like you'd mentioned earlier? Okay, that punch you just bounced off my head tells me that ship may have sailed. Was it a pirate ship? Haha, just a little joke. I am in quite a bit of pain right now. It's not too late, though, in my opinion, to salvage things. Perhaps a truce might be the best way to go here, for all involved? Cooler heads prevailing and whatnot. Hmm, I see that you're gearing up for your famous uppercut finisher. Oh boy, that's no good. Seems like it's time for Ole Jolly Roger to dig deep and make one last comeback. Fine by me. This is all exactly what I wanted. Someone's about to walk the plank. And unless I miss my guess, I think that— Arrrggghhh!!

DOOMSDAY, DESTROYER OF WORLDS

BEN FOWLKES

TERRITORY:

North American Championship Wrestling

(Tennessee, Alabama, Kentucky)

1985

Goddamn Internet

Thing I can't stand now is these message boards. People on there, they just beat all. Act like they know everything about everything. Elise tells me that if it bothers me so much I should let it alone, don't go on there. She's right, same way she is about most things. But there's one of these message boards where they only talk Memphis wrestling, and so I pop my head in there every once in a while to see what they're saying. Sometimes they post links to videos. Sometimes it's stuff I plum forgot about.

I don't tell anybody on there who I am. I don't need that kind of attention. But the things people say on there, it gets hard to keep my mouth shut.

The other day they had a thing going about all the wrestlers who got their start in Memphis and then went big nationwide after. It always surprises people to hear some of the names. I don't know why. I suppose they can't picture how different things were then. Or maybe Memphis just sounds like some redneck backwater to them.

Back when Terry Austin had the whole territory humming in the '70s and '80s, though, people thought different. I know the boys all did. There was real money in Memphis wrestling then. Our phone rang every week, people wanting to come work in the NACW. Still these knuckleheads on the message boards act like they can't believe it when they find out Mack Savage, J.J. Wild, Jason Cumberland and Hito Tanaka and about a dozen others I could name all came through there at one point or another.

Anyway, there they go talking about wrestlers who were nobody when they showed up in Memphis, then got big later. And one of these jokers brings up Doomsday.

How is it they had him in the mid-80s and couldn't do shit with him, he says.

Maybe because Doomsday always sucked even then, says another.

Another guy agrees with that one. Way overrated, he says. Nothing but steroids and face paint.

This comment, mind you, got about forty likes.

Still, the first guy says, one of the biggest stars Sonny Da Silva ever had. Memphis had him five years before that, and no one even knew about him.

I mean, can you believe that? No one even knew about him. You got to be kidding.

But that's the internet for you. The blind leading the stupid.

Hard Business

Know how long Dooms was in Memphis? Just about six months. Know how I remember that? It was basically the entirety of my time as a bachelor. Well, in my adult life, anyway. I was born and grew up in Corinth, Mississippi. Left home when I was 19 years old. Up till then my momma had cooked all my meals, washed all my clothes. One day I told her I was moving up to Memphis to become one of the wrestlers on TV, and she got this look on her face I'll never forget. Like I'd just told her I thought I could fly and was going to prove it by jumping off the roof.

"Don't you reckon that could be a hard business to make a living in?" she asked me.

I told her, momma, you know me. What wouldn't be a hard business? Dogcatcher would be a hard business for me. Garbageman would be a hard business. At least wrestling was something I loved. And at the time, I believed I understood it pretty well. You couldn't even begin to guess how wrong I was on that. I was as bad as these knuckleheads on the message boards now. Hell, I was worse.

Smart

My first job in wrestling, they told me be at the office tomorrow morning. You're going to drive Downtown Joe Dempsey to Tupelo and referee his match with Hito Tanaka and then bring him right back.

Referee! I couldn't believe my luck. Told myself, hell, you must be living right.

I remember Downtown got in the car and sort of squinted at me, this string bean kid behind the wheel of an old Ford Falcon. He asked me, "You smart?"

I wasn't a brainiac but I wasn't dumb either. I said yeah, I was pretty smart.

Downtown asked me what I knew about the finish for that night's match. Nothing, I told him. Match hasn't happened yet. How am I supposed to know anything about how it'll finish? He just looked at me.

"You ain't smart," he said.

That was all we said to each other the rest of the drive. Had my mind in knots all the way to Tupelo. Wasn't until I got in the locker room and heard some of the boys talking about their matches that I started to put it together. Did I think all this stuff was a pure shoot before that? I surely did. I know I'm not the only one, either. But the thing you have to understand is they played it all different back then. I was in need of an education, and on more than just wrestling, if I'm telling the God's honest truth. I had to get smart quick. Maybe I got some of that education a little too fast, but that part was different then too.

Year or so later I was married, baby on the way, working regular in the territory as "Rev 'Em Up" Eddie Ray. I asked Terry Austin where he came up with that, and he said, well, look at you.

"You're so damn high strung you make other people nervous just being in the same room with you," he said. "Might as well lean into that however you can."

I was a shade under six feet. I weighed maybe 140 pounds after a big meal. I'd check into hotels and tell them I was there with the wrestlers and they'd laugh and say, yeah sure, me too, kid.

What saved me was learning about the mental side of the business. Ring psychology, they'd call it now. I never missed a chance to listen to the old-timers talk about it. I was always watching how crowds reacted, what worked on them and what didn't, trying to pick up every little bit I could. One of the first things I learned was that, a skinny guy like me? If I work it right, the audience will end up dying to see me get flung from pillar to post. But you can't give that to them right away. You've got to make them wait.

So I'd dance around on the outside, throw out some open-handed slaps to a boy who outweighed me by 75 pounds. Pause every once in a while to look around at the crowd. I'd make a face, like see how good I'm doing? Then just when this ol' boy was about to get his hands on me I'd slip through the ropes or tag in my partner. Build that tension.

It was understanding some of those things that got Terry Austin to keep me around even after a lot of other promoters would've put me on a bus and told me not to write. One day Terry pulls me aside and out of nowhere starts telling me a story about a time when he'd asked his son's Little League coach if the boy was any good at baseball.

"That man thought real hard and told me, well, he has a good head for the game," Terry said.

Terry explained: This was what people said when you were smart enough to know how something should be done but not good enough to do it yourself.

"If someone were to ask me about you," Terry said, "I'd tell them you have a real good head for wrestling."

He let me sit with that for about three seconds, just long enough to see my heart breaking into a million pieces, and then he laughed. He told me, don't worry, he wasn't dropping me just yet.

"You think I'm telling you that you can't work in wrestling, but I'm not," Terry said. "What I'm telling you is, right now you're trying to do the wrong job in wrestling."

This was the start of my career as a manager, how I became Fast Eddie Ray, the smooth-talking city slicker who'd shake your hand and have you checking to make sure you still had all your fingers. Course, that's where I made my name. Anybody knows me now, that's what they know me for. What career I had, Terry Austin gave me right there on that very day.

But at the time? Well, I just about wanted to cry.

Lack of Appreciation

I remember one of the best angles I worked back then was with Hill-billy Ernie Shavers. We had this whole story about him needing money to save the family home up in the Smoky Mountains, and me signing him to this deal that would pay him an exorbitant fee, but all of it to come in the form of "precious jewels." One week on TV we're standing there and he brings out this supposed diamond necklace I'd given him and he starts showing it off during an interview with Steve Bath.

"Look at this here," Hillbilly Ernie says, "ain't it purty?"

Right away, all the crowd can see it's cheap costume jewelry. I remember we went to three different places trying to find one that would look fake enough even from the cheap seats. But Hillbilly Ernie is holding it up and grinning, talking about how ma and the kids ain't going to be hungry no more. I'm telling you, you could feel the crowd then. Boiling in their seats.

I'm standing there grinning behind my sunglasses, twirling my diamond-studded cane. I had to strain to hold it together as Steve Bath turned to me with that great comedic timing of his and said, "Oh really now, Fast Eddie Ray, this is lowdown even for you."

My first wife Loretta, she drove out to Gatlinburg with me one time and came and saw the show. Afterwards she kept asking me didn't it bother me how much those people hated me. I told her they didn't hate me – they hated Fast Eddie.

"But you're a con man," she said. "Taking advantage of this country hick."

I told her, honey, that's exactly the point. How many of those people in the crowd did she think had ever felt taken advantage of before? Whether it was some lawyer, some bank, some salesman on the telephone. They'd been there. They could relate to it. Now they had a place to put all those feelings, only here in our little world they'd get a payoff in the end.

She asked what the payoff would be. I told her, well, Hillbilly

Ernie would figure it out and then finally get his hands on me, but not until we'd filled houses with it all summer.

"And this is your contribution to the world," she said. It was more a statement than a question. "And you're pleased with that," she said, making this face.

I won't say I knew right then that we weren't going to stick together forever, but I will say it made me start to think real hard about the possibility.

Physical Realities

It's funny how I started off talking about Doomsday and then got on to the topic of ring psychology. Know how much Dooms understood about ring psychology? About as much as I know about heart surgery. He wasn't interested in learning, either. But then, maybe that's where necessity comes into the bargain. Dooms was six-feet-five and usually right around 250 pounds of solid muscle. Most guys that size back then were big body guys, big ol' lumbering heavies with some fat around the midsection. Dooms, he had abs you could play tic-tac-toe on. His veins looked like they were trying to escape out from under his skin. When he flexed he was like a damn anatomy textbook. We'd never seen anything like it.

If I'd had that to work with, would I have bothered learning the finer points of ringcraft? I'd like to think so, but the truth is I might have been down at the bar with my shirt off letting the girls feel my biceps instead.

I told that to Elise once, and she said well then it was a good thing God had dealt me a different hand then, wasn't it? When I said I don't know, I felt like maybe I could have worked with that other hand, she told me I would have had to do it without her.

"My mother taught me that any man asking you to look at his muscles is just distracting you from his missing brain," she said.

I had to admit that her mother got one right every now and then.

First time I met Dooms was backstage at an event in Knoxville. Terry Austin told me he had some new guys brought up from Florida he wanted me to look at. By then I was helping him book the eastern half of the territory, lightening the workload for him where I could, trying to show my value outside the ring. If you'd peeled my skull back to reveal my innermost thoughts at the time, what I was hoping for was to one day become Terry's partner, own a piece of the NACW. He must have known it, because he dangled that possibility out in front of me whenever he needed me to do something I didn't want to do.

Anyway, that night I was making the rounds before the show, and I turned a corner and felt like I'd walked into a brick wall.

Dooms was standing there. He had that sharp crewcut, real high and tight. He was wearing a tank top tucked into gym pants. He looked like an action figure come to life.

I told him, beg your pardon, didn't see you there.

"That's right," he said. "You beg my pardon."

I laughed, said well all right, he must be one of the new boys. I asked him his name.

"Doomsday, destroyer of worlds and conqueror of men," he said.

"You expect me to call you all that?" I said.

"I expect everything," he said and walked off.

Looking back, I'd call it one of the better interactions I had with the man.

My Contribution

What I didn't say to Loretta that night driving home from Gatlinburg, what I wanted to say but didn't have the words for yet, was that I know it's just a show. But so what? It's trivial, I guess some people would say. But so is damn near anything that entertains people and makes their lives a little more bearable. So was Shakespeare back when people were first paying to see it, and don't tell me it wasn't, because I've read it and even seen a couple in person. Believe it or not, this hayseed here went and got a little bit of culture under these blue jeans.

Point is, if it makes people smile, gives them a couple hours' worth of escape, isn't that good? Isn't that something?

Thinking about it now, Loretta sitting there and talking about my contribution to the world, I swear. As if everyone has to be a doctor or a teacher or a scientist. Plenty of people are happy just to get by, and a lot of them are barely even managing that. You think about the things people do for a living. I don't see there's anything so great about selling insurance, if we're all giving opinions on other people's work.

But I'm getting off in my own head again, thinking about me and Loretta. Arguing with the rearview mirror, as Elise calls it. And even if you win those arguments, what have you won?

Transitions

One thing people don't understand is just how big a star Billy Bayless was for us back then. They think they get it, because now everybody knows the name whether they know a single other thing about Memphis wrestling or not, but I'm telling you, in 1985? He was the whole ballgame. Had been for years.

Back then Terry Austin had a deal with channel 6 in Memphis. I still don't know how he pulled it off. Every other wrestling promoter in the country was paying for the privilege of being on TV. Terry was the only one who had a deal that actually paid him, even if it meant that every week we had to squeeze our ring into that tiny channel 6 TV studio. You couldn't fit more than two rows' worth of fans in there, and even then only on two sides of the ring. They had to shoot the whole thing from the other side to make it look like we had a full house.

For commentators, Terry got them to give him Bob Ellis, who was a newscaster for the station, and Steve Bath, who was the weatherman.

People still come up and talk to me about those Saturday morning shows. I'm not kidding. Just a week or two ago, Elise and I are sitting down to eat in Corky's, and a woman interrupts us to tell me she remembers me from those wrestling shows her daddy used to watch. Said she grew up out in Crockett Mills, and the only time in her life they got to eat in front of the TV was lunchtime on Saturdays, so daddy could watch his "rassling." Said her momma didn't like it but knew better than to argue with him about that.

I believe it. I ought to, many times as I've heard it.

Channel 6 loved Billy Bayless. Couldn't get enough of him. Every time he was out hurt, they acted like the good people of West Tennessee had all shotgunned their TVs and gone back to radio. Terry referred to this as "unfuckingsustainable."

"Bayless is damn near forty," he told me one morning, sitting in the little office he rented on the second floor of The Ambassador Hotel downtown. It was just down the street from The Peabody, where you could see those ducks come down in the elevator and walk the red carpet, which was always fun to watch after a couple drinks at lunch.

"You think any wrestler who ever lived started getting hurt less or recovering faster once he hit forty?" Terry said.

This is why he was so all-fired up about finding some new young talent. And it couldn't be just the same old stuff, either, he said.

"We're still booking these shows like it's 1979," he said. "People's brains don't even work the same way now as they did then. They're watching MTV, for crying out loud."

Terry was all the time going on about MTV in those days. I can close my eyes and see him now, sitting there behind that gunmetal desk, thick helmet of hair practically glued to his head with a part on one side like he'd done it with a razorblade. Sipping a NuGrape cola at ten in the morning and telling me what he'd seen on MTV the night before.

Terry'd been married a couple times. Had a son with his first wife, who I'll get to later, and a couple daughters with his second. It was his daughters that got him started on MTV. They couldn't get enough of it. He'd tell me, Ed, this is a whole new way of making television, and we'd better learn from it if we don't want to go the way of buffalo.

I believe it was this thinking that made him decide Dooms was going to be the star of the future. When he came up out of Florida, he was working some kind of barbarian gimmick. That Conan movie had come out a couple years before, and Dooms walked to the ring in all these furs, wearing some sort of Viking helmet. Terry doesn't get any credit for it now, but he was the one who put a stop to that. He said if you walked out there looking exactly like a movie character, you might as well tell the audience this was all made up. What you wanted to do was suggest a character. You wanted the audience to make the connection without knowing they were making it.

We both liked the name, though. Doomsday. It put me in the mind of nuclear armageddon. War with the Soviets, total devastation, this lone guy comes walking out of the rubble.

"I was thinking more Biblical," said Terry. "Book of Revelations stuff. But maybe we split the difference."

In the end we decided that we didn't want the furs or the helmet, but he needed something. A lot of our brainstorming sessions ended this way. Needing something, damned if we knew what it was.

Terry called me at home the next night and told me he'd got it, wanted me to drive out to his place near Brownsville so he could show me something. I said, Terry, it's ten o'clock at night. He asked me what was the use of being a newly divorced bachelor if I couldn't do what I wanted any time of day? I admit it made me look around my little apartment in South Bluffs, used furniture and nothing on the walls but an echo, and decide that maybe I could do with a brief change of scenery.

I get out there, and Terry is absolutely wired, holding up this Twisted Sister cassette tape he found in his daughter's room. His vision for Doomsday — that was his word, vision — was something like this, only crossed with Kiss and that David Bowie look from the Ziggy Stardust thing, then routed through hell and back.

"You're talking makeup?" I said.

"I'm talking face paint," he said. "A heap of it."

So that's how we came up with that look. The silver and the black. The glowing red lightning bolt across the eyes. It was decided then and there that I should be the one to introduce him on TV that week. Did Terry throw that in there just so I'd also have to be the one to explain the new gimmick to Dooms? Didn't even occur to me at the time. It sure did later on, though.

Revenge on All Mankind

"I don't do the manager thing."

This was Dooms to me, the first time I laid out our plan for him. Mind you, I hadn't even gotten to the face paint yet. I asked him what his objection was.

"I'm the only one who understands the character," he said.

"All right," I told him. "Explain the character to me."

That's when I got my first true window into the man's mind. God almighty. He gave me this whole thing about how Doomsday came from the nether realm, how he communed with the spirits of sky and earth, how this was the source of his power. He told me he was 10,000 years old and lived for centuries without a human form, just existing as a westerly wind on the open steppe or some shit. Then he was captured by an old witch who cursed him with a body, and for this he sought revenge on all of mankind. He went on like this for what had to be ten or fifteen minutes, or maybe it just felt that long.

I decided to bring us back to what you might call more immediate realities.

"You trained with all those bodybuilders down in Tampa, right?" I said. "Jimmy Redmond and Lenny Loomis gave you your start?"

He sat there blinking at me.

"In Sunshine State Professional Wrestling?" I said.

That got half a nod out of him. I asked him, how long have you been in this business? He told me about a year. I said all right, that means somewhere between six and nine months.

"I've been in it since 1972," I said. "I'm telling you from experience, wrestling fans don't want to hear any of that bullshit you just told me."

He got real mad then. Stood up and started huffing and puffing, pacing around the locker room. I figured, either this is someone we can work with, or it isn't. Might as well find out now. I laid it out for him then, what he had and what he didn't, how we were going to play it right out of the gate. If that didn't suit him, I said, we'd call Tampa and tell them to send us another bodybuilder. Sooner or later we'd get us one who could take direction. He sat back down then. I tried my best not to show how relieved I was.

"We'll try it your way at first," he said. "But in my heart, I will know that I'm still Doomsday, Destroyer of Worlds."

I told him that was just fine by me.

Then I thought, Christ, now you've got to tell him about the face paint.

Won't be Held Responsible

How we worked it that day for TV was, we let Sweet Daddy Silk walk to the ring first, doing his stutter step strut, taking forever to remove his robe, the whole nine. Then, when it came time for Doomsday to make his big entrance, I came out alone. I made sure to look real nervous, pacing and shaking my head. Steve Bath was already standing there ready with the microphone, asking me, 'Fast' Eddie Ray, what is the meaning of this?

"You're the one who's been telling us all week about this exciting new wrestler you were going to debut," Steve Bath said. "Now it's match time, Sweet Daddy Silk is ready, and you can't get your man into the ring?"

I made myself look all shook up as I explained how it wasn't that I couldn't get him into the ring, it was that I thought maybe I shouldn't.

"He's more than ready," I said. "I've got him locked in his dressing room backstage, and the minute I open that door, he'll come bursting right out here and head straight for that ring, there's no doubt about that. But Steve, I don't know. You haven't seen this man. I fear for people's safety, I really do."

Here the crowd started to rumble and groan. Another one of Fast Eddie's tricks.

We went back and forth like that a little. Finally Steve Bath said he was starting to think that I'd sold these fine people a bill of goods.

"Maybe instead of the savage wrestler you promised us, what you've got back there is a man who's scared to come to the ring and face Sweet Daddy Silk," he said.

Well, then I threw up my hands, shook my head. Said fine, that's the way you want it? I'd go back there and unlock that door. But one thing was for sure: I would not be held responsible for what happened to Sweet Daddy Silk or anyone else who got in this man's way.

Walking back through the curtain, I could feel it then, how I had them in the palm of my hand. They couldn't say what was about to happen next, but damned if they'd miss it for anything then. For me, that was always the best part. There's a place I want you to get to in your mind, in your feelings. I've got this little trap I'm going to set for you. And not only will you walk right into it and feel just exactly what I want you to feel, you'll think it was your idea. There ain't nothing better than that in the wrestling business. At least not for a skinny guy like me.

Debut

What I remember about that first match:
  – How the room got quiet when they saw him.
  – How Dooms did this slow, steady walk to the ring.
  – How Sweet Daddy really sold his reaction, doing his signature strut and then hitting a freeze frame thing in mid-stride, letting his mouth fall open.
  – How Dooms just about took Sweet Daddy's head off with that first clothesline. Then picked him up, tossed him off the opposite side ropes, and did it again.
  – How, in the locker room afterwards, we had to almost tie Sweet Daddy to a chair to keep him from going after Dooms, who he motherfucked up and down as he tore around the locker room, demanding to know who told this clumsy, potato-happy fool that he was a wrestler.

Memory

Jesus, Sweet Daddy Silk. When's the last time I thought of him? Now there's a fella that wouldn't take shit off nobody. You know he was mostly responsible for integrating the crowds at Memphis wrestling shows? Used to be they put the blacks up in the rafters and the whites down on the floor. Did it that way for longer than I care to admit, and most of us never thought much of it at the time. I'm ashamed to say that now, but it's true.

What changed it was when Sweet Daddy and J.J. Wild were the hottest tag team around – called themselves The Dominoes, one white and one black. One night Sweet Daddy said he wasn't going out there if they didn't move some of the blacks onto the floor. Terry didn't like it. He was worried it would mess with his money, as always. But then J.J. Wild sat down and said, well, you heard him. If Sweet Daddy doesn't go out, I don't either. And because J.J. was feared and respected in just about equal measure by all the boys in the locker room, pretty soon everybody was saying it.

What could Terry do then? That was the end of the blacks sitting up in the rafters in Memphis. Just like that.

Sweet Daddy Silk. Now there was a wrestler. Died of a heart attack on his own porch some years back. I start telling stories about the people I knew, follow them all the way to the finish, how many of them end like that?

An Honest Appraisal

Could Dooms wrestle? Not much, no. I know people said that about him even later, when he got big, but the truth is he was ten times better by the time most people saw him working for Sonny Da Silva. When he started with us in Memphis, he had maybe four moves, and he did them all just as stiff as an alligator's pecker.

But did he look good? Of course he did. He looked better than anybody we had. It was more than that, though. Just the physical facts of the man, he was a damned walking spectacle. Once you saw him, you couldn't take your eyes off him. A real shame he couldn't wrestle.

I asked him once, you ever think about slowing down, taking your time, maybe letting the tension build and learning a little ringcraft?

He said to me, you ever think about lifting some weights?

I told him yeah, I'd considered it, but as far as I could tell no matter how the weights got moved around, they always ended up back in the same place they started, so what was the point? He didn't think that was funny.

You know what really made Dooms pop, though, was the contrasts. Terry Austin, he understood something that a lot of these boys now don't. Sonny Da Silva sure doesn't. You turn on the TV these days, it's giants everywhere. And the ones that aren't are still monsters compared with regular folks. Flawless bodies, most of them. Greek gods just as far as the eye can see.

But you know what Terry used to say? If you got nothing but big guys, then you got no big guys. There's no contrast. No scale. The audience can't appreciate it.

Terry always believed in having a range of bodies in that ring. Short, tall, fat, funny-looking, muscles coming out of their ears, what have you. He said that the eye and the brain, they crave variety. I'm grateful he thought so. I wouldn't have had much of a career if he didn't, little old funny-looking guy like me.

"Don't knock funny-looking," Elise says. "Handsome gets boring, but funny is forever."

Her favorite was what she called my Donald Duck impression. I'd be all worked up and yelling at somebody, poking my finger in his chest, gesturing in all directions with my arms, so mad that it seemed like my feet both lifted off the floor at the same time and just hovered there a second.

"Even when you're not actually being funny," she said, "people look at you and they're ready to laugh."

I don't know if that's something I can really take credit for, but if she wants to give it to me anyway, I'll surely let her.

Pitfalls of Fame

Memphis. Union City. Dyersburg. Jonesboro. Johnson City. Gadsden. Jackson. Tuscaloosa. Louisville. Tupelo. Birmingham. Lexington. Montgomery. Meridian.

Everywhere we took Dooms, crowds went absolutely nuts for him. I mean, it was immediate. He showed up on Memphis TV as a nobody, and within a couple months they were standing outside the venues holding up signs with his name on it. I never saw anyone or any angle catch fire that fast. And he was just about the worst person it could have happened to.

Envy

One thing people might not realize is there's always a lot of jealousy in any of those dressing rooms. Hell, there's a lot of everything. Love, hate, fear, testosterone, paranoia. Place is overflowing with goddamn feelings. People look at wrestlers and see athletes or muscle freaks, but really what it is, is a traveling theater troupe. You think you could ever get that many actors together, mix in some steroids and coke and pain pills and every other controlled substance you can think of, then drive them all over the South and not have some problems?

Dropping Dooms into it was like kicking an ant hill. It wasn't just that the boys resented him for showing up and getting over right away. Though, Lord knows, it was also that. But also, when you've spent your whole life doing something and trying to get good at it, learning it inside-out and making it your whole world? Well, you see a lot of things in it that other people don't see. Details, is what I'm talking about. The finer points. You tell yourself those points matter, that maybe if you can get those just right you'll get the perfect opportunity and blast right off into space. Every wrestler tells himself that; don't let them fool you.

But when you build your whole world around that and then you see someone come in who's got none of those finer points, none of the stuff that you've been telling yourself means everything, someone too ignorant to even know how many pieces he's missing, and right away everyone loves him anyway? That'll do a number on you. I remember Hillbilly Ernie Shavers telling me once that seeing the crowds pop like that for Dooms, even after he botched spots left and right, made him think back to all the times they'd popped for him.

"It's like a woman telling you how good-looking you are," he said, "and then you see the fella she's married to and he's just ugly as sin. Now you don't know what to believe."

So what happened? Well, I guess you could say that some of the boys started to take certain liberties. It always starts like that.

One night in Mobile, I remember The Masked Convict went and potatoed him right in the eye. Thing swole up like a water balloon and took a week to go back down. The very next week, Sputnik Lee caught him with an elbow off the ropes that chipped a tooth. The worst was when Hito Tanaka, who'd come up through old-school judo dojos and had forgotten more holds than most of the boys knew, got him in a double-wristlock and really took his time letting Dooms work his way out of it.

But there's only so much of that you can get away with on a boy Dooms's size. What we needed was a locker room enforcer to keep the peace, someone like the Confederate Giant or Plowboy Daniels, one of those seven-footers, but we didn't have any at the time. In his prime, J.J. Wild could have done the trick. But by then J.J. was half-crippled and out of the business. That sort of thing leaves what they call a power vacuum in the locker room.

Dooms didn't have any technique, didn't have that technical know-how, but what he did have was sheer mass and strength. He worked stiff even when he wasn't mad at you. That night Hito put the stretch on him, when it came time for Dooms' finisher — a sort of running powerslam where he hoisted you up on one shoulder first and then walked you around like he was looking for the best place to put you down — he got airborne and really drove his shoulder down into it on the slam. Hito wouldn't admit it to anyone after, but I do believe he fractured a rib or two.

Sometimes what the boys would do, knowing Dooms had all those muscles and not much of a gas tank, was put the pace on him and just blow him all the way up. Get him running the ropes, no rest holds, just work, work, work. From ringside you could see his face changing colors. I remember one night in Clarksdale, he went twenty hard minutes with Ricky Steele, who'd been an NCAA champ wrestler and could flat out go. Ricky gave him no breaks, no mercy. By the end of it I thought Dooms might have a heart attack. He hit that running slam with the last ounce of energy he had, then walked straight to the back and threw up in a trash can.

"You've to do something before this gets out of hand," Terry Austin told me. "This isn't good for anybody."

"It already is out of hand," I told him. "But what am I going to do?"

He said talk to him. Said, he listens to you. I asked him what in the world had I ever done to give him that impression.

"Either you talk to him or you talk to everyone else in that locker room," Terry said. "Which do you think is likely to work out better?"

I had to admit he had a point there. On the subject of Dooms, the opposition was united. You had guys couldn't agree which way the wind was blowing, but they finally found common ground when it came to hating Dooms.

He didn't make it any easier on himself, trust me. I've never seen such a little sip of fame go to somebody's head so fast.

One night we're in Bells, Tennessee. He tells me he wants me to clear out the locker room before his match. I ask him why. He says he needs to commune with the spirits of the nether realm.

"So commune," I told him. "Nobody here will mind. They've seen weirder stuff."

Then he started complaining about the old Plymouth I had, the one I put 20,000 miles on in the span of a summer just toting him all around.

"I should be in a Cadillac," he told me.

"Why not ask the spirits of the realm to get you one," I said.

You could say our relationship was deteriorating.

Respecting the Business

"The way you talk about him now, people would think you hated him," Elise tells me.

I don't. I never did. Not even at the very end there, when you might say I had a right to.

I guess what bothered me was that he really did have something. I can't call it charisma, exactly, because it seemed to me that anyone who got to know him at all pretty quickly wished they hadn't. But some nights I'd walk out there with him, and you could just feel the crowd sitting there in the dark, caught up in some sort of rapture. He always had that, at least prior to the bell.

And once the match started, hell, if you didn't know any better, maybe you thought he was good. Maybe he could have been. But getting all that attention so quick, maybe he never really had a chance.

I tried to reason with him. Once we were on the road, headed to a show in Oxford. It was a pretty drive, and it had us both in a good mood, and I remember thinking it was as good a time as any to try to talk some sense. I told him, you know, chances are you're going to be a big star in this business. But the point at which you decide to stop learning, that's the point you'll always be stuck at, in one way or another.

He turned that big, square head of his to look at me. Always reminded me of one of those Easter Island statues. Sometimes there seemed to be about as much going on in his mind.

"So I should learn from you, huh?" he said.

I told him, among others. Learn from everyone you can.

"So I can get stuck where you are?" he said. "Or where they are?"

And what can you say to that? Maybe you know, but I sure didn't. Not then and not now, either.

"If you really want people to hate him," Elise says, "tell about how he was with women."

Truth is I don't know much about that, beyond the same rumors everyone else has heard. Most of that came later, when he was criss-crossing the country for Sonny Da Silva. Though, there was a dustup once at a motel in Montgomery. I remember a girl coming to the door to say she was fine, even though she didn't look that way at all. And one time a man was arrested with a shotgun in the parking lot of channel 6 after saying he was there to see Dooms about a personal matter. I never did get the full before-and-after on that one.

"Don't that just beat all," Elise says. "A wrestler can be a shit to women his whole life, and he's just one of the boys. But if he doesn't 'respect the business,' that's the thing y'all will never forgive him for."

And she might have a point there. It's true that, when you start thinking about stories you know involving wrestlers and women, there's not much there that you'd want for your own sister. How many guys I knew who beat their women, or worse? One whose name I won't mention even killed his. Got away with it, too. Least for a time. Everybody pretty much knew it, but I can't say he was shunned in the locker room because of it. So I guess there's another thing we got to be ashamed about, in case anyone's keeping a list.

But it's also true I'm mostly bothered by other things when it comes to Dooms. You know what most of the boys would have given to be plucked out of their own bodies and put into his? There ain't a deal with the devil that they wouldn't have signed right there on the dotted line. So why is it the people who get these gifts always seem like the ones least likely to appreciate them?

That eats at me still, if I let myself think about it too long. That, and some of that other stuff there at the end.

Plans and Backup Plans

Terry had a couple guiding principles when it came to promoting wrestling. One was that you never let good heat go to waste, no matter what. Another was that when you had something or someone who was really getting over, you leaned into it while you could.

"You've got to dip your biscuit in that gravy while it is still hot," he said.

So that's what he aimed to do with Dooms. Billy Bayless was set to return off back surgery. We'd build to a big blowoff at the Sports Arena between him and Dooms, Terry said. Have ourselves a full house and an ass every eighteen inches.

Only it didn't work like that. Billy, he wasn't a genius, but he wasn't dumb, either. He saw the way Dooms worked. He heard the other boys talking. Think he was going to come right in off surgery and put his health in that man's hands? At his age? Not if he didn't have to. And he knew he didn't. He was Billy goddamn Bayless. He was Memphis wrestling back then. To a lot of people walking around here now, he still is. I go into the city now, and I'll still see his face on billboards, selling cars or siding or some damn thing. Went into a hot chicken joint here not too long ago that had an autographed 8x10 in a frame on the wall right by the cash register. Only such picture in the place. You didn't know better, you'd think he was kin to the owner.

But Billy wasn't the confrontational type. He didn't tell Jerry no straight out. Instead he just kept saying he needed more time, doc said he wasn't ready, on and on like that. Meanwhile you'd hear about him going down to Ft. Lauderdale with a college girl or two, and it sure didn't sound like he was all that restricted by his medical woes, if you know what I mean.

"He just ain't going to do it, is he?" Terry said to me one day in the office.

I said no, I didn't believe he would.

"That's all right," Terry said. "I got me a backup plan."

I said I figured as much. He usually did.

Family

This is where Terry's son come into the picture, so I reckon I can't put off telling about him any longer. Luke was his name. Good kid. Tall and lanky, big mop of hair like his daddy's, only he didn't clamp it down with all that gunk Terry used. Had the personality of a golden retriever. You couldn't help but like him.

More than anything, Luke wanted to be a wrestler. People have asked me since if it was because he really loved the business or just wanted his daddy to love him, but that sort of thing is beyond my level of education. All I can tell you is that he worked hard and did whatever anybody asked him to, even if he did have some limitations as an athlete. Never looked for any free rides. Never tried to leverage his daddy's name for any special treatment. He and Terry both did their best to keep it a secret that they were blood relatives, in fact. I suppose Terry's thinking was that he wouldn't make life any easier on Luke if people looked at him and only saw the boss's son. I expect he was right about that.

I remember Ricky Steele one night knocked Luke unconscious putting his head into the ring post, then got mad at him afterward for laying there facedown on the floor and messing up the match. And Luke? He apologized, told him it wouldn't happen again.

Ricky said damn right it wouldn't, because he wouldn't try anything like that again if it was too advanced for him.

Advanced. Like he was doing backflips off the top rope.

I remember Luke looked at him, nodding all seriously, and then asked Ricky to please give him another chance at it. I mean, imagine that. Guy puts your head into a ring post and you're the one begging him to do it again. But that was Luke.

"I'll get it right," he said, and I could see he meant it.

That was the way he approached everything. He might not nail it right off the bat, but he was always game to try, always wanted to learn. But this business has a special way of being hard on boys like that.

Terry had it in his mind that, long-term, maybe Luke was the solution to the problem of Billy Bayless and those damned ravages of age. Maybe some of us should have tried to talk him out of that, but we didn't. When a man's own son is involved, lots of times he ain't all that open to constructive criticism.

So when Terry told me about the angle he wanted to work with Dooms and Luke, I said all right, we can do that. And then when I told Dooms he asked, are you out of your mind? I told him this one came straight from Terry Austin, and he asked, is Terry Austin out of his mind?

"This guy is nobody," he said. "Some tag team jobber."

"You were nobody in this territory five months ago," I reminded him.

"That's right," he said. "And now look. This guy's been here, what, years probably. And he's still nobody."

I didn't tell him it was Terry's son. I had more sense than that. He wrestled as Luke Dells, and at the time he was finishing up a run in a tag team called The Juke Joint Boys. I never did like the gimmick. He and his partner Will would come out in these sleeveless denim jackets, bandanas tied around their heads. The idea was that they were supposed to be tough guys from one of these roadside bars out in the country. I guess you could say the vision never came all the way clear for me. Were they the bouncers? Were they just guys who hung around the juke joints? They looked mostly like bikers, but when you saw them come to the ring they were all smiles, upbeat, fresh young faces without any scars. Crowds didn't know what to make of them. It didn't work for me, but Terry mostly kept them in his half of the territory, and I didn't say anything.

Now Luke's partner Will was going off to work for Danny Rich in Portland, and Terry wanted to give Luke a push as a single.

That week on TV, the plan was for Dooms to wrestle Will in a loser-leaves-town match. Then right as he's about to go for his big finish, Luke comes running out of the back trying to save his partner. Not exactly reinventing the wheel, as far as generating heat goes. But some things stick around because they flat-out work. At least as long as everyone does what they're supposed to do.

Whale of a Show

You can still find the match as one of those Facebook videos. They got the whole show from that week. Just hearing Steve Bath's voice during the intro gives me goosebumps even now.

"What a crowd we've got here today, and boy I tell you they are in for a whale of a wrestling show, aren't they, Bob?"

Were they ever.

Skip to about forty-three minutes in and you'll see me. I'm leading Dooms down to the ring. I'm twirling my cane. I'm stopping every few feet to point back at him. This man is the real deal, people! Consider yourselves lucky to get this close to him and live to tell the tale!

Luke's partner Will is already in the ring all by his lonesome at this point, standing there in his sleeveless denim jacket. The graphic on the screen just says, "Juke Joint Boy Will." Not exactly a great sign, as far as his chances for victory go.

Revisions

Watching it now, maybe Dooms isn't as bad as I remember him. Man alive, he is stiff, though.

See him clothesline Will up around the jaw. Body block him with a shoulder right on the bridge of the nose. Every time he goes to slam Will, he does it like it's never occurred to him to worry about how the kid will land.

He does look good.

Then comes the big moment. Dooms hoists Will up on his shoulder. You can hear the crowd sucking in their breath. Steve Bath calls out: "Wait a minute, who's that coming down the aisle?"

That's when the camera cuts to Terry's son Luke running down there and reaching through the ropes just in time to trip Dooms, who drops Will in a heap. Dooms falls down on one knee. He turns and glares at Luke, pointing at him. You.

Look in the background as Luke slides into the ring to protect his fallen partner and you'll catch a glimpse of my handiwork. I'm jumping up and down, pointing at the ref, doing my Donald Duck routine as the man in the striped shirt signals for the bell.

"Disqualification!" you can hear me shouting, loud enough to be heard on the broadcast. "That's a disqualification!"

Now, what's supposed to happen here is Dooms and Luke brawling it out just long enough to give the audience a whiff of a feud, then have Luke slide out with his partner once the ref breaks it up. It's not until Dooms puts a hand on the ref's chest and shoves him six feet back that I start to get the sense that he has something else in mind.

Fog of War

Watching it now, it's like it's happening all over again. How Dooms scoops Luke up on his shoulder and starts walking him around. How he points at me at ringside. What the hell for? I'm standing there. I'm just looking at him.

He gets that running start on the slam and he launches himself.

Up in the air and then driving hard down with the shoulder. On the video you can see the fear in Luke's face. I don't think it's fear of being hurt so much as fear of not knowing what the plan is anymore. Wrestlers can put up with just about anything as long as they know it's in the script. It's the unknown that really terrifies them.

Off the Rails

That first slam, you can practically see the air go out of Luke's lungs. He's laying there lifeless, letting his head loll side to side. Dooms kneels over him and looks back at me. He holds up an index finger. He mouths the words, one more?

I can see myself in the video, trying to give him a slight little head shake. No, man. Don't be an idiot. But I know the camera's on me, and so I can't let it show.

Dooms scoops him up again. That slow walk around the ring. Taking his time. He runs and this time he jumps up like he's slam dunking a basketball. It's a small room with a small crowd. You can hear the crack of Luke's collarbone snapping when Dooms drives him into the mat. You can hear him moaning in real pain as he's lying there. If you didn't know better maybe you'd just think, man, they are really selling it.

But that crack, that sound. Even now.

Then, see, I finally get smart. I move over to the other side of the ring where I'm not in the shot. I'm telling him now with hand gestures. Cut it out. Head for the dressing room.

He holds up that finger again. One more?

I'm off-screen but I can hear myself now, banging my palm on the canvas. The camera's in tight on Dooms as he looks at me and nods, like he's just doing what I'm telling him.

Okay, he says, one more.

"I can't believe it," Steve Bath is saying, just trying to keep up with the script all the way in the trash now. "Fast Eddie Ray is apparently not satisfied with the win by disqualification, and is insisting on his man Doomsday really making a point here today."

You can see his face paint peeling off under all the sweat. The crowd is losing their minds. Luke is laying there holding onto one dislocated shoulder as Dooms yanks him up by his hair. Even over all the noise in the room, and even on this shoddy old video posted to somebody's Facebook, you can still hear him whimpering in pain. Like a dog.

Improvisation

It's strange to watch myself now, sliding in under that bottom rope, hurling myself into Doom's enormous back, bouncing off him like a bug off a windshield. The way he does that slow turn to see me standing there, the way my face is giving off fear but also some kind of resolve, you'd almost think we wrote it this way.

"What is this?" Steve Bath says, and I know he must have been thinking the very same thing. Here he was adjusting on the fly with the rest of us, trying to make it make sense for the viewers at home. "It's as if Fast Eddie Ray is upset at his wrestler being so reluctant about pouring on the punishment!"

"Disgusting," says Bill Ellis. "But what else do you expect from Fast Eddie at this point?"

I knew by then I was committed. I also knew there was only one way it could end. Me shaking my finger at Dooms. Making it read to the crowd like, listen you big lug I'm the brains and you're just the brawn, so you do what I say. Him shoving me back against the ropes so hard I damn near got whiplash. Boy did they ever pop for that.

I waited just long enough to see Luke roll clear of the ring, leaving me alone with Dooms. I remember thinking, well, you're going to suffer either way, so you might as well make this one count.

Even on this little internet video you can hear it when I open-hand slap Dooms across his big ol' face.

They popped for that, too. Oh yes they did.

Questionable Strategies

Fella told me once that in car accidents it's always the people who tense up right before impact who get it worst. The ones who never see it coming, or the drunks who are already loose from liquor before the moment of impact? They don't feel nearly so bad the next day. So that's what I was thinking as Dooms scooped me up and took off running. Don't tense up waiting for it. Just let your body go slack.

Thing I'm proud of now is that, watching the video and looking real close at my face when he blasts off into the air, all you see is that slickster manager who's finally getting what's coming to him — and he's absolutely, satisfyingly terrified.

Scars

Luke went straight to the hospital. Dooms didn't even go back to the dressing room. Walked out to his car in all his gear, drove off without a word, headed straight out of Memphis and never looked back. Wasn't until later we found out he'd cut a deal with Vic Valley up in Minneapolis. Rumor had it that Vic paid him more than twice what Terry did. Also said he'd give him "creative control," which in Dooms' case meant letting him get on TV and run his mouth about the spirits of the nether realm every so often.

I've seen some of those promo spots he did in what little time he spent up there before Sonny Da Silva got him. Still got no idea what the hell he was talking about.

Me, I went to the bar in the Ambassador Hotel and drank until I couldn't feel whatever was happening in my chest anymore. Just being dumb and macho, I guess. Wanted to show I could take the bumps too when I had to. Trying to prove it didn't bother me, even though I felt like I was dying. It wasn't until two days later I finally broke down and went to the doctor for them to tell me I'd just about shredded all the cartilage in my sternum. If you don't think that hurts, well, that just tells me you ain't ever experienced it for yourself.

Course Terry Austin blamed me for what happened to his boy. What could I tell him? He kept saying I should have had better control over Dooms. There's a concept for you. Try telling a six and a half-foot steroid monster that he's a superstar, and then see how much control you feel like you have. But Terry just wanted to blame somebody. It wasn't going to be himself, though I suspect he did some of that too, in his private moments, especially later on. I couldn't tell you for sure if it was the reason I never got my ownership share or if that was just an excuse.

He asked me later if I ever told Dooms that Luke was his son. I told him I didn't, but I couldn't swear that no one else did. I'd say the odds of it are pretty good. I think what he was really asking was, how much of a grudge should he hold against Vic Valley because of it? For all we knew, Vic might have been the one to tell him. He could have even put it in Dooms' head to do something like that on his way out the door. I wouldn't put it past him. Not like he and Terry were the best of friends, even in good times.

But that's the thing about this business sometimes. There's all sorts of ways to get hurt, and you don't always know what's on purpose and what's pure accident. Sometimes guys can hate each other's guts but still take care of one another's bodies in there. Other times it's the guy who never meant you a lick of harm who cripples you for life.

Still, if he'd come right out and asked me how mad I thought he ought to be at Vic Valley, I'd have told him: considerably.

It was Luke I always felt the worst for. That boy didn't deserve none of that. Not even a little bit. I tried to do everything I could for him after that. Visited him in the hospital. Drove him to his physical therapy appointments. I got a lot more interested in carrying him to those sessions once I saw the therapist working with him. Took me four visits to get up the courage to ask her what her name was. She pointed to the little card on her shirt that said Elise and asked me, couldn't I read?

I told her yes ma'am, but I just wanted to hear you say it. That got a real nice smile out of her. I suppose I've been chasing that smile ever since.

Terry hung on for a while but lost his stomach for the business some years later. Got out, got back in. Got out again.

"Just burned out," Terry told me when I pressed him for answers on why he was selling. "You better hope to hell you never get like me, because once you do, I don't believe there's anything you can do for it."

I didn't know what he meant at the time. I found out, though.

Luke died in that car accident, must have been close to a decade later. Fell asleep behind the wheel coming home from a show in Macon. I heard it might have had something to do with those pain pills he got on and never all the way kicked, but I don't know for sure. There's another story that's a little too familiar in our business.

And Dooms, well, everyone saw how famous he got. Wasn't long before he was headlining those big pay-per-view shows for Sonny Da Silva. I even bought a couple, but I couldn't sit through them. Guess I'm still holding some grudges, too.

Elise likes to say that at a certain age we know ourselves by the scars we carry with us. I suppose that's true. If you gave me the chance to wipe mine clean, I'd probably turn you down. I came by them honestly. I might be afraid I wouldn't know what to make of myself without them. It doesn't mean they don't still hurt from time to time. Some days more than others.

ABOUT US

EDITORS

Chad Dundas is the author of the critically-acclaimed novels *Champion of the World* and *The Blaze*. His short fiction has appeared in the Beloit Fiction Journal, Sycamore Review, Sou'Wester and Thuglit. Since 2012, he has been the co-host of The Co-Main Event MMA podcast and is an executive producer on the award-winning history/true crime podcast Death in the West. He lives in Missoula, Montana with his wife and children.

Jonathan Snowden is the author of *Shamrock: The World's Most Dangerous Man*, *Total MMA: Inside Ultimate Fighting*, *The MMA Encyclopedia* and *Shooters: The Toughest Men in Professional Wrestling*. He works for the Department of Defense and lives in Ozark, Alabama with his wife and two children. He thinks about professional wrestling. A lot.

. . .

CONTRIBUTORS

Dan Brooks is a contributor to the New York Times Magazine, Harpers, Gawker, and other publications whose relationships to professional wrestling have not yet fully developed. He holds an MFA in fiction from the University of Montana and a BA in English and Theatre Arts from the University of Iowa. He lives in Missoula, Montana with his wife, son, and handsome dog.

Marco Bucci recognized two things at a young age. The first was that he wanted to become a professional artist. The second was that he couldn't draw. This delayed him for quite some time. At age 19 he began to study classical drawing, which led him to kindle a love for painting and illustration. He hasn't looked back since.

Marco's experience includes books, film, animation, games and advertising. His clients include: Disney, Marvel Studios, LEGO, LucasArts, Mattel Toys, and more. He lives in Toronto, Canada, with his wife and two kids.

Ryan Dilbert is the author of *Time Crumbling Like a Wet Cracker* and the flash fiction chapbook Mat Burns. He is a pro wrestling columnist and fiction writer whose work has appeared in NANO Fiction, matchbook, Smokelong Quarterly, BRAINBUSTER, and Wrestle Inn. He teaches fourth grade in Houston, Texas, where he lives with his impressively patient wife and two daughters.

Richard Fifield currently resides in Missoula, Montana, and is an author and artist. His previous novels include *The Flood Girls* and *The Small Crimes Of Tiffany Templeton,* and his short stories have been published in numerous magazines and anthologies, most recently *Evergreen: Grim Tales & Verses From The Gloomy Northwest*. Previously a social worker and activist, he volunteers his time as an advocate for women and teen girls, and self-published an anthology of their stories titled *We Leave The Flowers Where They Are*. A designer of clothing and interiors, he will not stop until the world is covered in rhinestones.

Ben Fowlkes is a former reporter and columnist for The Athletic and a co-host of the Co-Main Event MMA Podcast.. He's covered combat sports for outlets such as USA Today, Sports Illustrated, MMA Fighting, and others. His fiction has also appeared in Glimmer Train, Crazyhorse, and Best American Short Stories. He lives in Missoula, Montana, with his two daughters, his dog, and one ornery cat.

Carrie Laben is the Shirley Jackson Award-winning author of the novel *A Hawk in the Woods*. Their work has appeared in such venues as The Dark, Electric Literature, Indiana Review, and Outlook Springs; they've been a MacDowell Fellow and a resident at the Anne LaBastille Memorial Residency and Brush Creek Foundation for the Arts. They hold an MFA from the University of Montana and live in Queens. They miss *Lucha Underground*.

Nick Mamatas is the author of several novels, including *I Am Providence* and *The Second Shooter*. He has published dozens of short stories in venues including *Best American Short Stories, Year's Best Science Fiction & Fantasy, Ellery Queen Mystery Magazine*, and *Asimov's Science Fiction*. He's been following professional wrestling since Bob Backlund held the WWWF title.

. . .

Jason Ridler is a professional historian and writer. He's the author of the *Brimstone Files* series for Night Shade Books, has published over seventy short stories, and has written the celebrated noir wrestling thrillers *Death Match* and *Rise of the Luchador*. A former punk rock musician and cemetery groundskeeper, he teaches for Johns Hopkins University and Google.

Kevin Seccia is a writer from the great state of New Jersey. He's the author of the book *Punching Tom Hanks*, and currently he's a producer on the Fox animated show The Great North, which you can also watch on Hulu. You can follow him on Twitter (twitter.com/kevinseccia,) even though you probably shouldn't be on Twitter. He wondered if he used the word "great" too many times in this bio before sending it in. It's probably fine.

ALSO BY

SHAMROCK

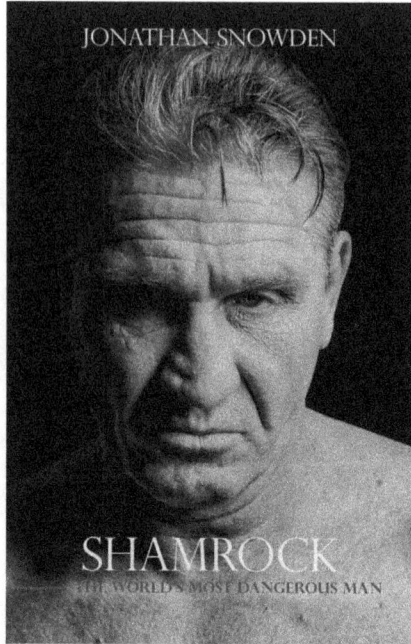

"It's one of my favorite sports books and the depth is incredible. The subject is so amazing. Honestly, this should lead to a movie."

--Dave Meltzer, Wrestling Observer

"This is, without question, the best book I've ever read on either pro wrestling or mixed martial arts."

--Jeremy Botter, Whizzered

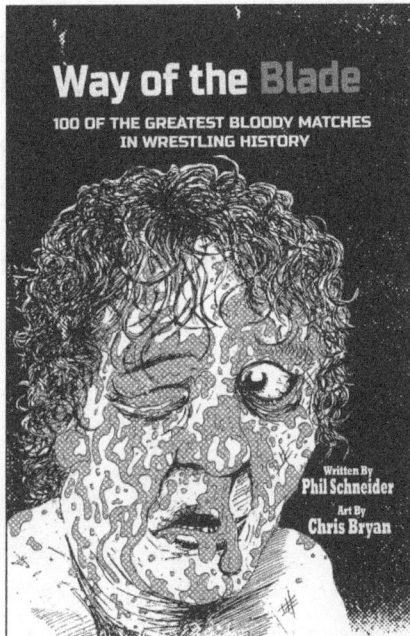

"*Way of the Blade* is a fantastic resource, and definitely a must-have in the collection of fans who appreciate that kind of hard-hitting violent wrestling action."

—Slam Wrestling

"*Way of the Blade* feels like a wrestling nerd, and I mean that in the most complimentary way, taking you on a trip throughout wrestling history."

—Voices of Wrestling

HYBRID SHOOT

Sign up to receive our free newsletter for sales, offers and thoughtful content about MMA, pro wrestling and boxing.

https://hybridshoot.substack.com/subscribe

CO-MAIN EVENT PODCAST

Since its humble beginnings in 2012, the Co-Main Event Podcast has provided listeners with the independent discourse they crave about the crazy, dog-eat-dog world of mixed martial arts fighting. Each week, veteran MMA journalists Chad Dundas and Ben Fowlkes put their own unique spin on the headlines, providing professional insight, uncensored opinions and terrible dad jokes for a diverse, worldwide audience.